THE FORGOTTEN ISLAND

DAVID SODERGREN

Cover illustration by Trevor Henderson
Graphic design by Heather Sodergren

Copyright © 2018 David Sodergren
All rights reserved.
ISBN: 9781718173460

For Heather,
for making me believe I could

PROLOGUE

P RACHYA RAISED THE BATTERED OLD WHISTLE TO HIS CHAPPED lips and blew three sharp bursts. The workers looked at each other, confusion etched onto the deep lines of their faces. Checking their watches, they saw it was just past ten. The hazy morning sun was still in its ascent, casting an orange glow over the sea that surrounded the island. It was too early for lunch, so what was old Prachya up to?

The men downed tools, glad for any respite from the day's labour, and shuffled past the bamboo scaffolding towards the foreman. Construction of the Man Wai Luxury Hilltop Resort could wait a little longer; they still had six months before the official grand opening.

Prachya stood away from the main building site, his back to the men, overlooking what would, once completed, be an outdoor pool. Right now it was a sorry-looking mess, a crudely dug basin next to a vast mound of dirt. Prachya, the site foreman since construction began three months ago, took off his baseball cap and wiped the sweat from his leathery brow. A cigarette dangled from his lips. This was bad news. It would set them back days, even weeks. Hell, it could shut them down for good.

The men trudged through the dirt towards Prachya. In six months this path would be a tastefully landscaped garden, flanked by sparkling white fountains, exotic flowers and Thai sculptures.

The kind of shit tourists love.

But now this.

The men stared into the pool, at the two frightened workers pressed up against the dirt walls, their spades and pick axes discarded.

And there, right in the middle, was the problem. A large hole, seven or eight feet in diameter, a thin, vaporous mist rising from it.

'What happened?' asked Prachya in Thai. 'Answer me,' he demanded when no explanations were forthcoming.

'It was Arama,' said one man. Like most of the workers, he was stripped to the waist, his young skin already showing signs of ageing from spending his life in the glare of the sun. His voice shook as he spoke. 'He was digging over there and the ground...it just opened up.'

Prachya put his cap back on, feeling rivulets of sweat dripping down the back of his neck. 'Where is he now?'

The young man gazed up at the foreman with fear in his eyes.

'It took him, sir. It swallowed him up.'

Prachya took a drag on his cigarette and crushed the tip between his fingers, then turned and spat and hopped into the pool, heading straight for the hole. A foul, primordial odour caught in his nostrils and made him choke.

The smell of death.

He lit another cigarette and peered down into the impenetrable darkness. Pulling a small torch from the pocket of his stained overalls, he crouched down and motioned for the men to join him, some of the braver ones reluctantly doing so.

From the other side of the construction site came the sounds of hammering and sawing and drilling and laughter. The radio was playing the one station it picked up, a mix of Thai and Western pop music.

All those other men, blissfully unaware.

He shined the torch into the hole. It was about fifteen feet of sheer rock face that opened out into a cave of indeterminate size. He let go of the torch and it fell, turning over and over, the beam flashing back and forth, falling, falling, falling. He waited for the sound of it hitting the rocks below, a sound that never came.

Several workers backed away from the pool. Prachya stared at them, his gaze rooting the men to the spot. He thought for a moment.

Was the whole hillside hollow? They were building the resort over some kind of cave network, that was for sure, but it couldn't possibly be as big as it appeared. Downing tools would cost hundreds of men their jobs, his own included. He thought of his wife and child and their tiny two-room apartment back in Bangkok, the roaches on the walls and the way the building rattled whenever the train roared past, waking the neighbourhood dogs and then, inevitably, the baby. By that point you could forget about getting any sleep.

No, he didn't want to stop construction. He put the cigarette to his mouth and noticed it had burnt itself out. It followed the torch down the hole and he lit another.

'I need a volunteer.'

Prachya searched for someone to meet his eye. The men muttered, coughed, shoved their hands in their pockets, but no one raised their hand or stepped up. Prachya shook his head.

'Superstitious bastards,' he growled. 'I'll do it myself.'

He instructed the men to fetch a winch while he looped the end of a thick piece of rope until it resembled a noose. He tugged on the rope to ensure it was attached to the pulley system, took a spare flashlight from one of the labourers, and slipped the loop over his foot. With a last glance back at his men — those cowards — he stepped over the lip of the hole and into the blackness. Two workers operated the winch, rotating the rusty handle and lowering Prachya into the gloom.

By this point it was almost lunchtime, and the faint whiff of boiling rice was replaced, as he descended, by a musty, fetid stench like a corpse buried in a basement. He abseiled the initial bottleneck, kicking away from the wall with his free foot until there was no rock left and he hung in the main cavern. He moved the torch back and forth. Water dripped from enormous stalactites that covered the upper part of the cave. Above him the entrance was getting smaller and smaller, a sapphire moon in the midnight sky. Only two men dared get close enough to watch, their heads silhouetted against the stark blue.

He swung the beam around trying to find something, anything. There were no walls. An unfamiliar sensation coursed through his body. He felt small, insignificant. There was no way they could continue. The whole hillside was a death trap, a tragic accident waiting to happen. On the other hand, he had potentially discovered a new geological marvel. The biggest cave in the world! Maybe they would name it after him.

Prachya's Cave. It had a nice ring to it.

Maybe he could even make some money?

He heard a noise and swung the torch, dimly aware of his heart hammering in his skull. Nothing there. He wondered how much rope remained and glanced up. The hole was little more than a pin prick.

The sound again. Scrabbling rocks falling as if someone had moved. Or something. He felt invisible eyes staring at him. He lifted the torch overhead and flicked it off and on again, signalling for the men to raise him back up. They would need to send a whole team down here with powerful halogen lamps and safety gear. Just as his eyes started to adjust to the darkness the rope jerked him back up again, the metallic creak of the winch barely audible far, far above him. A chill scampered up and down his spine. The cavern was as cold as a morgue and he wanted out.

That was when he heard the missing worker call to him.

'Help,' came a cracked and frightened voice.

'Arama?' said Prachya. 'Is that you?' Could Arama still be alive? He must have fallen hundreds of feet. Had something broken his fall? He searched around but the sound echoed and reverberated off the walls, coming from all around, impossible to pinpoint.

'I can't move,' he said. 'I can't move my body!'

'I'll send someone down,' shouted Prachya as he inched his way back up towards the light. He struggled to think of something to say, some reassuring words. A scream broke the silence.

It was the hellish sound of the forsaken, a high, gut-wrenching wail that split the darkness like a hatchet to the face.

'Oh god, oh god, what is that? *What is that?*' shrieked Arama.

Prachya shone his torch down, but it was useless, the beam fading away, swallowed up by the cave.

'Get me out of here,' he called. 'Hurry!'

Far beneath him Arama screamed in pure, desperate terror. Prachya's rope rose faster, as Arama's cries chased after him like spectral hands groping for his feet.

'No, no, no,' the man babbled. 'Help me!'

'Come on,' howled Prachya at his men as the rope juddered violently and he almost lost his grip, his foot slipping free from the loop. His hands grasped for the rope, the friction scalding his palms as he slid. His foothold gone, he coiled the rope around his forearm, every muscle in his body straining.

Below, in the murk of the abyss, Prachya thought he could make out movement. A lot of it. A low gurgling sound replaced Arama's screams and Prachya heard a slurping, tearing sound, like something was...*eating*.

The roof slowly came into view as he neared the well-like opening, the familiar faces of his men gawping over the edge, ashen with fear. Below him there came a steady noise, like stones thrown at a wall, a rhythmic sound that grew steadily louder.

Click-click-click.

Bile rose in his throat and he had a maddening sense that the cave was closing in on him and he released his bladder without even realising it as the clicking grew louder and louder and then suddenly there were hands on his shoulders and arms and he was being raised out of the hole by the men.

Several of the workers had already fled, rushing through the lush vegetation of the rainforest and down the hill to where the boats waited. Prachya sat up and the torch fell from his pocket, rolling towards the hole. It spiralled down, and out of instinct he leaned over and tried to grab it. It was too late, and he watched as the light disappeared into the abyss, but not before, for one brief, maddening, infernal second, it illuminated something.

Something in the darkness. Something moving, moving up towards him, towards the surface. And the noise, the scuttling that echoed throughout the cavern, that *click-click-click*, filled Prachya's ears with the dread sound that would cause him to wake screaming from his sleep until the day he died, as the devil from the pit emerged fully into the light, heading up, up towards Prachya and his men, up towards the daylight.

It was too much. He bellowed in horror and scrambled to his feet, knocking men out of his way, driven by one single-minded goal.

To get the hell off this island.

He crashed through the undergrowth, closely followed by several of his men, leaving the empty shell of the Man Wai Luxury Hilltop Resort behind. Without once looking back, Prachya reached the pier where two boats waited. Within minutes he and the men had split themselves between them and set sail for the mainland. Halfway through the seven-hour trip, and after several glasses of rum, Prachya remembered the fifty or sixty men back on the island, working on various aspects of the resort, digging power lines, mixing cement or just relaxing on their one day off at the hastily constructed workers' village.

With shaking hands he lit a cigarette and wept at the thought. No one commented on the streak of grey in Prachya's thick black mop of hair.

And no one asked him what he saw.

Prachya lived another twelve years, though those closest to

him say he was never quite the same. He would speak of that day to no one, not even his closest friends or family. Why would he want to think of that thing that tormented his dreams every night, that made him sleep with the lights on and wake drenched in a cold sweat, sometimes crying, sometimes physically frozen with terror?

It was on his deathbed that Prachya finally broke his silence. Surrounded by family and gripped by a fever that wracked his body, Prachya knew he was dying. He took his wife's hand and spoke for the first and last time of what he saw in the cavern, of the thing that had so profoundly haunted him.

The family listened, nodding in all the right places and smiling sadly. His brother caught the eye of Prachya's wife, who turned away, tears rolling down her cheeks. His son Boonsri simply shook his head, and when Prachya called his name imploringly, Boonsri looked back at him the way that Prachya had once looked at his own infant son.

We end our lives as helpless as when we begin them, he thought.

Prachya fell into a deep sleep, and the family agreed that he would soon leave them. None of them said it aloud, but they all felt it was time. As Prachya passed, he prayed that no other living soul should ever bear witness to the atrocity he saw that day in the cave, while his wife cursed the gods for conspiring to rob a proud man of both his sanity and his dignity.

'Even in death, a man should have his dignity,' she whispered as she wept alone by his bedside later that night.

As for Koh Wai Island? Well, it's still there, though you won't find it on any maps, the Thai government having quietly had it stricken from existence after the first and second rescue teams failed to return.

Almost thirty years later, any questions about its existence are met with polite confusion and smiles.

Time passed, the tracks of the diggers receding into the grass, the discarded tools rotting in the sun and vines creeping their way over the sun-faded walls of the resort, as nature slowly reclaimed what was once hers and would be again.

And whatever Prachya saw that day remained there, undisturbed, patient as death itself.

Waiting.

1

THEY WERE STILL SHAGGING.

Ana Logan stood outside the hostel bedroom she shared with her sister Rachel and Paul Cook, Rachel's boyfriend. She put an ear to the door, listening to Rachel's laboured panting and Paul grunting like a rutting stag.

'Fuck's sake,' sighed Ana as she ambled back down the crooked wooden stairs, her backpack slung over one shoulder. All she wanted was a shower; was that too much to ask?

The pair of them had been at it for over an hour now. Just thinking about it made Ana feel tired. She wandered into the hostel bar and settled herself onto a stool at the far end, ordering a vodka-lemonade. She looked around in dismay. They had flown twelve hours from Scotland to Thailand and here she was, surrounded by white people getting drunk. She could have left her house back in Edinburgh, wandered down the street to a pub and seen exactly the same thing any night of the week.

It would have saved a couple of thousand pounds too.

A German couple next to her argued boisterously in their native tongue while a group of English boys who didn't look a day over sixteen downed shots and cheered at the Premier League football on the big plasma screen that hung over the bar. Every time the commentator said the name Kane they downed their drinks and picked up another from the tray that balanced delicately on the edge of the pool table, almost daring someone to knock it over. In the far corner a lone guy in his forties, his hair tied up in a man-bun, danced erratically.

Drugs were pretty easy to come by, apparently.

The same faces every night for the last week, and the only thing that changed was how increasingly tired they looked. Ana caught her own reflection in the glass behind the bar and quickly looked away. Mirrors always made her feel vulnerable, and she avoided them wherever possible. They reminded her of—

'You know, you'd be pretty if you smiled,' said the barman in a thick Australian accent, giving her a toothy grin, his pearly whites a sickly pink under the flashing neon HAPPY HOUR sign.

She gave him a withering stare. 'So fuck off and give me something to smile about.'

His grin faded and he slammed her drink down, the liquid spilling over the lip of the glass.

'Must be on the rag,' he muttered, shaking his head and turning away.

Irritated, she considered going for a walk, but decided against handling the 'Looky-Looky' men, those guys who followed you up the street trying to hawk sunglasses or towels or fried cockroaches or magic beans.

'Looky looky miss, finest bracelet for you! You have husband? You want to see ping pong show? Looky looky!'

It was too hot to make the effort, so she pulled a battered Richard Laymon novel from her backpack and laid it on the counter, the dog-eared pages stained with sweat and suntan lotion. Going on holiday to a warm climate was the cruellest fate a good book could possibly face.

The noise from outside bled through the thin walls, interrupting her concentration. The roar of engines, the peel of laughter from the drunk and the terminally high, the techno beats from the clubs and twenty-four-hour shops. Bangkok wasn't just a city that never slept; it was a city that never shut up.

'I never signed up for this,' she said to herself, re-reading the same paragraph for the third time.

'Excuse me?' said a guy standing next to her, a nervous expression on his face.

'Oh, no, I wasn't talking to you,' said Ana.

'Oh.' He smiled and turned back to the bar, trying to get the Aussie's attention, but the barman was too busy chatting up a group of young girls in bikini tops who looked like they just wandered off the set of a rap video.

Probably telling them they'd be pretty if they smiled.

'So who were you talking to?'

'Huh?' Ana looked back up at the man. He was handsome in a baby-faced way, a scraggly beard like wisps of smoke and a barcode moustache she imagined was his pride and joy. It was the facial hair of a classic Gap Year student. 'Oh, right. I was just talking to myself.' She smiled and lifted her book, the international signal for 'Leave me alone'.

'That's a sign of madness,' he said, really laying his American accent on thick. She sighed and put the book down exaggeratedly.

'Excuse me?'

'Talking to yourself. It's a sign of madness.' He smiled at her.

'Well I'm not mad, thank you. The voices in my head

would have told me if I was,' she said curtly and he laughed and held out his hand.

'My name's Ricky.'

She gave in and shook his hand. It was clammy and sweaty, but so was hers so she couldn't complain. Even with the air-con on full blast there was no escaping the pervasive tropical heat.

'Ana,' she said. 'Look, I don't want to be rude, but I'd rather just sit and read if you don't mind.'

'Understood,' said Ricky. 'Excuse me, can I get a beer?' he called to the barman, who was having none of it, his shirt pulled up so that one of the bikini girls could press his rock-hard abs and squeal in delight.

'You need to get your tits out,' said Ana, not looking up from her book.

'Excuse me?'

'Best way to get served, apparently.'

'Yeah well, I don't look good in a bikini.'

Ana nodded. 'I bet they make your arse look big, aye?'

Ricky laughed. 'They do, they really do.' The Aussie reluctantly left his makeshift harem and handed Ricky a bottle of Singha, snatching the payment from his hand and heading back over towards the girls, but they had already left to find the next muscular blonde Aussie barman. In Bangkok's backpacker district, they wouldn't have to go far to find one.

'You look like you're having as much fun as me,' said Ricky, taking a sip of his beer.

Ana smiled. 'Sorry. It's just that this has not quite been the holiday I'd planned on. I'm stuck here in tourist purgatory while my sister's upstairs riding her boyfriend all night, and if I go outside everyone wants to sell me sarongs or touch my skin. It's weird.'

'They want to touch you?'

'Aye, something about the combination of ginger hair and the Scottish complexion makes the locals want to poke and prod me to see if I'm real. This kid yesterday walked up and jabbed his stubby wee finger in my belly and said, "Look! She fat like Buddha!"' Ricky burst out laughing. Ana raised an eyebrow. 'Oh, you think that's funny do you?'

'I do, I'm sorry,' he said, but he didn't sound it.

'I mean, it's true. When I see how skinny most folk are here, and then I see my decadent Western arse in a mirror, I'm almost ashamed.' She sipped her drink. 'Almost.'

Ricky smiled again and Ana found herself smiling back. He raised his glass.

'A toast, then. To decadent Western butts.'

Ana clinked her glass off his. 'I'll drink to that.'

There was a cheer from behind as one of the football teams scored, followed by the smashing of glass as the tray finally fell from the ratty old pool table.

'Mind if I sit?' asked Ricky.

'What a gentleman,' she said sarcastically. She sighed. 'Sorry, sometimes I can't help myself. Go ahead. I can't stop you anyway.'

He heaved himself up onto the stool, his legs dangling off the floor like a garden gnome on a toadstool. Ana called the bartender over and ordered another round, packing her book away for safekeeping.

'My sister says I use sarcasm to keep people at a distance or something. She reckons she's a fucking psychiatrist, but really she's just seen too many episodes of Frasier.'

'Ha, I do the same. Humour as a defence mechanism. Only problem is I'm not very funny.'

'That is a problem.'

'Sure is.'

'Well, your *crippling* anxiety didn't seem to affect you when you strolled up to me like ol' Johnny Big-Baws out on the pull.'

Ricky raised his eyebrows so high they almost popped off the top of his head. 'Well, I've never been called *that* before.'

'So what sets you off, you great big bag of nerves?' asked Ana wryly.

'Are you making fun of me?'

'What do you think?'

Ricky smirked. 'Fine. You know what I can't stand? Someone walking behind me in high-heels. The clicking sound stresses me out so bad I have to stop and pretend I'm checking my phone until they've gone past.'

Ana nodded. 'I can understand that.' She took a sip of vodka-lemonade and could only taste the vodka. The measures here were out of control. 'I hate when someone behind me on the bus is laughing. I always think they're laughing at me, or putting gum in my hair or gluing me to the seat or...'

'You've given it a lot of thought.'

'A girl should always be prepared.'

'Speaking of being prepared, I'm early for everything.'

'Me too.'

'No,' said Ricky, getting quite animated, 'I mean really early. Like, an hour early for everything. Cinema, drinks, whatever. I'm about five hours early to the airport.'

Ana laughed. 'Yeah, I'm like that! And then you get annoyed when your friends turn up on time even though they are arriving exactly when you arranged to meet.'

'Precisely! I'm here with this pair of hippy assholes, and they refuse to turn up to anything on time. Just getting them to the airport was the greatest test of mental strength I'll ever face.'

'They sound great,' said Ana, making a face that said otherwise. 'Why the fuck are you with them?'

Ricky chuckled and stared into the bottom of his glass. 'Long story.'

'You got somewhere to be? I don't. I have to wait for Robocock upstairs to finish getting his end away with my sister. Apparently that takes...' She checked the time on her iPhone. 'Almost two fucking hours.' She opened her eyes wide in mock enthusiasm. 'So far!'

Ricky laughed. 'You swear a lot, don't you?'

'So what? Don't tell me, you think it's unladylike?'

'No, no, it's just back home, you don't hear too many girls dropping the f-bomb.'

'You should visit Scotland sometime. We use "fuck" as punctuation. Now stop avoiding the subject and tell me why you're shacked up in Bangkok with two arseholes before I lose interest and go back to my book.'

Outside a car alarm screeched and they heard someone loudly haranguing a tourist who stood on the roof of his car, refusing to get down. 'No wonder people hate us,' muttered Ricky. He turned back to Ana. 'So anyway, umm, yeah this was supposed to be a couple's holiday. Three weeks away with my girlfriend and her two buddies. Then a month ago she tells me she doesn't love me anymore and dumps me. So somehow I ended up going on this holiday with her two friends, who, by the way, I really can't stand. And that's it, I guess.'

Ana nodded. 'That your idea of a long story?'

Ricky grinned. 'Jeez, I just can't win, huh?'

'I'm kidding on,' she said. 'Listen, I'm in the same boat. No break up for me though, I've been single for awhile, so I guess that's why I'm on holiday with my sister and her fuck-monkey. The eternal third-wheel.' She hoped Ricky believed her. He didn't need to know the truth.

'Wow. We're a real pair of losers.'

Ana laughed and raised her glass. 'Another toast? To the two biggest losers in Thailand.'

'To the biggest losers.'

They bumped glasses and downed their drinks, the booze going to their heads but neither minding.

'You know,' said Ricky, 'You're pretty when you smile.'

He sat back, pleased with the compliment.

'Oh don't you fucking start,' she said. His smug grin vanished and she burst out laughing. 'And you were doing so well too.'

With a final gasp, Paul Cook screwed up his face and ejaculated, his body collapsing onto Rachel, limp and spent. His clammy, hairy chest chafed her breasts and she wanted him off, but he lay there panting, his breath hot and sticky against her neck.

'Paul?' she said. 'I need a shower. Ana will be waiting for us.'

'Don't kill my buzz, babe. Not yet,' he replied. 'Don't talk about your sister while I'm still inside you.'

Rachel bristled at his choice of words. 'Well, there's another way to solve that problem.'

'Just a moment longer babe. It feels so good.'

Rachel sighed. 'Paul, kindly extricate yourself from my vagina.'

'Fuck,' he said, pulling out too fast. Rachel winced. 'You know I hate when you get all clinical on me.'

'It's what it's called, Paul. My Va-gi-na,' said Rachel, as if she were teaching phonetic English. Paul sat up, sweat glistening on his back. She pulled the thin blanket over herself, listening for the snap of the condom coming off, only relaxing once she heard it.

'You can be such a bitch sometimes,' he said, getting up and padding his way towards the shower.

'Hey, I'm first in there,' called Rachel.

Paul ignored her and stepped into the glass cubicle.

'Arsehole,' snarled Rachel, checking her iPhone. Quarter to nine. Ana had probably been waiting for at least an hour.

'Can't she get her own room?' called Paul from the shower, the water dribbling pathetically down his body.

'What?' Rachel found her deodorant and sprayed it around the room to hide the musky odour of sex. She considered opening the window, but that would mess up the air-conditioning.

'Your sister. At the next hostel, y'know, to give us some privacy?'

'Paul, we suggested that but you wanted to save money.'

'Yeah, well I didn't think she'd be hanging around so much.'

'You're a real dick, you know that?'

'You love it, babe.' He peeked out the shower. 'Wanna join me?'

'I'll wait til you're done, thanks,' she said, the patented Logan sarcasm lost on the post-coital Paul. She thought of her sister, alone in Bangkok. It had been Ana who suggested she go for a walk, either to give Rachel and Paul some alone-time or because she was sick of Paul and his attitude. Though she had never said as much, it was obvious that Ana thought Paul was a jerk who wasn't good enough for her. Sometimes Rachel thought her sister might be right.

Tonight, she had lain beneath Paul, weathering his thrusts and licks and pillow talk, and thought about the past, throwing in the occasional moan and whimper for good measure.

'That's right, yeah, you love it you whore,' he would say.

'Yes, that's it, you're so good,' she would coo back while thinking about what to have for dinner. It wasn't that he was bad in bed, just that sometimes she needed a break from Paul's insatiable sexual appetite.

The air-con cooled the film of sweat that coated her naked body and she wrapped the blanket tighter around her. In the shower, Paul sang *'Don't Let the Sun Go Down on Me,'* changing the lyrics to *'Don't Let Your Son Go Down on Me'*.

Rachel sighed, something she found herself doing with increasing regularity these days. She shivered under the blanket and waited for him to finish.

In a way, that was the story of her life.

By the time Rachel and Paul made it down the stairs it was dark, and Ana and Ricky were properly smashed. They were exchanging numbers when Rachel spotted them, Ana squinting at the phone like Popeye and pressing one key at a time. The football had finished and the TV now displayed the Sylvester Stallone movie *Demolition Man*, the sound muted while a DJ in the corner pretended to mix records while actually skipping between two knock-off iPods. The bar had filled up, drawing the usual crowd of backpackers and prostitutes.

Ana was laughing and Rachel couldn't suppress a grin. It

had been a long time since she had seen her sister this happy. Or happy at all.

The four of them drank long into the night, and for once it was Rachel who suggested they wrap up and go to bed. Before they did though, she presented Ana with the idea of attending the Kho Phangan Full Moon Party, a monthly night of outrageous revelry that took place on the beach of a small island. Rachel almost fell out of her chair when Ana agreed to go along, provided Ricky and his friends came too, of course. They downed the last of their drinks and said their goodbyes.

'See you at the party,' slurred Ricky as he and Ana parted. 'Bring your bikini.'

'Only if you bring yours,' said Ana, shouting the words into his ear over the music. He leaned in to kiss her and missed and somehow kissed the bridge of her nose and then he was gone, weaving his way through the crowded streets as Rachel helped Ana up the stairs to their room.

By the time they got into bed it was 4am and the sun was threatening to rise before their heads even hit the pillow. Rachel sat under the covers in her tee shirt, clamping her thighs shut to fend off Paul's drunkenly amorous advances. She looked over at her sleeping sister and her heart filled with love for her.

Everything's going to be okay, she thought. *It's been a rough year, but we've gotten through the worst of it and everything is going to be fine now.*

She was sure of it.

2

THE RICKETY OLD BUS WOUND ITS WAY OVER TRACKS THAT snaked across the vibrant Thai countryside. Here, away from the tourist spots, the real Thailand revealed itself, the places the brochures gloss over in favour of five-star resort-hotels and smiling white people in front of temples. Flimsy wooden shacks with corrugated tin roofs dotted the countryside; homes and restaurants, grocery stores and petrol stations. Outside, old men reclined on chairs, smoking cigarettes and watching the world ease by. As far as retirement plans went, it appealed to Ana. Just sitting in the warmth reading a book all day, perhaps with a loyal dog snuggled at her feet. And a cocktail; definitely a cocktail. She waved at one of the men as they drove past and when he nodded back she felt inexplicably sad.

They passed forests and beaches, villages and temples, the sky a rich opal, unencumbered by clouds. Stray dogs darted across the road, narrowly avoiding the bus as it veered from side to side.

They commandeered a table on the lower deck, Ana

choosing to sit opposite Ricky rather than next to him. She didn't want to face Paul and Rachel making out for the duration of the drive.

Behind them sat Ricky's travel companions, Josh and Lillian, the quintessential American backpackers. Josh was impossibly handsome; he looked like he was carved out of solid oak, with a wooden personality to match. He wore his hair in matted blonde dreadlocks, and a shark tooth necklace hung round his neck in an apparent effort to tick every box of the stereotype checklist. And yet somehow he was the better of the two. Ana hated Lillian the moment she set eyes on her. She knew she shouldn't judge on first impressions, but where was the fun in that?

As blonde and tanned as Josh, she carried herself with the swaggering confidence that all Californians seemed to possess, speaking in mindless platitudes and gasping in patronising awe at everything they passed.

'Oh my gawd Josh, look at their little houses. These people are so precious.'

'I bet they could teach us a thing or two about spirituality,' agreed Josh, his hand nestled snugly between Lillian's thighs.

Ana leaned over the table and beckoned Ricky to her.

'I hate your friends,' she whispered.

'Me too. I told you so.'

Rachel nudged her sister. 'They're right behind us.'

'They can't hear us. They're probably meditating or healing their chakras or something.'

'Not a bad idea,' said Paul. 'It's gonna be a long day. And night,' he said, winking at Rachel.

'Get a room you guys,' said Ana. 'Oh wait, you do, and I'm in it too.'

Rachel smiled slyly. 'I'm sure you can find alternative accommodation.'

Ricky choked on his water and coloured. 'What a beautiful day,' he said, a spectacularly unsuccessful attempt to redirect the conversation. Ana just shook her head in that weary big-sister way. At twenty-eight she was only two years older than Rachel, but she liked to pretend she had wisdom far beyond her years, when really it had been Rachel who had saved *her* all those months ago.

A particularly fierce bump in the road jolted Ana from her thoughts, lifting everyone from their seats and spilling drinks all the way down the bus.

'You guys okay back there?' said Ricky to Josh and Lillian.

'Of course, man,' said Josh. 'What's a few bumps on the road to enlightenment?'

'Enlightenment? Fuck, I thought we were going to the beach,' said Ana.

'It's okay,' said Rachel. 'I'm told Enlightenment has a great cafe.'

'You can mock us if you like, we don't care,' said Lillian with thinly disguised distaste. 'We're on a journey of sensual pleasure, experiencing whatever the world wishes to throw at us.'

'I can think of a few things I'd like to throw at them,' said Ana under her breath. Only Rachel heard and she stifled a giggle.

'Check that place out,' said Paul, sitting forward and pointing like a child as they sped past another unspoilt white-sand beach. Out on the sea tiny fishing boats bobbed on the horizon, the men hauling nets out of the water.

'Can't we just go there instead?' suggested Ana. 'It looks

so tranquil. So peaceful.' She tried to snap a picture but by the time the camera was ready it was far behind them.

'Come on Ana, you've got beaches back home. Where else can you experience a Full Moon Party?' said Paul.

'Paul, Portobello Beach is covered in sewage and dog shit and it's about minus-twenty degrees all year round.' She gazed forlornly out the window. 'This is different.'

'It'll be fun Ana, I promise,' agreed Rachel. 'We're gonna make sure you have a good time, aren't we Ricky?'

'Uh, yeah, sure.'

'And stop staring out the window like that Ana. You look like you're auditioning for a music video.'

From the front of the bus the driver shouted in broken English that they would arrive in fifteen minutes. From there it was only a short walk to their evening accommodation. Ana had already checked the route on her phone and saved it to the offline maps and taken a screenshot just in case.

She put her head back, closed her eyes and tried to get some sleep.

It pained her to say it, but Paul was right. It was going to be a long day.

They rattled to a stop and the doors wheezed open, the sticky heat invading the bus. The occupants disembarked to a chorus of hoots and hollers, racing down the narrow aisle. Someone's elbow caught Ana on the side of the head and she winced in pain and annoyance, but mostly annoyance. A tall guy in a Hawaiian shirt fell off the bus and landed in a heap in the dirt. He was drunk already, his friends helping him to his feet, his legs wobbling and unsteady. The first casualty of war.

'Full moon!' he cried out, and someone else whooped in agreement.

Ana sighed and leaned back in her chair, happy to let everyone else off first.

'So this is what Hell looks like,' she said to herself. Still, it could be worse.

At least here she could get drunk.

3

THE SHABBY HOSTEL NEAR THE BEACH WAS ELECTRIC WITH anticipation. Wooden signs painted in bright neon directed revellers towards the party, promising 'Big PaRty tiMe!' and 'CraZy FuN'.

Ana stepped out of the shower and wrapped a towel around herself, feeling refreshed after a long day of travel. She knew it wouldn't last. Rachel perched naked on the edge of the bed, waiting for her straighteners to heat up.

Ana pulled the flimsy curtains shut and started to dry herself, the blast from the air-con pleasantly cool on her wet skin.

'No one can see in, Ana,' said Rachel.

'You never know. I've heard Thai perverts walk around on stilts, gazing through second-floor windows.'

'It's a chilling thought.'

'You wearing your bikini?'

Rachel ran the straighteners through her hair. 'Nah. Paul won't leave me alone for a second if I do, so unless you want him wandering about with a stiffy all night...'

'That's a firm no.'

'Firm indeed. Anyway, I'm not planning on swimming. How about you?'

Ana lifted out a pale-yellow long-sleeve dress with little black dinosaurs printed on it. 'This, I guess.'

Rachel nodded. 'Sleeves again, huh?' Ana was quiet. Rachel's eyes traced the ragged lines that ran from Ana's hands to her elbows. 'You can't hide them forever, sis.'

Ana blushed. 'Why not?' she said, turning away.

'He's gonna see them at some point.'

'Who?'

'Ricky. If you're gonna sleep with him, he'll see your arms. He'll see the scars.'

'I'm not gonna sleep with him.'

'Then why are you wearing those?' said Rachel, pointing at the matching lacy bra and panties Ana had laid out on the bed.

Ana faced her sister again. 'Look Rach, just give me time, okay?' She stared at the scars, as if the very act of doing so could make them go away. 'I don't care if Ricky sees them, or anyone else. I'm not hiding them from other people. I think I'm hiding them from myself.' She smiled sadly. 'You ever lie in bed and remember something embarrassing you said, y'know, five or ten years ago and you just want to curl up and die of shame?'

'Nope.'

'Well, it's like that. Every time I look down, there's this reminder of a time in my life I want to forget, but I can't, not ever. It's marked on my body, like I've been branded.'

'Time heals all wounds,' said Rachel softly.

'Go fuck yourself,' replied Ana, and the two of them burst out laughing.

～

The gang reconvened in the hostel bar where the festivities had begun hours ago, judging by the raucous noise from the patrons. A kiosk selling fluorescent wife-beater vests and shorts was rammed with customers, and several people were daubing matching war-paint on their faces. The soundtrack to this post-apocalyptic hellscape was a mash-up of several competing bluetooth speakers; a discordant yet strangely fitting racket.

'Want some paint?' asked a girl with a heavy Teutonic accent. Ana smiled and waved a hand dismissively, the same tactic she employed when dealing with the Looky-Looky men.

'Maybe later,' she lied, settling herself into a wicker chair next to Rachel.

'I do,' said Paul, jumping to his feet and taking off his vest, standing bare-chested while the girl painted spirals on his skin. He leaned forward and whispered something in her ear and she giggled.

Josh and Lillian were already suited and booted and ready for action. Josh wore a bandana, his shark tooth necklace and bright pink shorts, an enormous heart scrawled on his chest in lurid green. Lillian reclined on a sofa as Josh massaged her feet, hearts inscribed down her arm with a matching one above her left breast, wearing a red bikini that was several sizes too small. They were the best-looking pair of insufferable arseholes Ana had ever met. She glanced down at the long-sleeve dress that hid her entire frame and simmered in quiet jealousy. Still, at least her outfit had fuckin' dinosaurs on it.

One-nil to me.

'Bit warm for sleeves isn't it?' said Ricky.

Ana shrugged, prepared for the question. 'Us Scots burn easily.'

Paul strolled back over to Rachel, giggling all the way.

'Hey Rach, check it out.' He lifted his fluorescent vest to reveal a large arrow on his stomach that pointed towards to his crotch. 'In case you get too drunk later,' he said.

Rachel turned to Ana. 'He makes me so proud sometimes,' she said dryly.

'He's quite a catch.'

'Hey come on, I'm only getting into the spirit of things,' protested Paul.

'Speaking of spirits,' said Ricky as Ana groaned at the awkward segue, 'Who wants a shot?'

They all did. As Ricky fought his way to the bar, Rachel took Ana's hand.

'Hey, you gonna be okay?'

'I'm fine. Apart from being trapped in a neurotic's worst nightmare, I'm absolutely grand.' She gestured around at the hordes of drunken backpackers.

Rachel chuckled. 'Hey, it's just one day, okay? Then we can get back to doing that tourist stuff you love. You know, temples and shit. We can go see that skeleton you were talking about the other day.'

'It's a mummified monk,' corrected Ana. 'And he wears sunglasses.'

'You're so weird. If I wanted a holiday surrounded by antiques and corpses, I would have spent the summer with grandma.' She paused. 'Why is the skeleton wearing sunglasses?'

'I dunno. Probably just a real cool dude.'

'So when you gonna kiss Ricky?' There it was, the classic Rachel subject change. Ana fixed her with a withering stare.

'Never,' she said, her eyes betraying her.

'He likes you. Doesn't he Paul?'

'Huh?' said Paul fiddling with his phone.

'There you go. Paul agrees.'

'Thank God for that. I don't know what I'd do without Paul to guide me. He's so wise.'

Rachel smiled. 'Tonight is gonna be fun, I promise.'

'And don't forget to turn your tracker app on, okay?' interjected Paul. 'Even if you've got no signal, it uses satellite tracking. We can't lose each other as long as we're all using it.'

Ana pulled her iPhone out of her handbag and showed it to Paul. Rachel did the same, though she kept her device in a waterproof running-armband. Paul checked they were both using it correctly — they were — and grunted his approval. Ana grudgingly had to admit it was a great idea. Each phone transmitted a signal that showed up on a map, so that if they got separated in the crowd, they could locate each other. Ana made a mental note to get Ricky involved once he came back with the drinks, but then he turned up with a tray of shots and she quickly forgot.

The party had begun.

4

TWO HOURS LATER, AND ALREADY SEMI-DRUNK, THEY shambled out of the hostel, following the crowds along the well-worn trail to the beach. It was impossible to miss.

The sheer magnitude of the Full Moon Party was awe-inspiring, and a little frightening. Ricky took Ana's hand and she smiled at him.

'We can find a quiet spot if you like,' he said. She squeezed his hand in response.

'Yeah, I'd like that. I don't do well in crowds.'

'No problem.'

They walked together, hand-in-hand, towards the island beach of Koh Phangan, where over twenty-thousand bodies vied for space, dancing, drinking and partying. Ana saw the bus they had arrived on still sitting there, the driver leaning against the side, smoking a cigarette and watching her. Ana looked away, surprised to find her heart racing.

He's not staring at you. No one is. There's nothing wrong, she told herself. But still, she let go of Ricky's hand and checked to see if her dress was tucked into her knickers. It wasn't.

'You okay?' asked Ricky.

'Do I have something on my face?' asked Ana.

Ricky looked confused. 'No.'

'Okay. I just...I feel like people are staring at me.'

'Everyone here is too drunk to stare. I doubt they can focus on anything.'

Ana looked back towards the driver. The still-smoking cigarette lay in the dirt by his feet. Beyond him stood someone else, only the side of their face visible behind the driver. It was pale and shrivelled, a bleached husk, the kind of face she was glad was hidden from full view. The sinister figure put a pale hand on the driver's shoulder, the ancient, powdery skin almost transparent in the sunlight. Ana couldn't see the thing's eyes, but they were definitely staring at her, she knew it. For real this time, no trick of the imagination.

Don't be so stupid, of course it's not. You can't even see the face.

But she could see the driver's. He mouthed something at her, seeming to move in slow motion, his words lost, drifting away on the wind. They locked eyes and Ana froze. The driver's mouth opened wide, his gaze fixed on her. Her heart pounded. The pale thing remained still as the driver began to shake, a trickle of blood running down his chin.

His neck bulged obscenely and his jaw slackened even further as whatever was inside him struggled to fight its way out.

The pale creature stepped out from behind the driver and Ana's stomach dropped.

It couldn't be...

'Ana? You okay?'

She turned to Ricky, her face phantom-pale.

'Jesus, what's wrong?'

'Nothing,' she said, gasping for breath. 'Nothing.'

She turned back towards the grisly scene, knowing full well that when she did, everything would be back to normal. The driver leaned against the bus, a half-smoked cigarette clamped between his teeth. He was fine. The figure was gone.

It's happening again.

It couldn't be. Not again. It had been a year. It was over, the past, a distant memory, a bad dream.

Should she tell Rachel?

Best not to. No sense worrying her, not now. She would wait until they got back to Scotland. It didn't matter, it was all under control now. She knew how to deal with the visions; she knew they weren't real.

It wouldn't be like before.

She wouldn't let them get inside her head.

'Ana, come on, what's wrong?'

She struggled to control her breathing. 'Nothing. I'm sorry Ricky, I thought I recognised someone. False alarm, thankfully.'

'You look pale,' he said, the concern genuine.

'I always look pale.' She smiled, surprised at how easy it was to slip into old patterns and even older excuses.

She took Ricky's hand and let him lead the way. Despite the heat, a cold shiver traced its icy fingernail down her spine.

This time she didn't dare turn back.

The noise on the beach was deafening, a near-constant cacophonous racket of crunching beats and stomach-churning bass bursting forth from massive speakers, while thousands of bodies pressed against each other, the crowd becoming one massive pulsating entity, a beating heart with alcohol for blood.

Shacks lined the beach; bars, street food stalls and more bars. On any other day it would probably be another stunning Thai coastline, all white sand and palm trees. But one night every month - this night - it became a weird backpacker carnival, where people took the "anything-as-long-as-it's-fluorescent" dress code very seriously indeed. All around bodies thrust and jerked in a bacchanalian frenzy, daubed liberally with glow-in-the-dark paint over every inch of exposed flesh.

'The paint factory must have exploded,' said Ana.

'What?' shouted her sister over the music.

Ana leaned right up to Rachel's ear, started to yell her comment into it and gave up. It was a lame joke anyway.

'Come on, I need a drink,' she said instead.

Rachel didn't need telling twice.

They pushed their way through the crowds, Ana gripping on to Rachel the whole way. A strobe light kicked in and the scene became a spectacle of twitching bodies. Ana felt the old sliver of anxiety creeping up on her like a spider. She always got this way around crowds.

Ten years ago, aged eighteen, her sister sixteen, she had accompanied Rachel to the New Year's Eve fireworks display in their native Edinburgh. Thousands of pissed-up Scots crammed onto the main shopping street to celebrate the end of another miserable year and the beginning of an even worse one. It was an excuse to get drunk, as were most events back home.

But there, trapped among hordes of drunks, Ana's throat had begun to tighten, her legs turning to jelly, a vast pit opening in her stomach. As the New Year countdown reached zero, she lost Rachel, separated by a group of boys pushing through. At that point a great cheer erupted and then everyone was hugging and kissing. Hands reached for her, groping and searching, brushing against her arse and breasts; one older man had leaned in and kissed her, the stench of alcohol on his breath making her retch. She had tried to retreat but there was nowhere to go, the people were packed in too tightly. She fought her way through the human quicksand in a panic, the throng surging against her at every turn. Then she must have blacked out, for the next thing she knew there was an EMT hovering over her in a mobile medical unit.

She had done her best to avoid crowds since then, but somehow here she was, of her own volition, at one of the busiest parties on the planet. It made the New Year's Eve party look like a visit to an old folks' home.

Great.

Rachel deftly picked her way through the crowd, not seeming to mind being bumped into, burned with cigarettes or having innumerable drinks spilt down her, and they emerged from the worst of it at one of many bars set up along the beach. At least the music was quieter here.

'Jesus Ana, let go of my hand. It's fucking sore!'

Ana slackened her vice-like grip and relaxed.

'Sorry.'

Rachel brushed a strand of red hair away from Ana's face. 'Listen, if you don't want to stay, you don't have to. I can get you back to the hostel if you like?'

Ricky and Paul emerged after them, followed by Josh and Lillian, who ambled through the crowd wide-eyed. Ricky scanned the area, spotted Ana and Rachel and made a beeline for them.

'It's fine, honestly. I'll just stick to the edges for now.'

'Okay. But if you change your mind...'

'Then I can make my own way back. Don't worry about me. Have a good time, okay?'

'I'm glad you came,' said Rachel. Ana smiled back, embarrassed. Rachel wandered off in the direction of the bar, where the drinks were served in small buckets like in a London hipster joint, the kind where food arrived on surgical trays and you ate peanuts out of a slipper.

Ana settled back against the wall of a dilapidated cabin that doubled as a body painting and henna tattoo area. An endless queue stretched around the corner and out of Ana's line of vision. Most people wore the requisite matching neon vests with slogans that made little sense. *'Same, same'* was the most common, whatever that meant. It reminded her of the t-shirts she would see at the local market back home; ones with *'Same shit, different day'* or *'FBI: Female Body Inspector'* written on them in Comic Sans. She had always wondered who bought those awful things, but now she figured they must be the UK's biggest export to Thailand.

'First impressions?' she asked Ricky.

'I fucking hate it.'

Surprised, Ana laughed, though it came out as more of a snort. She hoped the music had drowned out the sound.

They waited in silence as a circle formed around a man standing in the middle of the sand. He produced a long rope from a tub of gasoline, held up a flame to it and the whole thing ignited with a whoosh. Ana flinched. He snaked it around the sand like a burning serpent, entreating the assembled mob to back off slightly. When there was enough space, he spun the rope, first over his head and then in circles around his body, showering the crowd with sparks. Ana hoped the cheap neon vests were not as flammable as they looked.

Actually, would that be so bad?

Uninvited, a young woman shimmied her way over the sand and began to dance beneath the rope, tiny embers cascading over her body. This whipped the crowd up even more, and soon a familiar chant had begun.

'Get your tits out, get your tits out, get your tits out for the lads!'

Wow, thought Ana. *It's like I never left home.*

Unlike back home though, the chant seemed to work. It's amazing the things people will do when they're on holiday and don't have to face the consequences.

The girl began gyrating madly, sticking her arse out and shaking it, urging the crowd to chant some more, lifting her shirt up past her navel, dropping it back down, lifting it higher. It was like being at a strip club, except nobody was getting paid and the biggest danger was a different type of burning sensation. The man with the rope spun the flaming cord, and as the chant reached its apotheosis, the girl tore the shirt over her head and dropped to her knees in the sand, undulating wildly, as the crowd (mostly men, but some women too) roared their approval.

'Suddenly I feel overdressed,' said Ana. Ricky tore his eyes away from the topless dancing with some effort.

'If you want to join her, I'd be happy to hold your clothes for you.'

'I'm sure you would. Thing is, she's about eighteen and bounces in all the right places. When I move, it's more than just my tits that wobble. I wouldn't want to have put anyone through that.'

'I wouldn't mind,' squeaked Ricky, his voice breaking mid-sentence.

Ana shook her head, amused, as the same insistent techno beat that had played since they arrived came to a merciful end, only to be replaced by one that sounded exactly the same. It was the lift muzak from Hell.

Rachel arrived with the drinks and saw Ana's glum expression. 'There it is,' she said. 'The face where smiles go to die.'

'I'm having the time of my life,' said Ana, her stony expression unchanging. 'Can't you tell?'

'Shut up and drink this.'

Ana picked up the glass, a toxic green liquid sloshing about inside.

'Herbert West called. He want's his reagent back,' she said. No one got the reference and she immediately regretted it, mentally adding it to her *List of Mildly Embarrassing Moments*. She wondered how many hours of sleep she would lose thinking about this one.

'It's very...green. What is it?'

'Inexpensive.'

'That's not what I meant.'

Ana looked back at the man with the rope, the girl still writhing beneath him. She tugged the string of her bikini bottoms and they slipped off, the crowd roaring its approval as she got on her hands and knees and shook her bare arse for them.

Ana downed the drink, gagging on the acrid aftertaste, her throat burning. She looked to Ricky but he was distracted by the impromptu All Nude Revue. She couldn't blame him, the girl had a great body. Still, the joke was on her. She'd be picking sand out of her vagina for weeks.

She downed Ricky's drink. The sooner she got steaming, the better.

It didn't take long.

~

'Where's the DJ? I need a word,' said Ana, her words slurred. It came out as, 'wessa deeshay? Ah needa wurr.' She leaned into Ricky, resting her head against him.

'Why?'

'Rach, you promised me a "wide variety of music",' she said, pointing dramatically at her sister. 'Your words, not mine. So far all I've heard is this techno shit, *dun dun dun dun* all night.' She emphasised the point by pounding the table with each *dun*, the empty glasses bouncing with each strike, threatening to topple.

'Not true,' said Rachel, matching Ana slur for slur. 'At the start, they were playing *house*. Then, techno. This is more...rave.'

Ana sipped from the bucket. 'They all sound the same.'

'There's a reggae tent down the beach,' suggested Ricky, prompting Ana to splash some of her drink at him.

'Hey! I guess you guys are too *old* to appreciate good music.'

Rachel cocked an eyebrow. 'Hey Ana, did he just play the *old* card?'

'I think he did.' Ana stared straight at Ricky and said in her huskiest voice, 'And to think I was going to *fuck* you.' She shook her head as Ricky choked on his drink.

'How old are you anyway?' asked Rachel. 'You look about seventeen.'

'Actually, I'm twenty-one.' He paused in an attempt at dramatic effect. 'I'm twenty-one today.' And then, just in case they still didn't get it (they both did), 'It's my birthday.'

Ana was first to speak. 'Well Ricky, first of all, thank you for explaining how birthdays work.'

'And second, happy birthday!' said Rachel. 'That's it, a round of shots, and then we dance!'

'There's no amount of shots in the world will make *me*

dance,' said Ana, but Rachel wasn't listening. She got unsteadily to her feet, holding onto the back of Ana's chair for balance.

'Woah. I'm pretty wasted.' She reached down the top of her dress and hooked a handful of Thai Baht out of her bra. She noticed Ricky staring at her breasts as she did so, and handed the bills to him. 'You. Get the shots,' she commanded, slumping back down into her chair.

Ricky scurried off towards the bar, leaving the sisters alone for the first time since the hostel. Josh and Lillian were off dancing and Paul was somewhere, though no one knew where. It didn't matter, they could locate him with their phones if they needed to.

Or wanted to.

Rachel leaned in close.

'He likes you.'

'He likes your tits. Been checking them out all night.'

'He's a guy, he likes tits. Doesn't matter whose. Mine are more on show, that's all.'

'I guess. But Rach, he's twenty-one.'

'Yeah, but you're only twenty-seven.'

Ana considered. 'I think I'm twenty-eight.'

'Oh yeah.' There was a moments contemplation. 'He still likes you.'

The girls giggled.

'It would be one hell of a twenty-first birthday present,' cackled Ana.

'What would?' said Ricky, gingerly laying down a tray of shots on the table. As expected, he found no answers, only laughter.

Rachel raised a glass, and the others followed suit.

'Happy birthday Ricky. You'll get your present later,' she said, winking theatrically at Ana.

Ana started to say something, but Rachel quickly cut her off.

'To Ricky!' She downed the shot.

'To Ricky.'

'To me.'

The drinks were soon gone, but there were many more to come.

The night was just beginning.

Lights.

Music.

Dancing.

Drinking.

After a while it all blurred into one indivisible whole.

Ana let go, shedding her inhibitions, no longer in control of her mind or body. Time slipped by, drifting out to sea on a tide of unrelenting techno. The colours morphed, changed, the strobe light turning everything into jerky slow motion. Her own arms moved in front of her, above her head, but she didn't recognise them. She told Rachel she loved her and Rachel told her she loved her too. She was thirsty, but nothing satisfied. She noticed that when people danced, their limbs left a trail behind them. How odd never to have noticed that! Her eyelids were heavy, but sleep would be impossible. Her heart raced. She vomited. It made her feel better. Someone held her hair - Rachel or Ricky? Maybe Lillian? She took a drink of bright green liquid and gulped it down. She told Rachel she loved her and Rachel told her she loved her too. They met a group. More drinks. Someone offered her a pill. She refused, unaware she had already taken one. One minute she was dancing. Then she would blink and be at the bar, Ricky beside her. 'You remind me of a puppy,' she told him, but he didn't understand. Later, she stood by a tree and watched the sea roll in, the waves forming ethereal images. They frightened her. She felt like she had been here before, or would be here again. She considered wading in but was afraid that the tide would carry her out. How long had she been standing there? Rachel found her and Ana told her she loved her and Rachel told her she loved her too. They rejoined the party. No one knew where to find Paul. They walked along the beach and lay in the sand to watch the stars. Someone had a wild idea. Time marched on.

Lights.
Music.
Dancing.
Drinking.
Repeat to fade.

5

'WHAT...THE...FUCK.'

Disorientated, Paul lifted his head, wiping grains of sand from his dry lips. He rubbed his temple and gazed out across the beach. It was morning, the woozy sun peeking up over the horizon, and so peaceful he could hear his dehydrated mouth click when it opened. He forced himself up like an ancient mummy rising from the grave and tottered forwards, feet sinking into the scorching sand. Head swooning, he found his way to the nearest stall. The owner, a middle-aged Thai woman with tired eyes, was packing up, the night's festivities having drawn to a close many hours before. Paul fished a crumpled note from his pocket and bought a Coke, making sure to collect his change. It was warm, but helped soothe his scratchy throat. He checked his other pockets, relieved to find his phone and wallet still there.

Miracles do happen!

He looked at his iPhone and soon wished he hadn't. Through the spiderwebs of the cracked screen, his iPhone displayed thirty-three missed calls from Rachel and seven from Ana. Oh boy, Rach was gonna be pissed. He tried to recall the last time he had seen her and couldn't. They had gotten a drink at the start, Ana trailing along behind them like the little lapdog she was, then he had gone to the toilets and found a pool hall. Well, a shed with two pool tables in it. He remembered some English cunt challenging him to a game. That was the initial catalyst. A small bet. Paul, a sucker for a wager, particularly one he knew he could win, hustled that poor fucker for everything he owned. He had been unstoppable, and when some snot-nosed American kid started bad-mouthing him, Paul bet his winnings on a best-of-three. He threw the first game, letting the confidence go to the kid's head, and slammed all his money on the table. The kid failed to match his bet, so Paul made him a different offer and the dumb bastard took him up on it.

Paul, of course, won the next two games with ease. The kid looked crestfallen, *devastated*, but his girlfriend didn't seem to mind.

Paul looked back over his shoulder to the tree where he had woken up. The girl lay there still, snoring gently, her bare breasts rising and falling, an imprint of his body on the sand next to her. Paul admired her naked, sun-dappled form. She had been one hell of a prize. He wondered where her clothes were.

'Shit,' he muttered under his breath. He considered listening to the myriad voicemails, instead opening the Tracker app.

Not again, Paul, he thought, staring at the sleeping girl he had spent the night with, her legs splayed out in a most undignified fashion, giving him quite the view.

Not again.

He tried to be faithful to Rachel. He really did. But what guy in his situation wouldn't have done the same thing?

Rachel was cute, and she was great in bed, but sometimes a man wanted a little more, a bit of variety. He cast his mind back to last night, as he and — Christ, he didn't even know her name — had fucked in the sand, surrounded by hundreds of laughing partygoers, most holding up phones, snapping photos and filming them. He remembered taking her from behind, smacking her ass with his bare hand as she ground her hips into him and he yanked on her hair, the cheers from the assembled throng music to his ears.

Had the videos hit YouTube already? That'd be a great thing for Rachel to see, her own boyfriend in a live sex-show on the beach. At the time it had been exciting.

Actually, it still was. He decided to find the video later, to see if it was as good as he remembered. He wondered if the nameless girl would be as cool about it as he was. Kinky bitch had been pretty wasted. Her boyfriend would get quite a shock too, no doubt. The idea made Paul smile.

Sorry, Rach. A man's gotta do what a man's gotta do.

Checking the Tracker, he saw there was a signal coming from further up the beach, identified by the initials AL. Ana Logan. Funny that Rachel's initials weren't registering. No matter. He took a last look at the girl, dusted the sand off his shorts and followed the signal, leaving her naked and alone in the shade of the palm tree. As he stumbled along the beach, he decided to tell Rachel the truth about where he had been all night.

Hustling people at pool.

He had the money to prove it, several thousand Baht, however much *that* even was. The whole winning-a-girl-friend/live-sex-show thing he would skip. She didn't need to know every damn detail. After all, what's a relationship without a few secrets?

Paul stepped over a young guy lying prone on the sand,

one of many sleeping off last night's wanton debauchery, curled up on the beach like bodies washed ashore from a shipwreck, their skin visibly blistering under the intense glare of the sun. Plastic bottles and buckets littered the sand along with countless items of clothing, the waves slowly encroaching on them. Soon they would be swept out to sea forever, to fulfil their ultimate destiny of choking a dolphin to death. The smell of frying meat sizzled in the air and Paul felt his stomach grumble. He licked his lips. It would have to wait. He had to find Rachel soon before she went totally radge at him.

According to the app they were much further down the beach. The sun was low, casting long shadows across the sand. He rubbed his bleary eyes. The hangover was bad, but not apocalyptic. His balls ached more than his head, but that wasn't the drink's fault.

As he walked, the beach got more and more deserted until finally the stalls came to an end, giving way to the thick jungle that ran parallel. They must have walked some distance from the main body of the party, probably to get some sleep. Why hadn't they just gone back to the hostel?

Mind you, why hadn't he?

What if Rachel hooked up with some guy? The idea infuriated him.

She'd better fucking not have.

Paul wasn't normally a violent man, but he was possessive. And if Rachel thought she could get away with banging some arsehole behind his back...

The golden sand curved all the way to the horizon. There were several sets of footprints leading down the beach. He shielded his eyes from the sun and felt the sweat dripping down his brow. If only he'd bought a second Coke, or even a beer. Hair of the dog, and all that shite. In the distance a silhouetted figure wandered the beach. Paul sped up, found running in sand to be a lot more difficult than Rocky Balboa made it look, and slowed when he saw it was a wiry old Thai man in a turquoise tracksuit.

Here the footprints ended in a pile of discarded clothes, bags and sunglasses.

Paul checked the app; he should be right on top of them.

The Thai man smiled at him and went back about his business, which was either tidying up or stealing the abandoned garments. Paul didn't give a shit either way, so he opened his Contacts and called Ana. The strains of ELO's *Sweet Talkin' Woman* emanated from the pile of clothes in front of him and the old man dashed forwards and grabbed the yellow dress with the dinosaur print, rummaging in the pockets.

'Hey, that's mine,' said Paul wearily. Not a morning person at the best of times, today he wanted as little human interaction as possible.

The man took the phone from a pocket in the dress and answered it.

'Hello?' he said, then chattered excitedly in Thai.

'What are you doing?' asked a dumbfounded Paul. The man held up a palm as if to say, *Wait, I have to take this, it's Tokyo and the deal's gone through*. Paul put his own device to his ear. 'Give me the phone you stupid old bastard,' he said into the mic, listening to the man's voice through the crackly speaker.

The man turned to walk away and Paul strode forwards and shoved him. He landed on his back in the sand and Paul wrenched the phone from his surprisingly strong hands.

The man shouted something in Thai, picked up as much of the loose clothing as his arms would allow and scuttled away. Paul let him. He recognised the print on Ana's dress —

those stupid, childish dinosaurs — but couldn't recall what Rachel had been wearing.

If she was dumb enough to take her clothes off and leave them, then she can bloody well walk home naked.

Ana's phone had a picture of her and Rachel posing in front of a golden Buddha on the lock screen. Paul had taken it only yesterday on the neighbouring island of Koh Samui. He saw Rachel's smiling face and felt a momentary pang of disgust. Then he ran his hands through his hair and quickly got over it. More footprints led away from the abandoned clothes and into the sea. It took Paul a while to do the maths.

Oh shit, they must have gone skinny dipping!

Man, he wouldn't have minded seeing that. Particularly if Lillian was there too. He chuckled to himself, realising he had just let some old bastard run off with all their clothes.

There was something odd about it though; there were no footprints leading back out of the water. He looked left and right, scanning the beach but the only other set of tracks belonged to the old man.

The smile died on his face. Had they drowned? He checked the app again. No sign of Rachel's signal. He pinched the screen and zoomed out, widening the map until it covered the whole island. Still nothing. Heart beating faster, he tried again and found her.

A flashing symbol surrounded by blue, the letters RL above it. He sighed. She was okay. Thank fuck for that.

But two questions remained; what was she doing out in the middle of the Gulf of Thailand, and who the fuck was she with?

6

IN HER DREAM, ANA WAS BACK IN THE BATHROOM OF HER mum's cosy Edinburgh flat. It looked nothing like the actual bathroom, but she knew it was nonetheless. She stood naked by the sink, the strains of classical music from the radio leaking through the thin walls.

Mahler's Requiem.

It would be fitting, if it wasn't such typical grandiose dream bullshit. In reality, it had been Ariana Grande or one of those interchangeable pop muppets that had been playing over the tinny speakers. But dreams thrive on drama, so Mahler it was.

Whatever.

She had spent the day sorting through her mother's belongings, looking for information on the funeral that her mum had pre-bought back when Ana's father had died. She arranged an appointment with the funeral director, found the address of the registry office to inform them of the death, and fended off endless phone calls from both well-meaning friends and morbidly curious distant relatives.

The only person who hadn't called had been Rachel.

With the administration of death out of the way, she lounged by the fire in her mother's old easy chair and flicked through photo albums she had found tucked under the bed. Birthdays, holidays, trips to the park and the zoo and the beach. She tossed the album aside, the faded photos making her feel like her mum had been dead for years already.

She sat by the window, watching the world carrying on as if everything was normal. There was Mr Lang mowing the lawn for the third time that month, and old Mrs Croft gossiping with a neighbour she didn't recognise. A kid rolled by on a BMX, popping a wheelie, seemingly unaware that one day he and everyone he knows will be dead.

Ana laughed bitterly and texted Rachel again.

The voices rose in her head, speaking dark and terrible things in a primitive language. They were always there these days. Sometimes they spoke in respectful silence, but recently they were getting louder, more boisterous. If only she could understand what they said.

What they wanted.

Unable to think, she staggered to the pantry and slammed two paracetamol down her throat. It was a token gesture. The voices were here to stay. She leaned her forehead against the wall for a moment, dragging her nails down the wood-chip, one of them snapping off, leaving the soft flesh exposed and bloody. She never noticed. She drew her head back then rammed it forwards into the wall. Her body juddered and her legs buckled but it didn't help so she tried again. Still the voices called to her, hissing in serpentine tones.

'*Ana.*'

This voice she recognised, knew all-too-well. Her mother.

Her dear, dead mother.

'You're not my mum,' she said. 'I don't know what you are or what you want, but you have to leave me alone.'

A thousand voices, laughing all at once. Ana braced herself. If she felt a hand on her shoulder, she would surely go mad.

But aren't you already?

Now she stood facing herself in the bathroom mirror, her clothes neatly folded on the laundry basket, razor blade in hand. She could smell the gin on her breath as it fogged the medicine cabinet mirror.

Her arms itched so she scratched at them, harder and harder until the skin burst and her nails dug into muscle. She saw her forearms pulsing, something squirming beneath the surface. She took the loose flap of tissue between her fingers and peeled it back over her arm, removing the skin like a glove. Her forearm muscle parted and a spider crawled out, then another, and another. Ana slapped at her arm in terror, unable to scream. She gagged as something came up her throat.

It wasn't vomit though; it was something much, much worse.

She heard a splashing sound from the sink and looked down to see blood gushing from her wrist and splattering the white ceramic like a Rorschach test pattern, the silver blade catching the light. There were no spiders. She swapped hands and drew it down her other forearm, wrist to elbow, the most effective way to guarantee death. She was numb to the pain by now. She tried to swap hands again but the razor clattered uselessly into the sink as she fell back against the wall and slid down. A fat-bodied spider forced its way out of her mouth, dropping to the floor in front of her and scurrying towards the bathtub, leaving a trail of blood — *her* blood — across the tiles.

Ana raised her arms. They were crawling with arachnids, biting and rending flesh from bone.

Blood continued to flow from the gaping wounds in her arms, spraying her nude body. Her legs were leaden.

She heard a key in the lock and thought that her mother wasn't actually dead, it had all been a sick cosmic joke that she had fallen for, haha lol jks u got me gud xoxo.

The bathroom door started to open, a thin crack of red light emanating from within. A dark shape appeared and she looked away, back down at her wrists, at the bloated, corpulent spiders erupting from the gashes in her arms.

Oh, they're back, she thought as her consciousness ebbed like the moonlit tide.

'Ana,' said a familiar voice, and then the dream ended, just as it had in real life, with Rachel coming home, hopeful that her old key would still let her in, pretty sure that the lock would remain unchanged, not expecting to find her sister bleeding to death on the chilly tiles of the bathroom floor.

When Ana woke she thought she was dying.

She was curled into a ball, trying to stem the rising tide of nausea that threatened to drown her, her head throbbing, limbs aching. A headache enveloped her entire cranium, starting from the top of her spine and spreading out to her eyes like a demonic hand holding her head underwater.

The room swayed, so she kept her eyes tightly shut, hoping to fall back into the warm embrace of sleep until it had all gone away. She dimly recalled the dream and checked her arms, her scars, held her palms to them to make sure they were okay, that there was nothing else...*in* there.

Her pulse gradually slowed as she relaxed.

It was just a dream, a stupid dream. An exceptionally vivid and awful dream, but a dream nonetheless. Harmless. Not like the ones she used to have.

Just a dream.

And now she was awake and at home in bed, where nothing could hurt her.

Then she remembered that she wasn't home.

Her flat was thousands of miles away, and she was in Thailand with her sister. Vague memories of the previous night danced through her subconscious, making hazy suggestions without fully committing to an answer.

The nightmare faded back into her subconscious.

Against her better judgement, Ana's eyes flickered open.

She had no idea where she was.

Shit. Fuck shit fuck.

A boxy little room, sparsely furnished. She lay on a single mattress strewn across the floor. Bright morning-light streamed in through a round window, illuminating a pin-up calendar, the date of which read May 1995. The portrait was of a young Thai girl smiling demurely, her hands covering both breasts, eyes vacant and dead. A wooden ashtray lay in the corner, overflowing with pungent cigarette butts.

'Morning,' said a groggy voice next to her.

Ana would have screamed if she hadn't felt so utterly wretched. Instead, she slowly turned her head towards the source.

Ricky. He lay beside her under a flimsy red blanket, eyes half closed, resting his head on one hand like he thought he was Cleopatra or something.

Ana closed her eyes but the room kept spinning. No, not spinning but *rocking*. A gentle but insistent rocking like they were...

'No fucking way,' croaked Ana. Sickness crept up from her stomach (*a spider it's a spider*) and she fought it off, rising on unsteady legs. She looked out the window at the vast expanse of ocean that spread out all around. She was on a boat. A fucking *boat*.

Correction; *they* were on a boat. Her and Ricky. Where was Rachel? What even *happened* last night? Ricky propped himself up and looked at her oddly, like she was a strange sea creature in an aquarium, and Ana realised she was standing in her bra and panties, her nipples visible through the semi-transparent lace.

'Fuck, don't look,' she cried, dropping to her knees and wrapping one arm over her breasts, the other shielding her crotch. The sudden movement made her retch and Ricky pointed to the corner, uttering the magic word.

'Bathroom.'

Ana suddenly didn't care about her state of undress; there were more important matters to deal with. She crashed through the thin wooden door and vomited. The room swam woozily as her guts threatened to spill out through her mouth, the dull hammer blows in her temple rising to an apex of pain, the bitter taste of last night's wine coating the interior of her mouth.

Satisfied there was nothing left to come up — at least, not for now — Ana wiped the spittle and stomach acids from her chin and stumbled back into the small room where Ricky lay.

With that excitement over, she became conscious of her clothing situation again. Ana shrank into the corner, using her arms to cover her navy blue underwear.

'Where are my clothes?' she said, though it came out as more of a sigh. She was too tired and unwell to be as humiliated as she thought she should be.

Ricky looked like how she felt, his blonde hair plastered to his forehead with sweat, the light from the window turning his eyes into black pools. He seemed to take an eternity to answer, and Ana slipped down into a crouch to hide her body from his gaze, though she couldn't be sure he was looking at her.

'Don't you remember?' he said at last, each word garbling into the last like syllables had gone out of fashion overnight.

Ana's heart thumped miserably in her chest. She felt anger rising, anger at Ricky and his stupid questions, anger at herself for even being in this situation.

'Remember...what?'

Again the seconds turned to minutes as Ricky considered his response, Ana feeling more and more exposed as the time dragged on. Her skimpy underwear covered so little of her, she may as well be naked. She cursed herself for wearing it. Why couldn't she have put on her usual tummy-tuck knickers? They had served her well so far this holiday.

'Last night,' he finally said, like it was the dumbest question he'd ever heard.

Well guess what asshole, here comes an even dumber one.

'What. Happened. Last. Night?' said Ana, spitting out the words like salt water.

Ricky must have sensed her frustration. Was he taking pleasure in it?

'We took them off. When we swam for the boat. Remember?'

Ana shook her head dully, recalling none of this. Ricky regarded her like she was an idiot.

'What's the last thing you remember?'

Ana thought hard, but her brain felt like it had been involved in a twelve car pile-up. 'Your birthday,' she said, as the first piece of the puzzle was put in place. 'Aye, your birthday. We did shots. Then I think we danced. After that... almost nothing.'

'Wow. Okay, you missed a lot. Well...'

Ana shushed him. 'First things first.' She shivered, glancing down at her underwear. 'Did we...' She didn't need to finish the sentence, unless Ricky was even more of a dingbat than she suspected.

'No. No we didn't. We just ended up in here together. But nothing happened, I swear. I mean, you were pretty out of it...'

'Aye, no shit Sherlock.' Ana's body shook slightly, from cold or nerves or fear, she wasn't sure. Without warning, salty tears ran down her face. She instinctively made her way towards the mattress, wrapping herself in the sheet that had covered them as they slept.

But not together, she reminded herself.

'Hey, it's okay,' said Ricky, who had never been good at consoling crying women. This was obvious to Ana, who thought he was one step away from patting her on the head and saying, 'There, there.' She sat huddled in the sheet, leaving Ricky crouching in his baggy grey boxers and voluminous yellow neon vest.

'You look ridiculous,' she said.

'Yeah, whereas you're dressed for tea with the Queen.'

She forced a smile.

'Where's my sister?'

'Upstairs, I think.'

'She's here?'

'Yeah. They all are.' Ricky exhaled through his teeth. 'You really don't remember, do you?'

But Ana was already rushing towards the toilet, the gorge rising in her throat.

Rachel would just have to wait a minute.

There were more pressing matters to attend to.

It was with great effort that Ana managed to wrap her body in the red sheet and climb the five stairs that led to the deck of the boat. Every limb screamed in protest, her eyes struggling to focus. This was unlike any hangover she had ever experienced.

But it wasn't just a hangover, was it, her mind screamed at her. *You've been drugged. Roofied.*

No. She didn't know that. Not for sure, anyway.

She'd been careful all night, buying her own drinks, or at least letting Rachel buy them.

Rachel.

No. She wouldn't have.

Would she?

Rachel knew that Ana wouldn't enjoy herself at that party. And Ana knew that Rachel took drugs recreationally. Or at least, she assumed she did. Was it so hard to believe that Rachel would have slipped something into one of her drinks? The old Rachel, the one Ana had grown up with, wouldn't have done that. But did she even really know her sister anymore?

Of course she did. Rach would never do that to her.

Probably.

Maybe.

Ana forced open the wooden hatch and the sea breeze

jolted her. They were on the ocean alright. Fucking hell, were they ever. There was nothing but water, the waves surging all the way to the horizon.

The sky was the bluest thing she had ever seen and that omnipresent sun winked down at her, making her squint. She shielded her eyes and looked for a familiar face.

The boat was bigger than expected, one of those tour ships done up to look like an old Chinese junk. It must have been about fifty foot long, with a great wooden mast dead in the centre, the white sail furled. There were others on the boat too, their bodies strewn across the deck like discarded dolls.

'Ana!'

She turned to find Rachel shuffling towards her, her hair blowing freely across her face, wearing nothing but her polka dot underwear and the waterproof armband, her phone safely tucked inside. They embraced, sinking into each other's arms. Ana had rarely been so glad to see her sister. As they held each other Ana became dimly aware of other presences, but the only one that mattered right now was Rachel.

'Hey, you trying to kill me?' she said. Ana relinquished her grip, but only slightly.

'Sorry. It's just nice to see you.' She noticed Rachel had been crying.

'Paul's not here.'

'Have you checked your phone?'

She nodded. 'His phone is back on the island, but I've no signal and I'm low on battery. How about you?'

'I don't think I have it with me. Or my purse. Rach, I don't remember anything. Why are we on a boat in our fucking knickers?'

'You too?'

Ana nodded sheepishly, hugging the red sheet tighter around her. Rachel pulled at it.

'Let's see.'

'No! Fuck off!' said Ana, gripping tightly onto the blanket, but she had never been a match for her sister, who easily wrestled it off her, exposing Ana's pale flesh to the harsh Thai sun. As Rachel laughed, Ana grabbed the sheet back and covered her body. 'What did you do that for? Are you fucking high?'

A new voice spoke up.

'Mellow out, babe. We've all got bodies. We're all *one*, and we're all beautiful in the eyes of nature.'

Ana breathed deeply.

Oh good, Lillian's here. Can this day get any better?

'Aye, cheers pal,' said Ana, feeling worse for seeing Lillian's perfect body, making her own milk-bottle white complexion and chubby arse stand out even more.

'Here, if it makes you feel less self conscious...'

Lillian unhooked her bikini top and let it fall to the deck, baring her tanned breasts and standing unashamed as if this was a totally normal thing to do.

Ana was speechless and Rachel tried her best to fill the gap.

'Emmmm, you *really* don't need to do that.'

Lillian flashed them a smile that would have made Tom Cruise green with envy. 'No problem guys.' She raised two fingers at them in the international gesture for peace and sauntered back over to Josh, who looked like an 80s porn star in his skimpy black briefs.

Rachel squeezed her sister's arm. It was a subtle gesture the two of them had shared since childhood, meaning *did you see that?*

'Did she just flash us the 'peace' sign?'

'I'm more concerned with what else she flashed us,' said Ana.

With that, the two girls dissolved into a fit of exhausted giggles, content in the knowledge that no matter what had come between them, at least they still shared that uniquely Scottish misanthropy.

Sometimes, it's the little things that matter.

Ana took Rachel's hand. 'Don't worry about Paul, he'll be fine. You sure he's not on board?'

'Definite. It's just me, you and Ricky, Josh and Lill, and these three Aussies we apparently met last night.'

'You don't remember it either?'

Rach sighed. 'Not really. I think I remember someone pointing out a boat, and we decided to swim out to it. That's why we all took our clothes off.'

'Shit. How are we gonna get back without clothes, money or phones?'

'I don't know.'

They sat a moment, looking out to sea, the sun sending golden sparkles cascading across the water.

'Rach, I think we were drugged.'

'Oh, for sure. No doubt. This is no ordinary hangover. I feel like hammered shite.'

'I'm glad it's not just me. What are we going to do?'

Rachel shrugged. 'Do you think that Paul will find my signal?'

'Maybe.' She saw the disappointment in Rachel's face and changed her tone. 'Of course he will. Pretty soon he's going to parachute in from a helicopter like Rambo or something and be all like, "Come on girls, I'm taking you home!"'

'That sounds about right,' said Rachel, a little smile creeping into the corner of her lips.

Ana saw Rachel was staring at something. She looked

down and saw her bare arms were exposed, the thin white lines running from wrist to elbow. She quickly stuffed her arms back inside the red sheet and stared out to sea.

'I'm sorry Ana...'

'It's okay. I sometimes forget they're there, you know. Sometimes.'

That was a lie. As if she could ever forget the day she tried to take her own life.

'Come on, let's go and see the others. We can get some sunbathing done while we wait for Paul to rescue us. Like you say, he's probably on his way right now.'

Ana faced her sister and smiled softly. 'Yeah, you're probably right. Let's try to make the best of this. At least we can get a good anecdote out of it, right?'

'Right,' agreed Rachel, but she didn't sound convinced. She just wanted Paul.

She hoped he was safe.

7

'SO...DOES ANYONE KNOW WHERE THE FUCK WE ARE?'

Rachel's question hung in the air like a bad smell, no one eager to acknowledge it. They sat in a circle on the deck, the boat bobbing and swaying without clear direction, the mast creaking ominously.

There was Rachel and Ana and Ricky. Across from Ana sat Lillian, still topless, and Josh, still in his black underpants. They pawed at each other, seemingly unable to help themselves and not caring who saw. Ana had donned Ricky's yellow vest, which he had so *gallantly* given to her. It didn't cover much, but it did make her feel less self conscious. She crossed her arms to hide her scars and tugged the hem down over her crotch.

Across from her sat the Aussies; Darren, Bret and Lisa. These three seemed to be old friends the way they carried on, the gravity of the situation apparently lost on them. They, like everyone else, were clad only in their underwear.

'We are...exactly where we are,' smiled Lillian in answer to Rachel's question.

'Okay, that's really fucking helpful,' said Rachel, unwittingly echoing her sister's thoughts.

Josh stepped in. 'It's true. It doesn't matter *where* we are, as long as we just *are*.'

Rachel decided not to pursue this dead-end line of questioning.

'Right. Anyone have anything useful to add? Like what we're all doing on this boat?'

'Well, I remember it,' said Ricky, somehow now one of the most sensible voices onboard. 'Not in detail, but bits, y'know. We were all partying, drinking shots, dancing and stuff. We broke off from the main beach, looking for somewhere to make the party a bit more,' he searched for the right word, '...private.'

'Aw, I remember that!' Said Darren in an Australian accent, his curly black hair hanging over his face. All eyes fell on him, waiting for more. 'Ah, that's all guys. I just remember it. That's all.'

Ricky nodded slowly. 'Oka-a-ay. So we spotted this boat, took our clothes off and swam to it. There was a fridge full of alcohol, and that's where it ends for me, I guess.'

'So how did we get *here*?' asked Ana. 'In the middle of the fucking ocean, I mean.'

Bret raised his hand sheepishly. 'That was us, I think,' he said, gesturing at Darren and Lisa. 'We *defo* raised the anchor.'

'Yeah,' agreed Darren.

'But we couldn't find any keys.'

'No,' said Lisa.

'So this mad fucker hot-wired the *shit* out of it!' said Bret, pointing at Darren, who suddenly remembered.

'I did! I *did*!' The two of them high fived.

'And now we're lost at sea. Nice going,' said Ana, getting

up and going to sit in the shade. Her pale Scottish skin wouldn't last five minutes under the blistering sunshine. She wished for sun-screen. Maybe there was some on the boat?

'What's her deal? Panties on too tight?'

'Fuck off, Darren,' said Rachel, joining her sister.

'I reckon they are,' he continued. 'They're halfway up her bum!'

'Would everyone just chillax,' said Josh. 'We're on a *journey*. We're *meant* to be here, *together*.' Josh had a maddening way of overemphasising certain words that drove Ana crazy. She took Rachel's hand, her cheeks burning in embarrassment at Darren's comments.

'Rach,' she whispered conspiratorially.

'Yeah?'

'I can't deal with this.'

'Me neither. It's like a bad reality TV show.'

'Which one would you make walk the plank first?'

Rachel thought carefully. 'Lillian. Earth Mother. If she comes out with one more piece of cosmic bollocks...'

'I'd make Josh go last, 'cos he's the only one who's under-wear is skimpier than mine.'

Rachel agreed. 'You really can see everything, can't you? Every vein, every hair...'

'Stop it!' laughed Ana. She didn't want to think about Josh's dick right now. She felt sick enough as it is.

'Those other three don't seem much better,' said Rachel.

'What, the Aussies?'

'Yeah. Mr Misogyny 2018 and the other two.'

Ana laughed, though it hurt her head to do so. She thought she might still be under the influence of last night's libations. 'At least they're normal, I guess. What're their names?'

'Darren, Bret and Lisa, I think. The girl doesn't talk much.'

'Small mercies, I suppose.'

Overhead the unyielding sun continued to rise, the water lapping at the side of the boat. Apart from that, everything was still. The engine had cut out hours ago, either due to lack of fuel or Darren fucking something up when he hot-wired it.

They needed a plan, even just to stave off the boredom.

'Has anyone searched the boat yet?' asked Ana, loud enough for most of the occupants to hear.

'We did,' said Darren as he lay dozing beneath the shadow of the sail. 'But then we found the booze stash and stopped.' He raised a beer at her. 'Want one?'

The thought of drinking — of ever drinking again — curdled Ana's stomach.

'No, that's the last thing on Earth any of us need right now.'

'Speak for yourself,' said Darren, popping the cap with his teeth and glugging the amber liquid down.

'Ana's right,' said Ricky, standing up to create the illusion of importance. 'We should check the boat and gather together all the supplies. Look, I hate to say it, but we've no idea how long we'll be stranded out here. We may need to ration things so that we don't run out.'

Darren shrugged. 'Okay boss. We'll search above deck, you guys check below. How's that sound?'

'Sounds good,' said Ana, already heading down the ramshackle steps below deck, Rachel following close behind. She took Ana's arm.

'You don't really think we could be stuck out here, do you?'

Ana did, but thought it best not to say. 'Of course not. Paul will have the coast guard searching for us already.'

Rachel smiled. 'Yeah.' Then, more definitively, 'Yeah.'

'Come on, let's get looking. And take your time. The longer we're away from those arseholes, the better.'

Lisa leaned back against Darren.

'You got any joints?' she asked.

'Nah. Must've left them on the beach. You not still high?'

She snuggled into the nook of his armpit. 'Little bit. I've got a pick-me-up for when we start coming down.'

'Good.'

She glanced over at Bret. He was snoring softly in the shade, his baseball cap pulled down over his eyes.

'It's like that film,' she said after a while.

'What one?' yawned Darren.

'You know. The one on the boat.'

'*Zombie Flesheaters*?'

She shook her head, her hair rubbing against Darren's chest. 'Nah, the Sam Neill one, where they're stuck on a boat with a maniac.'

Darren draped his arm over her shoulder. 'Ah, *Dead Calm*.'

'Yeah, that's the one. Wouldn't mind *him* coming to our rescue.'

'He's an *old* bastard now.'

Lisa considered this. 'Oh yeah. Well, maybe if he came from the future.'

'Then he'd be even older.'

Lisa nodded again. 'Oh yeah.'

She looked out across the deck. Josh and Lillian lay

entangled in each other's limbs, Josh passionately nuzzling on his girlfriend's neck, his hand on her bare breast. She saw him look over towards her and they briefly made eye contact. He smiled at her, then went back to Lillian. She could see his erection straining against his tight black underpants and he worked it loose with one hand.

'Hey look, they're fucking,' she said to Darren.

'Oh yeah,' he said, barely interested. 'Good for them.'

Lisa sighed and stretched and watched them, feeling nothing. The drugs had all but annihilated her sexual desire over the years. She knew Darren was a good looking guy, and under different circumstances they might have hooked up at least once in the last four years, but it had never happened and probably never would.

Not after that night.

It was six, maybe even seven years ago now. It hadn't been her first time — Lisa had lost her virginity age fifteen to her then boyfriend, Trev, and it had been terrible for different reasons. No, this was years later, a random hookup on a night out in Brisbane, before she had ever met Darren or Bret.

The guy was nice. A lot older than her, but sweet. Oh, and loaded. The drinks were on him all night, and he plied her with enough booze to kill an elephant. They snorted some lines in the loo and went out dancing. There, they snaffled some pingers and lost track of time. They retired to the guy's hotel room and snorted more lines, rubbing the residue on their gums, letting nothing go to waste.

The rest of the night she only remembered in elliptical flashes.

The man sliding her jeans down her legs.

His body pressed against hers, his face all sweaty.

The creeping sensation like a snake coiling into her guts.

Her own hand reaching for her bag as he fucked her, looking for something.

His red face buried between her breasts.

That thing inside of her.

The switchblade springing into life as she pressed the round silver button.

The surprise on his face as she cut it out of her.

Then there was the mess on the bed as she stood on the hotel balcony gazing out over the city, a half-smoked joint in one hand, a severed penis in the other, the face in the moon winking at her from the night sky.

She had woken up the next morning in her own bed, unsure of how she had found her way back, or if anything she remembered last night had even happened.

She stayed in bed all day, only getting up when her bladder could take it no more. By this point, she had convinced herself it was all a dream, the product of some pretty wild hallucinogens. She peed, then staggered naked through to the kitchen, where she hid her stash in a biscuit tin. As she stood by the breakfast bar rolling a joint, she noticed the smell. There was a brown paper bag on one of the wooden chairs. It was soaken wet, the red liquid seeping through onto the white cushion—

'Hey Lisa,' said Darren.

'Huh?' she replied.

'I said, should we search the boat? We told them we would.' He pressed a hand to her forehead. 'You okay? You're looking a little spacey.'

'I'm fine,' she said. She smiled at Darren to put him at ease. 'Just on a comedown I reckon.' She fished into her bra and pulled a small baggie of pills out.

'Want one?'

Darren said he did.

8

PAUL SLOGGED HIS WAY THROUGH THE SAND TOWARDS THE remnants of the Full Moon Party, the ceaseless heat prickling his bare skin. At this rate, he would either sweat his hangover out by lunchtime or die of dehydration. Most of the tourists and partygoers had gone back to their hostels by now. A few determined stragglers still danced in the sand, but the stalls were being packed away.

'Hey, anybody? I need the police,' he called out half-heartedly in a raspy voice.

Either no one heard him or cared to listen. He lumbered towards one of the stall-holders.

'Excuse me,' said Paul. The local smiled at him indifferently and walked away. 'Wait, please. I need your help. Police? Where can I find the police?'

The man shrugged and kept walking, eager to get away from this crazy white guy. Paul gave up, hoping to find someone more helpful. Sweat trickled down his back and he stole another Coke from the unmanned kiosk. The frozen can felt good in his hand and he rubbed it across his forehead.

'Won't somebody help me?' he shouted.

'Shut up,' called a voice from the beach.

'Trying to sleep,' said another.

'My friends have gone missing. I think they're in a boat out there…somewhere,' he said, his protestations falling on deaf ears. He looked out over the sea, then along the beach, past the prone bodies and the litter and the speaker system. There, through the haze of the sun, a pier shimmered in the distance like a mirage, at least a dozen boats of differing sizes moored to it.

A plan formed in Paul's sleep-deprived mind.

Rach was at sea. Ahead of him were some boats.

Rach.

Sea.

Boats.

Sure, he could get the police involved. They would send out a boat to find Rach and bring her back to the island. If he was lucky, they might let him tag along and revel in the second-hand glory.

However…

What if *he* was the one who rescued Rachel? Paul imagined himself as the captain of a vessel, navigating treacherous waters in pursuit of his woman. Just imagine her face when she saw him coming for her!

She'd be so grateful, and he would be a hero.

With any luck, he and Rachel would sail away and "accidentally" leave Ana behind.

The whingeing cow.

Realising who he really needed to speak to, he abandoned the Full Moon Party and headed off in the direction of the pier. He had to hurry. Time was of the essence.

That said, he was pretty hungry, so he stopped and bought some noodles and a beer, paying with his pool winnings. Feeling generous, he even left the woman a small tip, something he normally resented. He parked his arse down on the sand and slurped his noodles, eyeing up young ladies in thong bikinis as they staggered past.

With lunch out of the way, Paul resumed his journey, eventually reaching the long wooden walkway of the pier, the planks warped and twisted by the elements.

Several boats were docked, but most sat lifeless and empty. Tour boats, fishing boats, they were all deserted. He strolled casually along the pier, checking out each boat as he passed, wondering where everybody was. Could he steal one if necessary? The wooden beams creaked alarmingly beneath his feet, getting worse the further out he travelled. He spotted activity on the ship docked at the far end of the jetty and made a beeline for it, eager to get on board and out of the sun's harsh rays.

A young Thai man in shorts and a Beyonce tee shirt sat on the deck untangling fishing nets. He must have been about the same age as Paul, early thirties or so. An older gentleman reclined against the rails, smoking a cigarette and eyeing Paul warily. The younger man noticed the tourist and glanced up.

'Can I help you?' he said.

'You speak English? Thank God,' said Paul. He hated going to other countries and finding the locals didn't speak English.

Lazy bastards.

Uninvited, he stepped cautiously onto the deck. It was a good size, about thirty feet, twice the length of the others. It reminded Paul of the boat from *Jaws*, a film he hated; the special effects were just so unrealistic. The young man kept sorting through the nets, separating them and checking for rips or tears.

'My friends have disappeared. I think they may have stolen a boat, or been kidnapped. I need someone to take me out there after them.'

The old man barked something in Thai from the other end of the fishing boat. The young guy replied and Paul wondered if they were father and son. He turned back to Paul. 'Sorry, my friend. We're busy today. Fishing season. You understand.' He smiled and got back to work.

'I can pay you.'

He looked up. 'Not enough,' he said, still smiling.

Paul smiled back and pulled a wad of notes from his shorts pocket. His pool winnings. As Paul counted the notes out he saw the guy's eyes widen in disbelief. Sixteen-thousand Baht. According to Paul's calculations, that was approximately three-hundred and fifty pounds. He made that in a day back home, where he worked for a video games company. But to a Thai fisherman, it was the jackpot. The lottery.

The motherlode.

'Please wait here,' said the man, and he ran over to the older fellow. After a brief but animated discussion, the two of them came back to him. 'We can help you find your friends,' he said excitedly.

'Oh my God, thank you. Thank you!' Paul grinned. This was too easy.

'My name is Chakrit. This my uncle, Tan. He doesn't speak English. Doesn't have to deal with the tourists like I do.'

He held out his hand and Paul shook it eagerly.

'Paul.'

'Pleased to meet you, Mr Paul. Last night, someone stole old Prama's boat. He said there were eight or ten of them, all white, all in their underwear. That sound right?'

Paul shrugged. 'I guess so. I wasn't there. I was, uh, busy.'

Chakrit nodded. 'Okay. Well, we can sail out and head east. See what we find. But I tell you, the ocean is big. Very big, my friend. Maybe we won't find them.'

'Don't worry about that,' said Paul, a little too smugly. 'I'm tracking them.' He handed Chakrit his phone, pointing to the flashing dot on the little world map. Chakrit's eyes narrowed. He took the phone from Paul and showed it to the older man, who yelled something in Thai and stepped back, almost losing his balance, the colour draining from his face. He started shouting at Chakrit, then took the money from his pocket and thrust it back into Paul's chest, shaking his head.

'Hey, what's going on?' said Paul, as the old man held up the phone and pointed at the dot, ranting madly about something. 'What's he saying?'

Chakrit ignored Paul, shouting back at the old man. Paul scratched at the back of his neck and stared off into the distance, uncomfortable. His neck sizzled at the touch. After a while the conversation ended, the old man pocketing the money again and stalking off towards the navigation bridge.

Chakrit turned to Paul and smiled again. 'We find your friends.'

'What was all that about?' asked a bewildered Paul.

'My uncle. He's a good man, but like many Thai, he can be a superstitious fool.'

'Superstitious about what?'

Chakrit clapped Paul on the shoulder. 'Don't worry, my friend. Old stories.' He removed his Beyonce shirt and handed it to Paul, then started untying the rope that moored the boat to the dock.

'Put it on. You need it more than me,' laughed Chakrit, pointing at Paul's reddening skin.

Paul put the shirt on as the engine spluttered into life with a choking sound like someone strangling a robot, and soon the little wooden pier was fading into the distance. Through the window of the cockpit he watched the old man counting the cash again.

Money talks, thought Paul. *And luckily, it's bilingual.*

Something soft brushed past his leg and he recoiled, almost falling overboard. Chakrit grabbed his arm and pulled him back.

'Thanks,' said Paul, watching as a little pug dog scampered out from under his seat. It sat and stared at Paul, his big eyes framed by a wrinkled face.

'Don't mind Grub,' said Chakrit. 'He likes to know what's going on.'

Paul stared at the dog and the dog stared back at him. Grub yawned and wandered off to find some shade, resting his chin on his paws. Paul shook his head.

'I know the feeling, pal. I know the feeling.'

Chakrit lit a smoke and offered Paul one. He accepted, then looked at the old man, who left the cockpit and sat next to the pug, scratching his scruff. He spoke in Thai to Chakrit, who snorted and waved his hand dismissively.

That old guy looks really worried, thought Paul. *In fact, he looks scared out of his mind.*

'He okay?' asked Paul.

Chakrit grinned at him, the sun reflecting off his sweat-slicked muscles. 'I told you. Old stories.'

Paul nodded, wiping sweat from his brow. 'Yeah. That's what you said.'

After a while he joined the old man and the pug in the shade. As he did so, the old man got up and went back inside. Paul decided not to take offence; he wasn't in the mood for a chat anyway. He checked his phone. They had barely made any progress. Hardly surprising, considering Rachel had about a ten-hour head-start on them.

Probably shouldn't have stopped for that lunch.

But it was so tasty!

He tried to brush a speck of dust from the screen, and when it wouldn't budge he realised what he was looking at. Zooming in on the miniature map confirmed his suspicions. He hadn't been able to see properly before, with the glare of the sun on the screen, but now, here in the shade, he could see it clearly.

Rachel was heading towards an island.

It was too perfect. They would stop there, then Paul would arrive to save her and perhaps spend some time on a desert island. He smiled as things started to fall into place.

'Everything's coming up Milhouse,' he said.

'What's that?' said Chakrit.

'It's a *Simpsons* reference,' started Paul. 'Actually, forget it. Doesn't matter.'

Chakrit nodded and lit another smoke. The pug walked over to Paul and clambered onto his lap. The old man grumbled in Thai and looked back towards the distant memory of the shore. And all the while, the great sun in the sky beat down with righteous fury. Paul realised he could no longer see Koh Phangan beach, just the panorama of crashing blue all around him. He leaned back, closed his eyes and fell asleep.

They sailed on.

9

'Okay. So we have two flare guns and five flares. Twelve bottles of water, twelve cokes, and a fridge full of booze. One map, one machete, three life jackets and this,' said Ricky, holding up a harpoon gun.

'So no food?' asked Ana. Ricky shook his head.

'Why don't we just look at where we are on the map?' asked Lisa, her voice as limp and insipid as her expression.

'Well why didn't I think of that,' said Ricky, tossing the map over to Lisa. 'Here, tell us where we are.' Lisa looked at the map for a while, then threw it back.

'There's no need to be rude,' she said. Then, under her breath, 'Wanker.' Darren held her hand protectively.

'At least we have plenty of water,' said Ana, trying to cling onto the only modicum of good fortune she could find. Ricky snorted.

'For a day or two, maybe. Who knows how long we'll be out here.'

Rachel agreed. 'We're just drifting. Does anyone even know we're out here? There's no radio, and our phones are lying on a beach somewhere.'

'They've probably been sold on the black market already,' said Ana.

They looked to the three Aussies for ideas, and were met with blank stares.

'Got a hit?' Darren asked Lisa, who fished into her bra and pulled out the small baggie of pills. She took one and offered them to the rest of the group. Darren and Bret took one each, while Ana, Rachel and Ricky stared in disbelief.

'Really? You're gonna get pilled off your tits while we float to our deaths?' said Ana.

Darren dry-swallowed the pill. 'That's right. You got a better idea?'

She didn't.

The hours passed slowly, a hospital waiting-room without a hospital.

Ana scanned the horizon for boats, or a rescue helicopter. She could go mad out here. Blue sky, blue sea, nothing else. Nothing to take her mind off their situation. Rachel hunkered down in the shade next to Ricky, resting her head on a life-jacket. Darren, Bret and Lisa lay spaced out on the deck, occasionally engaging in the sort of meaningful conversation reserved for the terminally high.

'Guys...if I was to eat myself...would I disappear...or become twice as big?'

Josh and Lillian were below deck. Ana didn't even need to look; she could hear the wet slap of flesh on flesh as they fucked.

As much as she told herself she disliked Lillian, she secretly wished for some of the girl's confidence. That *whatever happens, happens* attitude. She figured that you had to be born with it, preferably in America.

No chance.

She smiled sadly to herself and looked down into the

deep blue, looking for answers where she knew she wouldn't find them, watching the boat carve its way through the unending waves.

And then she looked up and saw it, her eyes widening.

'Guys! *Guys!* Oh shit, come here!'

Rachel heard her sisters voice calling. She pushed herself up and padded barefoot towards Ana, the soles of her feet burning on the sunbaked wooden deck, making her hop across the boat.

She saw it too and her heart skipped a beat.

'Oh my God...'

A shape on the horizon, rising up like Atlantis. The rest of the crew - even the stoners - joined them. Lillian and Josh arrived last, reeking of sex, and the eight of them stood in hushed, reverential silence, half expecting to blink their eyes and find that it had vanished, a trick of nature, a cruel façade.

It was an island.

'Is that Koh Phangan?' asked Ricky. 'Did we get turned around?'

'I don't think so,' said Ana, unable to articulate exactly why she thought that.

As they floated closer, they were able to make out the general lay of the land. Ana was right. This was not the island they had left behind. White sand beaches gave way to the lush vegetation of a thick jungle. It carpeted the island, right up to the steep hill that towered over all, casting a shadow over the crystal waters of the lagoon. There was, however, no sign of life.

'It's beautiful,' said Josh, wrapping his arm around Lillian and cradling an ass cheek with his palm.

'We need to signal someone,' said Ana. She hurried to the pile of provisions and grabbed the flare gun. Snapping open the barrel, she inserted a flare before rejoining the group.

Darren snatched it out of her hand.

'Quick love, give it here would ya?'

'I can do it myself, you—'

He pointed it in the air and fired. Ana threw her hands up in annoyance as the scarlet flame erupted from the barrel and crested the sky before burning out against the brilliant blue, the sparkling embers drifting casually to a watery grave.

'Now what?' asked Lisa in that infuriatingly passive monotone.

'I guess...we wait,' said Rachel, huddling closer to Ana, watching as the island inched ever closer, almost as if it were moving towards *them* and not the other way round.

And so they waited.

They waited for what felt like forever, but there were no rescue vehicles forthcoming, no boats hurtling through the water, no helicopters hovering overhead. Just the omnipresent, claustrophobic roar of the ocean. They drifted onwards, the tide pulling them in. No one spoke, a heavy silence of expectation descending. Angry clouds hung over the hill, the first ones Ana could remember seeing since they arrived in Thailand. They looked out of place, as if they had been Photoshopped in.

After a small eternity their boat reached the shallows, coming to a stop with a soft thump as the underside struck the sand about thirty foot from the shore.

And yet strangely, no one felt compelled to move. They stood waiting, gazing out over the untouched white sand. It was Ana who said what they were all thinking.

'What if there's no one here?'

The only movement was the branches of the trees

dancing in the light breeze. The whole scene felt like it had lain undisturbed for centuries. Lisa, in a rare moment of clarity, broke the silence. She scanned the island, her eyes drawn to the top of the hill, to the skeletal remains of the Man Wai Luxury Hilltop Resort.

'Look. Up there, in the distance. A building.'

'I can't see it,' said Ricky.

Ana pointed at it and was surprised to find her hand was shaking. Ricky adjusted his eyes and found it atop the massive hill, mostly buried under thick vegetation.

'Jesus,' was all he muttered. He took Ana's hand and gently squeezed it.

'Looks like it's abandoned,' said Rachel.

'You can't stop nature,' said Josh.

'What did you say?' asked Ana.

'Nature. I mean, we can cut it back, build on it, civilise it if you like, but nature always wins. She always reclaims what was once hers.'

'What was *always* hers,' added Lillian.

For once, it sounded less like hippy bullshit to Ana and more like a lopsided kind of truth. Maybe it was the drugs wearing off, but this place had an atmosphere she didn't like. Despite the stifling glare of the sun, she broke out in gooseflesh.

'So what now?' asked Ricky. 'Do we head on up there?'

'No,' said Darren, appearing to fully sober up for the first time that day. 'We head into the jungle.'

'Why?' asked Lisa.

'Because someone's got a barbie going.' He pointed at the far edge of the island, where a thin wisp of black smoke rose from somewhere in the middle of the jungle. He nodded to himself. 'Someone's here.'

Again, a chill skated down Ana's spine.

'I don't like this,' said Rachel.

Ana silently agreed.

'Okay then,' said Ricky. 'I guess we should set off towards the smoke?'

'Someone should wait here and keep an eye out for passing boats,' said Ana. Her eyes flicked from the ruined building on the hill to the trail of smoke and back again. Something wasn't right here. Something was amiss. She turned to the Aussies. 'How about you guys keep watch? The rest of us can trek towards the smoke.'

'Fuck that,' said Bret. 'I'm starving. If someone's cooking up snags, I wanna get involved.'

'Damn right,' agreed Darren. 'You can stay and watch for fucking boats. We're getting something to eat.'

She shrugged to show she didn't care either way. If anything, she was trying to do them a favour. She was more than happy to sit on the boat and await rescue. The jungle had always creeped her out. Before leaving Scotland, she had spent an entire evening Googling what spiders and snakes were native to Thailand. It was a form of strange masochistic therapy for her. Even the act of scrolling down the page had filled her with dread, afraid to see which eight-legged monstrosity would reveal itself next. It had all proven fruitless so far; the only bugs she had seen were the mosquitos, and they were more irritating than frightening.

'Fine,' she said. 'Me, Rach and Ricky will stay here. The rest of you go and get help.'

'We're not going anywhere,' said Josh. Ana sighed.

'Why not?'

'We're in an area of unspoilt natural beauty,' explained Josh patronisingly. 'For you, the journey has brought you here. For us, the journey is just beginning.'

'We're going to explore our surroundings,' said Lillian.

Ana wished to god that she would put her bikini top back on. 'We'll bathe in the tranquil waters,' she continued. 'Laugh beneath the trees. Make love in a waterfall.'

'Okay,' said Ana, just happy that they weren't going to stay on the boat with her. Let them make love in the waterfall, at least then they wouldn't be shagging on the boat all afternoon. 'But don't go far. There could be anything out there.'

'Love is in that jungle,' said Lillian, but Ana had already tuned her out.

Darren picked up the machete from the pile of supplies. He hefted it in his hands, testing its weight, looking at his reflection in the rusted blade.

'I'll take this,' he said, as Ricky dispensed water bottles to Bret, who passed one to Lisa and held onto the other two for himself and Darren.

'The most important thing is to make contact with someone. Try to find a radio or a phone,' said Ana.

'At the very least, find fuel or a boat. Even a compass would help,' added Ricky.

Darren wasn't paying attention. He was too busy swooshing the machete through the air, living out his Indiana Jones fantasies, if Indiana Jones had been a blonde Australian twenty-something in a pair of stained Calvin Klein jocks. Bret nodded in the affirmative.

'Don't worry guys, we'll be back in a jiffy.' He smiled a crooked smile that no one trusted. 'Lisa, you got any left?'

Lisa pulled out the baggie from her bra again. 'One for the road?'

'Guys, I don't think you should have anymore,' said Ana stepping forward and reaching for the bag as Lisa pulled it away.

'What the fuck do you think you're doing, bitch?'

'I said you don't need anymore,' snapped Ana.

Lisa tucked the baggie down the front of her black panties and sneered at Ana.

'Come and get it, bitch. Just you fucking try.'

No one spoke. Even Lillian and Josh were taken aback by the venom of Lisa's words. Ana backed off, her cheeks colouring. 'I just think—'

'Don't fucking tell me how to think, bitch. Don't you fucking ever.'

As Ana tried to stutter out a response, Rachel instinctively stepped in front of her. 'Okay, it's time you guys were off now,' she said, trying to keep her voice calm, despite the anger boiling inside her at the treatment of her sister. And there was something else too.

It might have been fear.

Lisa stared at Ana for a moment longer, then smiled. It was not a pretty smile. 'Relax guys, can't you take a joke?'

No one was laughing.

Ana and Rachel hung back while the threesome clambered down the small metal ladder into the cool water and headed for land. Standing on the deck, Ana couldn't help but worry that her life was now in the hands of those three idiots. She watched as they reached the shore and trudged their way through the sand, the sunlight glinting off Darren's machete. They were tiny specks in comparison to the hill that towered above them, the strange overgrown buildings perched atop like some kind of monument to man's arrogance. She felt like someone was watching her and she pulled the baggy yellow vest down to her thighs. She was being absurd.

Wasn't she?

Lisa's attitude had rattled her for sure, but it wasn't just that.

There was something about this island she didn't like.

The three explorers made their way across the sand and stood at the edge of the undergrowth. Of the three, only Bret turned back and waved. Ana raised her hand delicately and stood a minute longer, then walked back to sit by her sister's side. In the distance, she heard the sounds of Josh and Lillian splashing around in the sea.

She had no idea they were being watched.

10

'I DON'T WANT TO GO BACK. LIKE, *EVER*.'

Lillian lay on the deck at a right angle to Josh, her head resting on his thigh, staring up at the sky. Much to Ana's chagrin, they had made their way back to the boat for a drink of water. Lillian was, of course, still topless. Ana had surreptitiously left her bikini top lying on the deck in the hope that Lillian would see it and cover herself, but no such luck. She took small sips from a water bottle, trying to conserve the precious fluid but also battling dehydration from last night's boozy misadventures. Also, listening to Josh and Lillian prattle on made her nauseous.

'I know, babe. I feel like we've found our *path*, y'know?' said Josh. Ana looked at Rachel and shook her head.

'Just think of our friends back home,' agreed Lillian, 'Working their nine-to-five desk jobs.'

'Like sheep. A bunch of mindless *sheep*.'

'You know, where I come from, sheep don't get desk jobs,' said Ana. Josh fixed her with a withering stare. Ana was unperturbed. 'They live in fields. Eat grass. Make wool.'

'Do you mind? We're having a private conversation here?' said Lillian, but Ana wasn't done.

'Hey, that'd be a good slogan for you guys. Make Wool, Not War. You know, like sheep.'

Lillian sat up, irritated.

'Mindless *sheep*,' continued Ana. Rachel snickered behind her.

'Why are you doing this? What gives you the right to kill people's buzz?' said Josh. Ana noticed he was clenching and unclenching his fists. She shrugged.

'Just killing time.'

'Well don't.'

Ana fell silent for a few moments, then Rachel spoke up.

'What're their working conditions like?'

Josh swallowed hard, anger welling inside him. He took a long time to respond. 'What?'

'The sheep. I'm just wondering...are their working conditions baa-a-a-d?'

'Are you fucking serious?'

Lillian touched his arm, urging him to ignore the comments. He brushed her hand away.

It was Ana's turn again.

'The thing with sheep is, it's too easy for bosses to pull the wool over their eyes.'

'Stop it,' said Josh, his voice deepening.

'I guess the computers in America need more *RAM*?'

'I said *stop* it.'

'Hey Josh, if they're in finance, do they work on Wool Street?'

Josh stood up, stomping his foot on the deck like a petulant child. 'Shut up! Shut up, you fucking whining Scottish bitches!'

Rachel and Ana shared a brief glance - any longer and they knew they wouldn't be able to contain their laughter.

'Come on Lill, let's leave these sluts alone with their pimp.' Josh pointed at Ricky. 'If you can't control your bitches, I might have to teach you a fucking lesson, do you understand me?'

Ricky looked around in surprise. 'What'd I do?' he asked, but Josh and Lillian were already disembarking. They splashed into the shallows and headed for the beach. The girls started laughing. 'Do you have to get in a fight with everyone you meet?' said an exasperated Ricky.

Ana got herself under control, giving Ricky an exaggerated wink. She lay back against the rail and closed her eyes.

'Just killing time,' she said.

Josh stormed ahead of Lillian, but soon realised it was difficult to walk angrily on a beach when your feet kept sinking in the sand. He waded up to his ankles in the water then stopped and let Lillian catch up to him. She pressed her breasts against him and ran her hands over his muscular yet hairless chest.

'Don't let them get to you,' she said, playing with his shark's tooth necklace. 'They're just jealous. Jealous of what we have, of our lives, our experiences, our journey.'

His chest puffed out in anger and he snorted. 'They couldn't possibly understand.'

'That's right babe. They're lost. Lost souls, that's all. Don't be angry, it's such a wasteful emotion. Show pity instead. Show them love.'

Josh's breathing was calming, Lillian's words having the

desired soothing effect. The water sloshed around their ankles and he took her face in both hands.

'You really get me, babe.'

'I know, babe.'

'They've stopped,' said Ana, watching Josh and Lillian from the prow of the boat. 'I think she's trying to calm him down. She's rubbing his chest like she's waxing a car.'

'You really pissed him off,' said Ricky, a trace of annoyance in his voice. 'And it wasn't *you* he was going to hit.'

'Relax Ricky, it wouldn't have gone that far,' said Rachel, playfully flicking Ricky's ear as they sheltered from the sun in the small staircase that led down to the sleeping quarters. From their vantage point, Josh and Lillian were out of sight, but Ana was keeping them up to date. 'What's happening now?'

Ana squinted into the sun at the two figures in the surf.

'They're just talking. He's— oh shit, he just pulled down her knickers! Guys, you gotta see this.'

Rachel frowned. 'I'm not sure I do.'

Lillian stepped backwards out of her bikini bottoms. She bent to pick them up but Josh held her wrist.

'No,' he cooed, 'Let them go. Let the sea wash away our ties to decadent Capitalist fantasies.' He stroked her face and gave her his most profound stare as her swimsuit washed out to sea. Lillian nodded and slid her hands down to the V of Josh's stomach, slipping her fingers into the waistband of his briefs. She could see he was ready.

'Are they fucking yet?' called Rachel from the stairs. It was too hot, even in the shade. She needed to get below deck.

'No, not yet,' replied Ana. 'But I can see why she's with him now. I can finally understand what she sees in that boring slab of ham.'

'What's that?' asked Ricky.

Ana turned her head in their direction.

'A massive dick.'

They faced each other, naked, as Josh took Lillian into his arms, his erection pressing into the tight flesh of her abdomen. He leaned in to kiss her, but she pulled back.

'Not here, Josh. They're watching.'

'Then let them watch. Let them see love in its *purest*, most *sensual* form. Let them *learn*. Let them *understand* what happens between two souls that are so *deeply* entwined.'

'No Josh. They'll ruin it, with their laughter and their jokes. Take me, please, but not here. I want it to be special.'

She took Josh by the hand and led him towards the trees, Adam and Eve in their very own Garden of Eden.

'Ah, they're off into the bushes,' said Ana. 'Probably for the best.' She turned and realised no one was there, Ricky and Rachel having gone below deck several minutes ago, leaving her alone. She watched as the naked pair disappeared into the trees, only their fluorescent paint still visible.

'I guess this is my life now,' she sighed to herself.

They proceeded into the jungle, just far enough for the boat to no longer be visible, out of sight of prying eyes. Lillian leaned back against a tree, spreading her legs apart slightly. Josh came to her, kissing her, his stubbled cheek scraping her mouth and neck, but he struggled to get Ana and Rachel out of his head; their laughter, their barbed comments. How could they understand what he and Lillian shared? *They* were the sheep.

Stupid, ignorant sheep.

It was the same all over the world, wherever they travelled on their voyage of self-discovery. People laughed at them, their tiny minds unable to comprehend the wonders of a spiritual journey.

Those people, with their mobile phones and their Twitter accounts and their obsession with technology. They made Josh sick. They knew not the pleasures of making love in the rain, of dancing in the moonlight with your soulmate, of spending a week toiling in the fields of a monastery. No, they were too concerned with money and reality TV and how many 'likes' their latest social media post had. They were weak-willed and ignorant. All of them. Especially Ana and Rachel. The Brits were always the worst, with their sarcasm, every sentence dripping in that ironic humour of theirs. He hated them with every fibre of his being, and made a mental note to upload a video about them to his YouTube channel when he got back.

Lillian put her hands on his throbbing cock, tracing her fingers up and down the shaft. Josh's breathing intensified and he stepped back and spun her around to face the tree, kicking her right leg to the side and pushing down between her shoulder blades, arching her back.

Lillian felt like she was about to be frisked by a cop.

Without warning he positioned himself on bent knees and thrust at her, eliciting a gasp that was either pain or pleasure, he didn't care.

'Josh—'

'Quiet,' he grunted, his hips working now, his thighs slapping off her ass.

Those bitches would never understand. They were stuck in the mire, bogged down with the unnecessary complexities of modern living.

He pushed harder and Lillian smacked her brow off the soft bark of the tree.

'Josh, you're—'

'Shut up,' he snapped.

They would never know true love.

'Those sluts...' he said, not even realising he was speaking.

'Josh, *stop!*'

But he couldn't. Not yet. Not until he had shown them that his way was the right way.

Those bitches.

Those cunts.

'Josh, stop, please!'

'I'm almost done,' he growled in a voice she barely recognised.

'Josh wait, I hear something, *someone's coming!*'

'You're damn right I am!' he shouted, his body pumping away in an animalistic frenzy as he neared release.

He never noticed the movement behind him. Not until it was too late, and even then he never fully understood what was happening. A hand, filthy and calloused, grabbed him by his dreadlocks, pulling his head back and exposing the glistening skin of his neck, veins pulsing from the exertion.

He felt the cold steel against his throat and heard the ghastly ripping sound as the serrated blade cut deep into the skin, tearing arteries to shreds, not stopping, sawing through muscle and sinew until the blade scraped across the bone of his cervical vertebrae. He tried to scream but all that came out was a vile gargling sound. His body stiffened for a second then went limp, but not before disgorging a spray of blood onto Lillian's bare back.

Lillian felt Josh make one final thrust into her before sliding out completely. Hot liquid splashed onto her skin - a quite extraordinary amount. She held onto the tree, panting.

'For fuck's sake Josh, what was that? That wasn't love-making, that was—'

She turned round and came face to face with Josh, his face caught in a silent scream, blood oozing thickly over his chest. His lifeblood jetted from the savage wound, an arterial spray that hit her clean in the face. His body collapsed at her feet and as hands reached out to grab her, Lillian managed one final, throat-shredding scream.

The scream echoed across the beach.

Ana stood up, walking back to the prow and scanning the beach. There was no trace of Josh and Lillian.

Rachel's head poked through the wooden hatch.

'Was that Lillian?'

Ana nodded, barely hearing her. The scream carried out to sea on the wind, where it died out, leaving nothing but brooding silence in its wake.

'I told you,' she said quietly, her eyes scanning the edge of the jungle. 'That dick was *huge*.'

Rachel raised her eyebrows and whistled, before

ducking back down into the cool below deck. Ana stayed where she was, looking out over the solitude of the island as the sun dipped behind the welcome shade of a passing cloud, the boat bobbing silently in the water.

And once again all was still.

11

THE WIND RUFFLED PAUL'S HAIR AS THE FISHING BOAT PICKED up speed, bouncing across the waves of the choppy sea. Chakrit sat cross-legged on the deck rolling a cigarette. He finished and handed it to Paul, who carefully lifted the pug from his lap and took the cigarette. Grub grumbled in frustration and toddled off to rest his belly elsewhere.

'Thanks,' said Paul. He found some boxes in the shade and sat down, lighting up.

'Not a good place to sit,' said Chakrit.

Paul held the lighter an inch from the tip of the cigarette. He depressed the button and the flame vanished. 'Why not?'

Chakrit smiled broadly and pointed at the wooden crates. 'You're sitting on dynamite.'

'Fuck,' yelped Paul, leaping to his feet and moving to the other side of the boat. 'You could have told me.'

'I just did.'

'Yeah, but...fuck.'

The old man laughed from on top of the boat, a throaty cackle that was surprisingly infectious. Paul shook his head. Daft Thai bastards.

'Dynamite, huh? I thought blast-fishing was illegal?'

Chakrit finished rolling his own cigarette and lit it unhurriedly. He puffed and looked at Paul. 'Nobody around,' he said, gesturing with his hands, spilling ash onto the deck. 'Quick way to catch fish.'

'Yeah, but doesn't it damage the, umm, coral or something?'

Chakrit said something to the old man and they both laughed. Paul didn't bother asking for a translation. He sat down next to the pug again and lit up. 'Sorry pal,' he said, stroking the snuffling dog's spine. He checked his phone and noticed the battery was low. No problem there. He pulled a power pack from his pocket and plugged it in, giving him another twelve hours of battery, or so the packaging promised. It would be enough time to find Rachel, anyway. He opened the tracker app, the dot flashing either on or next to the island. He had a sudden fear that she had been kidnapped and taken to this remote island. But by whom and for what purpose? He wanted to rescue her, but not at the cost of his own safety.

'Hey, Chakrit,' he said. 'This island, the one we're headed to. Are there any, y'know, pirates there?'

He expected another laugh and was disappointed when there was none. It meant the question was not as absurd as he hoped.

'No pirates, no.'

That seemed to be the end of the discussion, so Paul tried a different tactic.

'That old guy your dad, huh?'

'Uncle. My parents died many years ago. My uncle looks after me, gave me a job on the fishing boat. Feeds me.' He patted his belly and grinned. 'Good food.'

Paul leaned back, enjoying the cigarette. He had to

admit, it wasn't an unpleasant way to spend the day after the Full Moon Party. Some tourists pay good money for this sort of thing. Then he remembered how much he had paid them and inwardly grimaced. He jerked a thumb in the old man's direction.

'What's he so afraid of? What's this "old story" you were talking about?'

Chakrit wiped the sweat from his eyes and moved into the shade next to Paul and the pug. 'Today's too hot, even for Thai,' he said. He flicked his burnt out cigarette butt overboard and started to roll another. Paul waited.

'My uncle thinks island is, you know, cursed.'

'Cursed?'

Chakrit nodded, a wry grin etched onto his features. Paul wondered how old he was. He looked young, with babyish features and kind eyes, but working at sea can prematurely age a man, and his skin was tough. He carried numerous scars on his body and arms. Paul's only scar was on his inner thigh from when he had chickenpox as a baby.

'Yes. Cursed. Many old Thai believe this. And some young ones too.'

'Do you believe it?'

Chakrit smiled again. 'I hear legends. There is some truth, I think.'

'So tell me.'

'You will think I'm crazy.'

'You're smoking next to dynamite. I already think you're crazy.'

Chakrit laughed. 'I like you, Mr Paul. So I'll be honest with you. This place we're going...it's dangerous.'

'In what way?'

'People don't come back. Thirty years ago, the island was

bought by a big construction company to open a hotel, luxury stuff, a real tourist place, understand?'

Paul nodded.

'They took over the whole island, many men living together, building the hotel. Then one day, something went wrong. A hole opened in the ground and bam! Men disappear.' Chakrit laughed. Paul realised he was clenching his jaw. 'So they say, anyway. The men who made it back. You see, something happened and panic! Everyone ran away. But there were not enough boats, you see? So many men were left there. The men who make it back, they told the police, but no one believed them. Everyone just laughed. So they sent a boat out to bring the men back. That boat never came back. They sent out another boat, full of army men, to find the men from first boat. And guess what?'

'They're never seen again.'

'That's right! You sure you never heard this story?' asked Chakrit, still smiling. 'Anyway, no one ever came back from the island. Others try, land there, but they do not come back either. Afterwards, Thai government make decision. They take the island off the map. They say it's not there anymore, gone. They say bye-bye, island. Bye-bye.'

'It's on my map,' said Paul.

'Yes, satellite map show it. Can't hide that. But Thai map?' Chakrit shook his head. 'No more. Gone.'

'So the men who were left behind...are still there?'

'Yes. Or, they were killed by monsters.'

'I don't believe in monsters,' grunted Paul.

'Neither did they,' said Chakrit. Paul dragged deeply on his cigarette, suddenly wishing he was back at the hostel.

'You don't believe that shit, do you?'

'In monsters? No, that's kid stuff. But I know people don't

come back from island. Only the ones who make it off first time. The lucky ones.'

Paul ran his hand down the soft fur of the happily snoring pug.

'So tell me, Chakrit. If you think that no one returns from this island, then why are you taking me there?'

For the first time Chakrit's smile faltered. His features darkened as if covered by a black veil. His kind eyes grew smaller. 'I want to go, but Uncle would never let me. He only understands one thing; money. To him, money is stronger than family.' Chakrit smiled again, but this time it was forced and uneasy. 'You see my friend, my grandfather was foreman on the island.'

'Oh shit,' said Paul.

'He's one of the few who made it back. What he told us, my family...no one believe. He was a good man, old Prachya. Strong man. When he came back, he had changed.' Chakrit tapped a finger to his temple. 'Up here. What could do that to a man, Mr Paul? What happened on that island that broke my grandfather's mind?'

'I don't know. But I guess we're going to find out, huh?'

Chakrit shrugged, the easy smile returning, brightening his features.

'Part of me hope so. Part of me...'

'Yeah?'

Chakrit took a draw on his cigarette.

'Part of me hopes we never find out.'

12

LISA WATCHED DARREN SWINGING THE MACHETE WITH reckless abandon, enjoying his new toy as he hacked at the foliage to create a path. The further they ventured in, the tougher it got. The trees seemed to be closing in on them. Was it possible to get claustrophobia outside? Lisa thought that it was. A bunch of city kids, they were unused to being surrounded by so much nature. She hadn't expected the jungle to be so...*jungly.*

Unfamiliar sounds chirruped and squawked and screeched, her bare feet sinking into pools of mud that sucked at her ankles. She remembered a World War I documentary she had watched where the soldiers had gotten trench foot. The thought made her shudder.

Sunlight dappled through the thick canopy of trees, blinding her anew with every step, while phallic flowers bloomed in luxuriant reds and purples, and vines dangled from lichen-coated trees like so many slumbering serpents. The plants were unlike anything she had ever seen. Bulbous stalks that rested on stumps resembling human feet, the blooming heads swaying as if following her, soft grape-like fruit swinging like eyes on stalks. The trees twisted and contorted away from the sun, seeking shelter from the rays in the dank solitude of the jungle, as flowers the colour of freshly spilled blood burst forth from the bark, splitting it open and sending a putrid sap oozing from the wound. Through the narrow gaps in the fauna creatures darted furtively, yellow eyes peering at her with malicious intent.

She hated nature, hated wildlife, hated this godforsaken jungle. That snooty bitch Ana was probably sunning herself and sipping on a chilled coke right now, laughing her fat arse off. She thought she was so much better than Lisa, telling her not to take any more pills. Funny, she hadn't said that last night when she'd been dancing around the boat in her undies, her pupils dilated like saucers.

Stuck-up bitch. She'd been trying to hide her scars all day, but they had all seen them last night. When she next saw her, Lisa decided to tell her just that.

The leaves and ferns stroked her skin like razor blades and her body shrank into itself to avoid contact. She tripped on a root and fell to her knees but forced herself back up, trying to keep pace with the others. A butterfly bigger than any she'd ever seen brushed past Lisa. Its wing span was roughly that of her outstretched palm, with colours so vivid they didn't appear natural. She held her hand out, willing it to land. The delicate insect floated through the air, the gentle flap of its wings slowing as it came to rest on her outstretched palm. Lisa clamped her hand shut, crushing the colourful creature. She uncurled her fingers and looked at the damaged mess. She brushed off the remains on her leg and kept going.

'Could do with some mozzie repellant, eh?' said Bret, happy to hear someone's voice, even if it was his own. Like the others, he had stripped down to his shorts for the swim to the boat, and now found his entire body a playground for mosquitos, nipping and biting at his tender skin. They seemed to flutter before his very eyes, always one step ahead of his swinging arms. In the distance he heard a bird caw mocking him.

'Daz, you know where you're going, right?'

'Yeah mate, I reckon it's straight on.'

From behind, Lisa snorted.

'You okay back there, Lee?' shouted Darren.

'Whatever. Just get us where we're going already.'

'I'm trying,' he said. Part of him wished Lisa had stayed on the boat, but he knew she was a liability, and only he knew how to handle her. Lisa liked precisely two things in life; drugs and B-movies. Their supply of pills rapidly dwindling, coupled with the lack of a telly, meant that Lisa was liable to snap unless Darren could steer her away from the other occupants of the boat. She was prone to irrational bouts of violence and paranoia, and Darren had once seen her stab a girl with a pen because she thought she was a ghost.

He hacked at a vine as thick as his arm and foul-smelling green liquid spilled out, splashing his feet. He looked down in disgust, wiping the goop against a tree, the bark as soft as rotten fruit.

Only his machete punctuated the silence, slicing through the air and chopping at branches that extended out like arthritic limbs. The air grew thicker, clouds of insects misting in front of their eyes. Darren batted some away and checked his watch. It was almost three. Funny how the day gets away when you're trapped on a desert island.

'When does the sun set?' he asked.

'Bout seven, I reckon,' said Bret from behind him.

'We'd better make tracks man. I don't wanna be stuck out here in the dark.'

'Want a pill?' asked Lisa.

'Not now, mate,' said Darren. 'Maybe once we get there.'

Darren stepped out into a small clearing. He sniffed the air, the unmistakable scent of a fire wafting through the putrescent stench of the flora.

'Guys, come here. I can smell burning.'

'I don't smell anything,' said Lisa, but something had captured Darren's attention. Bret looked at her and shrugged, then followed Darren.

'Holy shit...' he said.

It was a digger, an old backhoe loader, nestled in amongst the trees. The three walked towards it, the once-yellow vehicle now a filthy greyish-brown, vines snaking over the metal body, nature claiming the vehicle as its own. The rear of the digger was hidden from view by the wild foliage, and the glass around the driver's seat was cracked in several places. It reminded Bret of a spiderweb, and he shuddered.

'Someone's been here alright,' said Darren, climbing up the decaying footholds that led to the driver's seat.

'Not recently,' said Bret. 'This hasn't been used for years, mate.'

Darren sat himself at the steering wheel and placed his hands on it. Bret was right. The vines had fused themselves to the interior and plants grew through the floor. The keys were in the ignition but when Darren turned them, nothing happened. He wasn't surprised. To his right there were more hidden vehicles. Diggers, an old 4x4, each caked with rust and caught in the fetid and unshakeable grip of the jungle.

Abandoned tools barely visible beneath the undergrowth baked in the sun like rotted bones after a cemetery flood.

'Why would they leave all this shit behind?' asked Lisa.

'Guess they left in a hurry,' said Bret.

'Yeah, but why?'

'Maybe that hill's a volcano or something?' suggested Darren, making his way from the driving seat back onto the jungle floor. He turned and spat, then took a water bottle from Bret, finished it and kicked the empty container into the bushes. Now only one bottle remained.

'I don't like this,' said Lisa.

'It's just the pills.'

'No, there's something else. Like we're not alone here.'

'Good. We're meant to be looking for help, remember? If we're alone, we're in big trouble.'

'Guys, check it out,' said Bret, pointing beyond the digger. 'Tracks.'

Sure enough, the remains of a dirt road meandered through the trees. Many years ago, the path had been forged by the relentless march of the vehicles. Now, with no one to wander it, the track had all but vanished, only the vague outline remaining.

'There we go. Problem solved,' said Darren, hoisting his machete up again. 'Let's follow the yellow brick road, what do ya say?'

'Where do you think it leads?' asked Bret.

'Where do you think, you drongo? To whoever built that fire! Now come on, let's get going before it gets too dark to see.'

Bret looked up at the sky, hidden behind the trees. Darren set off along the track, determined to get something to eat to placate his rumbling belly.

He looked up just in time.

'Holy shit, look at that fucking thing,' he said, spreading his arms wide in a Christ-like posture to stop the other two getting past him.

Lisa and Bret caught up with him and stopped. It was hard to discern anything at first. Trees, ferns, and then more trees and ferns. Then Lisa spotted it and involuntarily gasped.

The web was huge, and thicker than any she had seen before. It stretched at least twenty feet across, from one tree to another and about ten feet high, the leaves and greenery caught up in it acting as a form of camouflage. In the centre was a monkey, twitching in a desperate attempt to escape. It clawed at its legs with one free paw, its coat matted and bloody. Bret took a step closer and Darren held him back.

'Wait. Don't you see it yet?' he whispered.

Bret scanned the web, looking for the source of Darren's interest. When he saw it, his stomach lurched violently.

It couldn't be real.

A spider, but bigger than any he had ever seen. Living in Australia, Bret had seen plenty of spiders, big and small. One summer spent on his uncle's farm had taught him to shake his shoes every morning before putting them on, to avoid any unwanted surprises. Black widows, funnel webs, redbacks; no creature with eight legs had ever fazed him. As long as you respected them and kept a safe distance, chances are they would leave you alone. But nothing on Earth could have prepared him for the sheer size of this monster. It must have been at least eighteen to twenty inches wide. It wasn't right. It wasn't *natural*. Thick fur covered its body, but the legs were bare and white like bony fingers protruding from the grotesquely bulbous frame.

Bret turned to Lisa, who was frozen to the spot in horror. The arachnid sat at the top of the web. Was it watching them? It left its perch and crept towards the monkey, who was now thrashing wildly, with each movement finding itself more and more ensnared in the deadly trap. The frightened beast screeched in terror.

Unhurried, almost as if it was putting on a show, the great spider stalked towards its prey.

'Fuck me,' said Darren. 'It's as big as that poor monkey.'

'Bigger,' whispered Bret, as icy tendrils of fear caressed his neck. He suddenly felt very itchy. The spider stopped just above the thrashing monkey and reared itself up, and for one horrifying moment Darren thought it was about to leap at him. He gripped the machete handle, his hands slick with sweat, his throat constricting. Instead, it dove down to the helpless simian, enveloping the entire body in its bone-white legs and forming a cocoon-like grip. It bared two enormous fangs, then plunged them into the soft dome of the monkey's skull. The creature's shrieks took on an eerily human aspect, like a child trapped at the bottom of a well, as a geyser of blood spurted from its head, spraying the web a dark crimson. The spider gripped tighter, pushing its fangs into the monkey's head, harder and harder until the skull shattered and the head collapsed like a burst balloon and the awful screams mercifully stopped, replaced by a horrid slurping noise.

It was a nightmare, an aberrant horror.

Darren motioned for his friends to back up, ever so slowly. He started to move and found his legs frozen. He looked back at the spider, poised over the now-desiccated carcass, the blood drained from the mummified monkey. The sounds stopped and he could swear - swear on his mother's *life* - that it had looked at him, that it knew what he was and why he was here.

Adrenaline surged through his body and he willed his

feet to move, walking backwards, not taking his eyes off that monstrous creature until he was a safe distance away.

He saw that Bret and Lisa were already way back out of reach.

'Let's get the fuck outta here,' said Darren. 'Right. Fucking. *Now*.'

13

'HOW YOU DOING, SIS?'

Ana opened her eyes and saw Rachel looking down at her. She stretched and forced herself into a sitting position, unscrewing the cap from a water bottle and taking a long sip.

'Jeez, I must have dropped off,' she said, wiping the liquid from her lips.

'Lucky you were in the shade. You redheads don't do so well in the sun.'

'Looks like it's setting anyway. Fuck, I feel rough.'

Rachel sat down next to her sister. She too felt like shit, but she was used to it. The last few years had been a blur of drink, drugs and sex. Living the rock 'n' roll dream. But Rachel was no rockstar. One day you wake up and wonder where your life has gone.

'Where's Ricky?'

'Downstairs, sleeping like a baby.'

'He didn't try it on with you?' smiled Ana. Rachel laughed.

'It's you he likes. Must have a thing for the older woman.'

'I prefer to think of myself as *experienced*.'

'That makes you sound like an old prostitute.'

Ana nodded. 'True. Okay then, I'm distinguished.'

'I don't think women are allowed to be distinguished. That's only for men who're going grey.'

'I've got grey hairs,' Ana protested. She held out her hair for Rachel to look at, the thin strips of grey nestled in amongst the ginger strands. Rachel nodded grimly.

'To men, that just means you're old.'

Ana yawned. 'That's okay, I can deal with that. Maybe Ricky has a fetish for greying prostitutes.'

'You'd better hope he does,' chided her sister.

Ana laughed. It had been a while since the two of them had spent so much time together. Things were finally starting to feel like before, how she remembered it.

'I've missed you,' she said, catching Rachel off-guard.

'Umm, missed you too,' she said.

'Where did you go?' said Ana.

'What?'

Ana grimaced internally. That had come out wrong. She wasn't trying to start an argument. She just needed answers, and now was as good a time as any, wasn't it?

'I don't mean...' She struggled to say what she meant. 'You know...I wish I was like you sometimes,' said Ana, changing tack. 'Living free, not a care in the world.'

'Hey, I care about things.'

'Yeah, but—'

'Look, if you have something to say, just say it.'

'No, I'm sorry Rach, I shouldn't have brought it up. Forget it, okay.'

But Rachel wouldn't let it lie. 'No, no, I'm curious. What're you getting at? Is this about mum?'

And just like that, it was all out in the open. Ana chose

her words carefully, then thought *fuck it* and said, 'Rachel, where were you? Where the fuck *were* you?'

Rachel stood up and walked away from her, running her hands through her hair.

'I knew it. I *fucking* knew it.'

'What did you expect, Rach? You disappeared! Our mum was dying and you just up and left!'

'It's not that simple—'

'Oh, but it is, *sis*. She got sick, you couldn't handle it and you left me there. You left me there to deal with it by myself.'

'Deal with it? You make it sound like a spider in the bath.'

'I *needed* you!'

'I—'

'*Mum* needed you.' Ana felt the trickle of warm tears down her face.

Rachel just stood, silhouetted against the setting sun. It was for the best. Ana didn't want to see her face.

'I was there for her through the chemo. I went with her to every appointment, listened to the doctors' diagnoses. I watched her give up, Rach. Give up on life, give up on hope. You know she asked me to kill her? She wanted me to unplug the equipment while the doctor was out the room. Can you believe that? I was by her side when she died. I held her hand. *I was there when she asked for you!* What was I supposed to say? That you were off getting high somewhere? That you were out fucking some random? I couldn't answer, because I didn't know. I didn't...know...'

Rachel was silent. Her head ached. 'Look Ana, let's talk about this tomorrow. We're in a stressful situation, we're not feeling well—'

'*BECAUSE OF YOU!*' Ana exploded. 'Because you drugged me, you fucking cowardly bitch!'

'I...what?'

'Oh don't act innocent, I know it was you. You fucking drugged me...your own sister. You know I hate that shit.'

'Well you didn't seem to hate it last night,' said Rachel, her words cutting through Ana like a butcher knife.

Ana curled up, retreating into herself. 'Fuck you.'

'So that's what you think of me, huh? Fascinating. You know what Ana...I hate you. You're so perfect, the perfect daughter. Well, she still died, didn't she? You couldn't help *that*, could you?'

Ana got to her feet and stormed over to Rachel.

'Look, Ana, I'm—'

Ana struck her hard across the face as Ricky emerged from below deck.

'Guys, what's going on?' he said, the dictionary definition of poor timing.

The two girls faced each other. Rachel put a hand to her reddening cheek. Ana drew back her left hand and slapped the other side of Rachel's shocked face. Rachel turned on her heels and ran to the ladder, stopping as she reached it.

'I was there for you, Ana,' she said without turning round. 'I was there for you when you gave up and slit your fucking wrists. Or don't you remember?'

She clambered down into the sea and swam towards the shore.

'Wait, Rachel, come back,' called Ricky. 'It's getting dark, come on, we can work this out!'

'Leave it Ricky. Let her do what she wants. It's what she's best at.'

'Are you serious Ana? We don't know what's in that jungle! Darren and the others aren't back, and we've not seen Josh and Lil for hours!'

Ana slumped down onto the deck.

'I don't care. I've finally realised that I just...don't...care.'

Ricky didn't understand. He saw Rachel arrive at the shore, the dying light casting a warm orange glow on the water. She stepped onto the sand, following the footsteps of the Aussies. The only sound was Ana sobbing. As Rachel vanished into the trees, Ricky cursed his luck.

There goes the best looking one, he thought.

Still, he supposed, Ana would have to do for now. She was upset and emotional. She needed comfort, a shoulder to cry on. A warm embrace.

A good fuck.

Rachel found it easy to follow the trail of destruction Darren had left in his wake. Leaves and ferns coated the ground as she carefully stepped over fallen branches. She wished for some clothes. A comfortable pair of shoes, some jeans and a long-sleeve top. The essentials for trekking in the Thai jungle. Instead, she was wearing nothing but her bra and panties. She felt tiny wings fluttering against her skin, and the sharp pain of stingers piercing her flesh. She tried to swipe the insects away, but it was a losing battle.

Fuck!

She was furious. With Ana, but also with herself. Shame commonly manifests itself in anger. She had lashed out at her sister, when it was herself that was to blame. Partly at least. On the boat, she had felt that old familiar guilt rise to the surface. Instead of acknowledging it, she had forced it back down. And when Ana had brought up the drugs, it was the perfect excuse to attack her. It hurt Rachel to know that her own sister thought she would secretly drug her. But then, they hardly even knew each other anymore. Why would Ana suspect anyone else?

'I'm sorry,' she said to herself. She stopped and sighed, letting the last of the tears fall, unaware of the eyes that tracked her as she walked.

Above her the sun hung low in the sky.

It would soon be full dark.

14

IT WAS A GIRL, ANOTHER ONE. HE HADN'T SEEN ONE IN A LONG time. Months, years even. Time ran differently here. Now there were at least two on the island, maybe more. A boat floated nearby in the sea. More girls? If he brought them back, his people would reward him. They would be pleased.

His God would be pleased.

She was vulnerable. Defenceless. Often, the interlopers carried weapons. Guns, as he had once called them in another life, a life nearly forgotten. Not this one. Her posture was slumped. Defeated. She carried nothing and she wore little. A long time ago, his reaction would have been very different. At the back of his mind a thought struggled to the surface, lustful and decadent. Something about the way she walked, the way her body moved, the softness of her exposed flesh...

He cast the thought aside and watched her from the bushes, little more than a shadow. His hands clutched the knife, the blade sticky with blood.

He hadn't wanted to kill the other girl. She would have been a fine specimen to return with, but she had fought back unexpectedly, and he had defended himself. Now she lay in a pool of her own guts. It was all he knew anymore. All any of them knew.

Survival.

Survival and worship.

Seeing this girl brought back more memories of a time long gone. A distant past that may as well have been a different lifetime. Perhaps it was? Her young face stained with tears. Had he known someone like her once? A sister? A daughter?

A lover?

He thought he had a daughter once, about her age or younger. He tried to recall her face, but nothing came to him.

No, he was mistaken. There had never been a daughter, nor anyone to care for. There was nothing in his life except survival and worship.

Survival and worship.

That was all that mattered.

15

'WE'RE HERE.'

Darren emerged from the jungle into a spacious clearing, the remains of the dirt track creeping towards a deforested area roughly the size of a football pitch. Six large two-storey buildings lined the perimeter, three per side, and in the middle, the smouldering remains of a recently extinguished fire.

Shelter for the night. A sigh of relief escaped his lips and he allowed himself the comfort of a smile.

Bret and Lisa followed, taking in the sight. Some of the structures were almost invisible, dressed in vines and creepers, stray trees sprouting haphazardly beside them. There were a couple of vehicles, all-terrain types, but they looked just as useless as the old digger, the wheels hidden by long grass, the shattered windows crying bloody tears of rust as the wind spat icily through empty frames.

'I don't like it,' said Bret. 'What was this place?'

'I don't know man. Somewhere for the workers to live while they built that thing on the mountain? What do you think, Lisa?'

'I don't know,' she said, surveying the derelict scene. It looked like no one had been here in decades. And yet a fire had been lit and then put out. Recently. But by whom? And where were they now?

'I guess we should take a look inside,' said Bret.

'Yeah mate, good idea,' replied Darren. 'Me and Lisa'll get the fire going again. You check out some of those buildings. Gotta be something useful in one of them.'

'Why me, man?'

'It was your idea. What's the matter? You chicken?'

Bret bristled at the suggestion. 'Nah mate, it's just...what if there's another one of those spiders or something in there?'

'Then I'd rather find it before it gets dark.'

'Fuck,' breathed Bret. There was no point arguing. Darren had always emerged as the natural leader of their small but tight-knit group. It had been Darren's idea to come to Thailand. Darren's idea to go to the Full Moon Party.

Come to think of it, maybe Darren wasn't always right.

Bret strode purposefully towards the nearest building, a two-storey monolith. Above the doorway was a sign in Thai, now barely legible, the letters scratched and faint.

About five foot away, he stopped, facing the door. Uneasiness crept over him.

It's just a door man. Go through it, he thought. *Yeah, easy for you to say, brain.*

He took tentative steps towards the doorway. His legs felt weak from hunger and exhaustion.

'Hurry the fuck up, mate!'

He looked back at Darren, whose armfuls of twigs and branches would hardly be enough to toast marshmallows, never mind keep a roaring fire going all night.

Something moved out of the corner of his eye. Over

there, in one of the buildings. Somebody at the window.
Watching.

Spying.

There was nothing there now, but Bret could swear he
felt eyes on him. He twirled around on the spot to try to
catch a glimpse again, but whatever he had seen was gone, if
it had ever really been there at all.

'Mate!' shouted Darren, failing to mask his exasperation.

'Alright, alright, I'm going in,' Bret called back. 'But I
wish I wasn't,' he mumbled. Dead leaves crunched beneath
his feet as he reached for the doorknob and pushed the sun-
faded door. At first he thought it was locked, but then the
hinges shrieked in agony and the door gave way. It shuddered open and he faced the narrow rectangle of darkness
and all the secrets therein.

The interior was pitch black and Bret waited for his
vision to adjust. No sense in blundering in. There might be a
big hole in the ground, or a low hanging lamp.

Or a giant fucking spider.

He began to pick out details. It was a hallway. Jackets,
damp and rotted, hung from the walls like pig carcasses in a
slaughterhouse, the smell dank and foul. He eased past
them, not wishing to make contact with his bare skin. He
stepped on someone's toes and looked down at rows of
work-boots lined up along the floor. Outside Lisa and
Darren talked, their voices distant, like a TV bleeding
through a hotel wall. He traversed the windowless hallway
as quickly as possible, treading lightly over feathers and
animal shit. Something squished between his toes and he
grimaced but kept moving.

Bret rounded the corner into what had once been the
living quarters. Sodden girlie magazines littered the floor,
while filthy plates and mugs adorned the table, the food

picked clean long ago. He wrinkled his nose at the rotten stench as the dying light streamed in through the windows, picking out tiny dust motes and buzzing insects, the ragged curtains billowing gently. He carried on, bumping his ankle on a low table, knocking an ashtray to the wooden floor. It shattered, disgorging its contents. He glanced down and saw an animal of some kind, its belly torn open and gutted, maggots festering in the open wound.

He walked on.

The kitchen was next. Water dripped from the ceiling, landing in shallow pools. Bret pinched his nose and inhaled through his mouth. 'Either they left in a hurry, or they really needed a cleaner,' he said, trying to talk away the rising fear that tightened like a knot in the pit of his stomach. The ground was carpeted in leaves, the trees outside swaying through glassless frames like haunted paintings. Dishes were piled recklessly in the sink, threatening to topple at any moment. Wanting out fast, he slid open a drawer hoping to find something of use, though he didn't know what. As expected, it contained some cutlery and little else. He lifted out a decent-sized butcher knife and held it tightly to his chest. The second drawer housed a snake which raised its head to stare sleepily at Bret, its tongue darting out. He slammed the drawer shut and left the room, and the snake, well alone.

Darren bundled the sticks onto the ashes of the fire. The light was beginning to fade, the sun dropping below the canopy, the restless shadows of the trees lengthening across the barren clearing.

'We need more wood,' he called to Lisa. She was staring

at a building, unmoving. 'Lisa?' She turned to face him. The spaced-out look in her eyes suggested that she had taken enough pills for today.

'Lisa, we need more wood.'

She nodded, stealing a last glance at the building and turning away. She followed the well-trodden track through the village, past the derelict buildings and vehicles.

It had to have been her imagination, but she could have sworn she had seen something in the window. She wrapped her arms around her chest and shivered. It was getting cooler now. Her skin was red and burnt and itched like hell, tiny pock marks and bites dotting her near-nude body.

At the edge of the village, where the jungle began again, she saw a wooden signpost, pointing off in various directions. Eight of them, in fact.

'That's weird,' she said to herself. It was the last thing she had expected to see. The setting sun blinded her and she half-covered her eyes.

'You find any, Lisa?' called Darren from afar.

'Yeah, just be a minute,' she shouted back. 'I see a sign.'

She liked the way Darren had taken charge. Wandering through the jungle in his jocks, swinging that machete around. She liked that too. Maybe tonight would be the night to get over her fear and hop in the sack with him. Could be fun, she reasoned. Be nice to forget about this fucking jungle for a while.

As she neared the signpost, the sun slipped from her view, settling below the tree tops.

She stopped and stared, her blood turning to ice and freezing her veins. Her jaw slackened and dropped open.

'Oh fuck,' she mouthed.

'Oh Jesus fucking Christ.'

Darren held the two rocks in either hand and bashed them together. He had seen this done in the movies plenty times. You hit two rocks together, they spark and voila! A fire. They always made it look so easy.

He stopped a moment, his eyes following Lisa as she walked towards the sign. Her panties were creeping up her ass and he sat and watched her until she was too far away.

'Hate to see you leave, love to watch you go,' he sniggered. He noticed the drop in temperature and cracked the rocks together again. Nothing. He wondered how Bret was getting on. The sun arced beneath the trees and Darren struck the rocks again, desperate to start the fire before the light completely vanished. He couldn't even make it spark. If he only had his clothes on, he could have grabbed his lighter and got this damn thing going in seconds. He tried the rocks once more.

'Ah, fuck this,' he said.

He heard gravel crunching, someone approaching from behind.

He turned, a goofy smile on his lips.

'Bret? How did you get—'

But he was cut short.

It was not Bret.

The staircase creaked with each step, the wood damp and mossy. Bret didn't even know what he was looking for anymore, but felt compelled to keep going. He did not want to come back to Darren with nothing to show apart from an old knife. Not when his friend was building a fire to keep them warm for the night.

He ran his fingers along the dusty walls until he came to three doors, one hanging at an angle from its hinges. Beyond it was a bathroom, the powerful odour assaulting his nostrils like toxic waste. In the centre lay a sizeable pile of clothes. He swallowed hard and entered, kneeling by the soggy mound of clothing. Bikinis, Hawaiian shorts, combat fatigues. It was an odd mix of swimwear and military garb. Several backpacks and handbags lay to the side. He rummaged through one of the bags and found an old Nokia phone and a purse containing several thousand Baht. Inside the purse he found a photo of a teenage boy grinning at the camera, the edges worn and mouldy. He tried another and found a Swedish passport belonging to one Lars Anderrson. Bret checked the last page and discovered the passport expired in 1997.

There were more bags, more passports. Jewellery, torches, even an old Polaroid camera. He picked it up and wiped a film of grime from the chunky machine. He pressed the button and the camera went off with a blinding flash, the antique device spitting out the photograph. Bret was astonished that it still worked.

'They don't make 'em like that anymore.'

Unnerved, he took the photo and slowly backed out of the bathroom. Choosing one of the other doors at random, he found himself in the sleeping quarters. The door slammed shut and he gave out a startled cry.

'Stay calm, man. Just stay calm.'

Bunk beds lined the walls, most of them missing mattresses, springs bursting forth from the remaining ones. Thick cobwebs trailed from the ceiling and one bed at the far end looked to be completely cocooned.

No way he was going anywhere near that one. No fucking way. He tried one of the numerous bedside cabinets, wrenching open a drawer, knife drawn. Inside were some socks, or at least what used to be socks. He tried another. A dog-eared porno mag and a leather-bound diary. It was written in Thai and completely useless to Bret.

He tried more drawers whilst shaking the Polaroid photograph, the spectral image gradually appearing.

Some jewellery. A watch. A pair of glasses. Some photographs of a young Thai woman smiling at the camera and holding a baby. In another, the same woman stood on a beach laughing. In this one she was heavily pregnant. Bret felt an unaccountable sadness. What happened here? Where did everyone go?

He shut the drawer gently and looked at the Polaroid, holding it up to the dying light. He laughed at his own startled expression, his eyes wide, face totally bleached out by the powerful flash.

'What a dork.'

He stopped laughing, his skin growing cold. He squinted hard at the photo. There was something behind him.

A shape, lurking behind the doorway.

No, *bullshit*, it was a shadow, a trick of the light.

'Fucking hell, mate, you're getting jumpy,' he told himself.

He looked once more at the photo, as if to try to convince himself. A shadow, that's all. Nothing more.

But shadows don't have gnarled, white fingers, not like the ones in the photo, the ones that wrapped around the wall, the ones that belonged to the figure in the photograph, the figure that had stood behind him, watching and waiting.

The figure that was still in here with him.

He was jolted from his thoughts by the sound of screaming.

Lisa.

She tried to run but couldn't, her legs refusing to work as if they had atrophied the moment she saw the signpost. Her stomach fell.

The post had been crudely hammered together, eight wooden planks jutting out, four per side in a roughly symmetrical pattern. To each plank had been nailed a skeletal arm, the hands dangling limply. Impaled upon the central spike was a skull, the sharpened point protruding out through the shattered cranium, pure white and picked clean of any remaining flesh by the birds and insects. It was like some kind of totem or idol, fashioned into the form a skeletal humanoid spider. The skull leered at her, the jaw hanging open. She stumbled backwards, her legs giving way and landing with a thump on her ass.

She heard screaming and realised it was coming from her mouth.

She couldn't seem to stop.

Seconds before, Darren turned to what he thought was Bret just in time to see the wooden club swinging through the air. It struck him on the side of the face with such ferocity that his cheekbone shattered on impact. He hit the ground and tried to crawl away, his vision blurred, his fingers clawing uselessly through mud and dirt. He lifted a flaccid hand to his burning face, finding a shard of splintered bone jutting out through his cheek. He tried to call out for Bret, but his mouth didn't seem to be working, his jaw only attached at one side. A sharp kick sent him onto his back, giving him a look at his assailant through bleary, tear-soaked eyes.

A tall man, gaunt, and deathly pale, chalky hair draped unflatteringly over his skeletal visage, loose pockets of flesh drooping from his wiry frame. The man's skin was so white it was like looking into a milk bottle, and Darren could have sworn he could see the veins running through the man's naked body like tapeworms. He wore nothing but a neck-lace, from which swung several small bones. He looked about a hundred years old.

Darren's first thought was cannibals.

Another man appeared, then another, each bearing the same sinister, almost transparent complexion. One of them wore what appeared to be a ragged pair of cut-off denim jeans. Another had on a faded grey tee-shirt with the *Black Sabbath* logo emblazoned across it. It was so absurd Darren wanted to laugh, but before he even had a chance, the men raised their tools and started to bludgeon him, bringing the objects down again and again. His ribcage gave way first, several cracked ribs plunging into his lungs. Darren began to choke, blood spilling from his mouth, raising his hands to protect his face. He rolled onto his front, trying to escape.

A steel bar cracked his lower spine, a plank of wood snapped his ankle bone in two. As his body went into shock, a severe blow crushed his skull, caving it in. His body stiff-ened then lay, a mass of useless bloody tissue.

The men turned their attention to Lisa, who sat watch-ing, shaking her head from side to side in confusion and horror, looking at everything but seeing nothing.

She never stood a chance.

From the second-floor window, Bret stood helplessly as his old schoolfriend was murdered, heart hammering in his chest, frightened and disbelieving. He saw Darren's body twitching, the jerky death spasms wracking his corpse as dark blood pooled around the body. He stood stock-still as the men reached Lisa, their long fingers grasping at her as she shook and screamed, fought and thrashed, but in seconds they had her by the arms and legs. They carried her back to the fire, laying her down next to the pulped mess that minutes before had been his friend. He watched as the men held her down, more appearing, one carrying a thick rope. How many were there? And where were they all coming from?

Too late, Bret realised exactly where they were coming from.

He spun around, the dirty kitchen knife in his hand, the room as quiet as a crypt, scanning for any trace of movement. He sidled away from the window, hoping those outside wouldn't notice him. His back slid across the wall and he froze, listening intently, becoming aware of a scratching sound in the darkness.

It was in here with him.

Bret ducked down, keeping to the shadows and avoiding the light, the cover of darkness his only hope.

Hope. Ha! Hope was just an acceptable lie people told themselves to get through the day. It had no real-world use, not for Bret, not right now, not ever.

In the far corner something moved. A chair, no more than a centimetre, but the scraping of wood was unmistakable. Bret blinked, trying to clear the window-shaped imprint of light from his eyes, to see through the murk.

Downstairs a door banged shut. Were they looking for him? Did they even know he was here? Obviously one of them did, but he hadn't been out in the clearing for very long, and if he could deal with that one...

Lisa's screams echoed all around. Bret closed his eyes, trying not to think of what horrors she was enduring out there. He gripped the knife tightly.

What were they? An ancient race of cannibals who objected to the intrusion of civilisation onto their island? Aliens from another dimension on a mission to colonise the Earth one small island at a time?

Focus, Bret. For fuck's sake focus.

Something dripped on his head, startling him. The gooey white mucus dripped from his fingers as he wiped it away.

'Leave me alone,' he whispered, clutching the knife, ready to strike should the need arise. Another globule of liquid plopped onto his hair and an overwhelming sense of dread shrouded over him. He raised his head and found himself staring into cold, dead white eyes. Bret howled in terror and thrust the knife up. The monstrosity above him jerked out of the way, leaping clean across the room. It landed smoothly, scurrying into the shadows, and then came for him, limbs thudding across the dirty wooden floor, scuttling like a crab. No, not a crab, like a—

It darted up the wall, climbing easily onto the ceiling, scrambling towards him and sending a light fixture crashing to the ground, the long-dead bulb shattering on impact. As it passed the window Bret caught a glimpse of the soft, gelatinous skin and the humanoid face before it launched itself forward.

In moments of abject horror, the brain switches to a cerebral low-power mode in a frantic attempt to preserve the sanity of its host. As Bret's mind twisted perilously close to breaking point, his survival instincts kicked in and he drove the knife forward with both hands, plunging it into the onrushing body of the creature. The impaled beast writhed in pain, its talon-like fingers clawing deep scars down Bret's face.

Bret kept his eyes shut, refusing to acknowledge the presence of the freakish organism. He hauled the blade up, disgorging the contents of the rancid stomach, the intestines landing with a plop on his bare feet. Venomous spittle sprayed across his face as the creature spasmed on the end of his weapon before sagging to the floor in a lifeless heap.

Bret opened his eyes, the room once again falling silent, save for a pitiful clawing sound coming from his left, a scratching that intensified by the second. He didn't want to look, didn't think he physically could.

'No, no, no,' he said, clutching the knife, one hand pressed over the blade, not noticing as it sliced into the skin of his fingers. There was a tearing sound, something soft being ripped apart, split open. The huge cocoon next to him rumbled ominously, something inside scrabbling to get out. He looked towards his escape route and saw two more of the creatures creeping along the ceiling, their movements calculated, methodical.

At the precise moment he lost his mind, Bret let go of the knife, letting it clatter to the floor.

'You win,' he said, smiling, holding his empty hands up in surrender. He took one step, then another, then broke into a run, heading for the nearest window. He didn't stop when he reached it, throwing himself through.

He felt weightless. Free. Absolved. He was safe. Everything was going to be okay.

Everything was going to be fine.

Bret's body flew through the empty frame, seeming to hang in midair for brief, maddening seconds before crashing headfirst down to Earth. The sickening crunch of his neck breaking reverberated across the clearing. He lay still, head tilted at an awkward ninety-degree angle. His chest continued to rise and fall as he savoured his dying breaths, the strange men looking at him in disinterest before turning back to Lisa.

Poor Lisa.

For her, the worst was yet to come.

16

RACHEL KICKED THE SAND IN FRUSTRATION. IF SHE HAD pockets her hands would have been thrust into them, but her underwear did not allow for such cliché body language. She stood at the edge of the beach, gazing into the impenetrable jungle, the air thick with concealed menace.

The boat was far behind her now, the outline only occasionally noticeable against the lunar glow that splashed across the waves.

What a mess. She knew she should apologise to Ana. She had gone too far this time. But would she get an apology back? After all, it was Ana who had been out of line, not her. It was Ana who had hit her.

But didn't she have every right to, for all the time she had spent with their mother while Rachel lost herself in a cocktail of booze and drugs and sex. Anything to avoid coming home and helping.

'You really fucked up,' she sighed, unconsciously swatting a bug on her forearm.

She looked for signs of life on the boat, but the night was drawing in and they had surely gone down below deck, where it was warm, and there was water and a toilet and even a mattress. That sounded pretty good right now. Suddenly she wanted to be back on the boat, among other people, to hear voices, anything other than the drone from within the jungle that rose and fell like a beating heart.

Then she saw it.

In her peripheral vision, a bright splash of neon, the unmistakable colours of the Full Moon Party. It had to be Josh and Lillian. She never thought she would be happy to see them.

'Lillian?'

There was no answer. They were lying down. Asleep? Having sex again?

As she listened, the dusky wind shook the trees and something deep in the jungle shrieked but there were no grunts or pants or squeals of delight.

'Josh?' She started towards them. 'You guys awake?'

She stepped cagily, her toes slipping comfortably into the sand, closing the distance on the sleeping hippies.

They didn't stir. To her left the foliage shook but Rachel didn't notice.

'Guys, hey, wake up.'

It had to be them. She could make out some bright pink and green and also red, lots of red. The palm leaves rustled softly, and she detected an unpleasant odour in the air.

She reached the jungle and pushed aside a luxuriant fern.

Her first thought was that she had caught them mid-cunnilingus, Josh's head buried between Lillian's legs as she sat on the ground, legs splayed. Her head was tilted towards Rachel, eyes wide and milky and staring.

'I'm sorry,' Rachel stuttered, until she noticed the savage puncture marks across Lillian's face and breasts. And Josh's head was not between her legs, it was resting in Lillian's hollowed-out belly, facedown in loose, stringy intestines that spilled out over the edges of the barbaric wound.

The blood rushed from Rachel's head and the next thing she knew, she was on her knees vomiting.

Ana paced back and forth across the deck, scanning the line of trees for someone, *anyone*. The wind whistled past her ears, the sky rapidly darkening as night's black cloak descended.

'No sign of them?' asked Ricky. Ana shook her head without looking at him. 'Come on, let's go below deck. It's getting cold.'

'No, I'm gonna wait. They've been gone for hours now.' She pointed into the distance. 'Look, the smoke has stopped. The fire's out. If they had reached it, they wouldn't have let that happen, would they?'

Ricky stepped closer and wrapped the red blanket around Ana's shoulders. She accepted it without really noticing. 'Maybe they found somewhere warm?' he suggested. 'They're probably at a bar right now, sipping on a margarita and talking about those suckers they left on the boat.'

'But why hasn't *anyone* come back?'

'They probably realised it was gonna get dark before they made it. It makes sense, they know we're safe here. Food, shelter and all the modern conveniences.'

Ana hugged the blanket tight, grateful for the warmth it provided. 'I guess so,' she said unconvincingly. 'But what about Josh and Lillian?'

Ricky thought hard, trying to come up with a good lie.

'Still having sex? Enjoying the healing properties of nature?'

'Yeah. Maybe.'

Ricky took Ana's hand in his. 'Listen, if no one's back by morning, we'll look for them. Together. Now come on, you can't even see anything anymore.'

'I just wish there was something we could do.'

'We could fire a flare?'

Ana finally turned away from the island and looked at Ricky.

'That way, if anyone *is* lost, they'll know where we are,' he continued.

'But what if somebody else sees it?'

Ricky was puzzled. 'Like who? We want anyone to see it, to come and rescue us, don't we?'

Ana shivered. Of course she wanted to be rescued. So why did she not want to fire the flare? Why was she afraid of giving away their position? She took a moment to ponder the thought.

'I know, Ricky. It's just—'

There was a rocketing sound like a firework going off, and the luminescent red beam pitched into the sky, briefly illuminating the boat and its occupants a bright hue of crimson. To Ricky, Ana looked like she was covered in blood. To Ana, Ricky looked like a devil; all that was missing was a pitchfork. As quickly as it appeared, the glow vanished and they were plunged into shadow again. It seemed even darker now. Ricky tossed the flare gun onto the deck.

Ana left her position and grabbed a cartridge from the small wooden crate containing their provisions, opening the flare gun and clicking it into place. It felt satisfying. She could tell Ricky was watching her and felt the need to explain. She had never understood her need to justify things to people, but here she went again.

'It's good to be prepared. If we see a ship or something, we don't want to be fumbling around in the dark looking for a flare,' she said quietly.

Ricky didn't answer, instead thinking about the phrase *fumbling around in the dark*.

'Okay,' he said. 'We're all set. We've fired it, it's too dark to see, and we can go looking in the morning. You can't sit here all night. Come on, let's go downstairs and try to catch some sleep.'

'I don't think I'll be able to sleep, Ricky.'

'Then we can talk. Come on, we need to hide from these insects. They're eating you alive right now.'

Ricky was right. She was exhausted. The comedown from the drugs had taken its toll on her, physically and mentally. A good nights sleep would help to shake off the cobwebs, she hoped. There was nothing she could do sitting here staring into the night. Ricky held out his hand and she took it, following him through the little wooden hatch and down the stairs. Ana took one last look out across the bay, the sea lapping against the beach.

A woman, pale and gaunt, watched from the trees.

'She isn't real,' Ana said beneath her breath. She rubbed her eyes. She was losing it again. A symptom of stress and anxiety her doctor had once told her, before suggesting she see a therapist.

They were there on the street, always far off through crowds of people, their faces gauzy and unclear. Sometimes they simply stood watch, like sentinels. Other times they beckoned to her, a siren call from the depths of insanity.

Stress. It had been stress before, and it was stress now.

Of course it was. What else could it be? The only alternative was that she really *was* nuts.

Often they came to her in dreams, nightmare visions that dissipated upon waking, leaving only the lingering sense of dread hanging over her like a black cloud. They spoke to her faintly in a language she didn't understand, the words giving her migraines that felt like dead fingers rooting around in her brain.

She hadn't told her mother about them, and she sure as hell hadn't told Rachel. Ana didn't want Rachel worrying about her; she worried enough for both of them.

She looked out over the sea to the island, a strange familiarity washing over her.

The spectral figure turned and disappeared into the jungle.

'Ana, you coming?' said Ricky from downstairs.

It's not her it isn't real it's not her it isn't real.

'Ana?'

She turned her back on the island.

'I'm coming, Ricky.'

She made her way down the steps, but the words kept running through her head.

It's not her it isn't real.

～

Rachel wiped away a long string of phlegm, thankful to the darkness for concealing some of the gruesome discovery.

But not enough.

The smell alone was enough to make her gag, catching in her throat like a fishhook. She had never seen a dead body before, and here were two of them. But not just dead. Disfigured. Mutilated.

Butchered.

She got to her feet. Head swimming, she staggered away from the stench and took several deep breaths to clear her lungs. She wanted a drink. Needed one. She had to get away from this place.

Ana.

She had to get back to Ana. To protect her, or to be protected?

What did it even matter?

The bushes shook. She stepped backwards, tripping as her feet caught in the sand and falling onto her ass as the leaves parted and the ghastly thing shambled out of the jungle, staggering towards her, a man, but horribly deformed, his skin as white as snow, features soft and jelly-like, its mouth opening in a snarl, saliva drooling from the lipless muzzle. It was naked, the genitals withered away to a nub, its limbs crooked and angular. It regarded her with black eyes.

So many eyes.

It towered over the defenceless Rachel, studying her.

In its hand it clutched a claw hammer.

'I wish Rachel was here.'

Ricky cracked his knuckles, the sound impossibly loud in the cramped confines of the room. 'She'll be fine. She looks like she can handle herself.'

'Yeah. She can. That's always been her problem.' Ana lay down on the mattress, trying to get comfortable on the worn, shapeless fabric. She wondered how many different people had slept here over the years, if it had ever been washed. She pictured the captain of the ship bringing hookers here, one in every port.

Each stain tells a story, she thought.

A horror story.

'I shouldn't have gone off on her like that,' she said, trying not to think about the sexual history of the mattress any more and failing. Poor Miss May 1995, trapped forever in the calendar, facing out on the sordid erotic adventures of the mattress. What tales would she tell, if only she could talk?

'Hey, you're sisters. Sisters fight. She'll get over it.'

Ricky seemed determined to have a serious talk, so Ana finally acquiesced.

'It's just a stressful situation, you know? We haven't seen each other for years, did you know that?' Ricky stayed quiet, letting her tell her story. He watched her, his eyes taking the scenic route up her bare thighs. Ana didn't notice, she was focused on Miss May 1995. There was a melancholy in the girl's eyes that she hadn't noticed before, or maybe she was just projecting. 'It was when I needed her most. Some sisters hate each other, but we had always been friends. Best friends. I looked up to her. Even though I was the eldest, she was the most popular, and everyone fancied her. I wanted even just a wee bit of her confidence. Her strength.'

'You're strong.'

Ana smiled sadly. 'No Ricky, I'm not. I get anxiety walking into a roomful of people. I won't answer the phone if I don't know the number. If someone pays me a compliment, I don't believe them. I look in the mirror and all I see is this...this fat loser.'

'Hey—'

'No *don't* Ricky. Don't tell me I'm wrong. All I ever

wanted to be was like Rachel. Then when our mum got sick, she just fucked right off. Left us.'

'Cancer?'

'Aye. The usual.'

'You didn't know where she was?'

'Ah you know, she'd call sometimes. Wish us the best. Say she hoped to make it along soon, but work was so busy. Too busy to visit her dying mum.' Ana started to cry, and she let Ricky wipe away a tear. He put an arm around her and she leaned into his shoulder. 'At the end, she was just lying there, this skeleton with skin stretched over it, and she asked for Rachel to be there. We knew it was the end. I tried to phone and—'

Ana broke off, putting her head in her hands.

Ricky waited in silence as the last remnants of sunlight were extinguished. The room was as black as a tomb.

'Is that why you...y'know,' he said.

Ana lifted her head. She traced her thumb down one of the puckered scars.

'No,' she intoned. 'It was something else.'

Her heart beat so fast she thought it might burst out of her chest. Was she going to do it? Could she tell Ricky the truth? Would he even believe her? She trusted him, that much she knew.

'I saw—'

Ana stopped.

What. The. *Fuck* was happening? Ricky's arm dangled loosely over her shoulder, his hand above her breast, fingers brushing against the lacy material of her bra. She froze as his hand probed, his skinny digits slipping beneath the material, finding the soft plumpness of her breast.

'Ricky,' said Ana, tears trickling down her face. 'What are you doing?'

'Relax. I'll make it all better,' he cooed, forcing his hand down further, cupping the breast, catching her nipple between two fingers and squeezing. She grabbed his arm and pulled herself free. In the darkness below deck, she slid away from him.

'Ricky, no,' she sniffed.

'Don't fight it, Ana.'

'I'll fucking fight you in a minute, you creep. Get off me!'

He pulled her towards him and planted a kiss on her salty, tear-stained lips. She shoved him away. 'Fuck off Ricky! Were you not listening to me? I'm baring my fucking soul for you and...and...'

'You fucking bitch!' he shouted, an angry voice screaming into the void. 'You and your sister. Jesus fucking Christ, a real pair of cock teases.' Ana was shell-shocked and unprepared for the violence of Ricky's words. 'And to think I wasted my pills on you sluts yesterday, when I could have been fucking anyone I wanted!'

Ana's temper flared. She grappled with her self-control. 'First of all Ricky, I don't know how we can be sluts *and* cock teases, so make up your mind you ignorant fucking prick. Second of all, it was you? You drugged me? You drugged *us*?'

'Well, I drugged Rachel so I could fuck her, but when I saw what a pain in the ass you were gonna be, I gave you one too.' Was he laughing as he said it? Ana couldn't tell; she was so angry she couldn't think straight.

She swallowed hard. She wanted to beat the living shit out of Ricky. But first she had to check something.

'So last night, when we woke up together...'

'Don't flatter yourself. I wouldn't want to fuck you anyway.'

'You just tried to!'

'Whatever bitch, go run and cry to mommy. Oh yeah...'

It was dark, and Ana couldn't be entirely sure where Ricky's face was, but she made a guess, clenched her fist and swung.

She had always been a good guesser.

Her fist connected with his ear and he yelped in pain.

A bunch of fives, to use an old colloquialism her mother had been fond of.

She swung again and missed, then tried lower and hit him in the chest. One more punch found his stomach. Winded, he crumpled in a heap, drawing his legs up to his chest, protecting himself from any further blows. Ana got up, imagining the cringing mass at her feet. She clenched her fists, anger and excitement surging through her veins.

'People like you, Ricky, are why I hate people.'

She left him prone on the mattress, gasping for breath and ears ringing, and stormed up the stairs. She threw open through the hatch, the evening wind doing nothing to calm her buzzing nerves. Thoughts raced through her mind and she stomped across the deck in an effort to work off the adrenaline.

What the hell was she going to do now, trapped here on this boat in the dark with a sexual predator for company? She ran her hands through her hair, taking deep breaths, trying to calm down. Her instincts told her to leave, but where could she go? She had, what, three flares left? Not enough to get through the jungle, anyway. She picked up the gun, considering her options. Part of her wanted to fire one into the little room where Ricky was nursing his wounds, shake him up a little.

Fucking creep.

The boat rocked gently and Ana stared into the sky. The stars were so bright out here, not like back home in Edinburgh, where the pollution masked them. In the distance, far away, came an ominous rumble.

'A fucking thunderstorm? Aye, that's all I need. Could this fucking trip get any worse?'

It could, and it was about to.

Rachel had only a second to think.

Apparently, when you're about to die, your life flashes before your eyes in a blur of nostalgic memories.

Not true.

Only one thought ran through Rachel's head as the creature hulked over her. It was a simple one, singularly lacking in the profundity expected of death-bed speeches.

It was, *Holy fucking shit, what the fuck is that?*

It stalked menacingly towards her, limbs jerking like a glitchy video, every movement an act of extreme pain.

The creature crouched down on all fours, tightened its grip on the hammer and leapt forward with surprising agility. Rachel threw herself to one side as it brought the blunt end down into the sand, the cold steel grazing her shoulder. She rolled, trying to get upright and away from this maddening scene.

The creature remained on all fours, pivoting to face her, inching forwards in an arachnid crawl. The desolate moons of its eyes betrayed not a hint of emotion as it scuttled over the sand towards her, its jaw slack and hungry. It wielded the hammer fiercely, lashing out towards Rachel's face. Just in time she threw an arm up to block it, the bell of the hammer striking her in the forearm with a sickening crack. She fell back and the creature lunged forwards, realising Rachel was on the defensive.

She kicked her leg up violently, catching the monster under the chin, her foot penetrating the soft, gooey flesh, her toes sinking deep into its throat. When she realised she could see her foot inside its neck she finally screamed, a mixture of fear and utter disgust. The creature did not seem to notice. It raised its hand high and brought the hammer down on her leg. Rachel shifted her position at the last moment and caught only a glancing blow to her calf. She withdrew her foot and watched as bilious white liquid oozed from the monster's throat.

She shuffled backwards as the thing put a stumpy hand to its throat to check for damage. Rachel took the opportunity to yell for help. She knew the boat was nearby. If she could just make it! The creature reared back on its haunches ready to strike and came for her again. Rachel kicked up towards it, sending sand up into the thing's face. It howled as it came down on top of her, dropping the hammer and wrapping both soggy hands around her throat, squeezing tighter and tighter, its legs wrapping around her body and holding her tight, its revolting penis pressed against her bare stomach, a thin trail of liquid dribbling out. She looked up through sagging eyelids and saw the moon through the creatures head, blood pulsing through rippling veins. Something moved inside; something inhuman, almost insect-like. The pressure on her throat increased, sapping her energy. She threw both hands up at the thing, punching and clawing at it. She remembered the self defence class her mother had made her attend when she was a teenager.

'Eyes! Throat! Groin! Knees!' they had chanted, throwing punches and kicks in the general direction of the appropriate body parts. They had laughed about it at the time, her and Ana. She wasn't laughing anymore.

She closed her hands over the thing's face and pressed

her thumbs into its eyeballs. They sank in deep, the orbs bursting, slime trickling down her forearms. It recoiled in agony, giving Rachel the time she needed to reach for the hammer and swing it towards the creature's head. It burst like a ripe tomato, disgorging its acrid contents onto Rachel's face. She clamped her mouth shut but not before some of the revolting goo had entered, the rancid taste on her tongue making her gag.

The body collapsed onto the sand as Rachel vomited for the second time that evening. And when she saw the spiders stream from the soggy confusion at the end of the creature's neck, she almost did again.

17

ANA AWOKE ON THE WOODEN DECK, THE STARS TWINKLING dully overhead, the gibbous moon indistinct in the night sky.

She sat up and glanced around, wiping a tear from her eye. How long had she been out? She half expected to find Ricky with his hand down the front of her knickers. Thankfully, he was nowhere to be seen. Probably still brooding downstairs. Or had he left her on the boat by herself? She sidled over to the rapidly diminishing supply pile, relieved to find the flare gun still there. She tore Ricky's vest from her body, suddenly appalled to have it touching her and sat shivering in her underwear, clutching the flare gun to her chest, her heart pounding. Where was everyone? Why hadn't anyone come back? Where was Rachel?

Something came back to her. A scream. She had been roused from her slumber by a scream. Or had it been part of a dream? She tried to calm herself by counting to ten. She thought about going to check to see if Ricky was still there. And what if he was? Would she rather be here alone or with a sex pest? What if he tried it on again? And what if this time, he didn't stop? She gripped the flare gun tightly. If the time came, could she use it? Could she pull the trigger on Ricky?

Another scream. This one was definitely real. She peered over the rail and scanned the coastline for the source. It was too dark.

'Ana!' came a voice from the blackness.

'Rachel?' Without thinking she raised the gun above her head and fired. The beach lit up momentarily and she could see her sister charging across the sand. Rachel hit the water running and dived in like an extra from Baywatch.

'What's going on?' said Ricky, emerging onto the deck and rubbing his eyes. 'Did you fire a flare?'

Ana ignored him. Rachel cut through the water like a shark, electing to swim rather than wade towards the ladder. She clung onto the rails and hauled herself up, throwing her whole body over the side and landing with a wet bump on the deck. Ana ran to her, cradling Rachel's head against her breast.

'My god Ana, we have to go, we have to get out of here, we have to go now,' she ranted breathlessly.

'What are you talking about Rach? You're safe now, you're safe here.' Who was she trying to convince though?

Rachel pulled away and drew her knees up to her chin. 'No, no, you don't understand, they're dead, they're all dead.'

The whole world seemed to tilt on its axis. Ana's heart plunged into the pit of her stomach. 'Who? Who's dead?'

'Rachel, what happened?' asked Ricky.

'Shut up,' snapped Ana.

'Josh and Lill. I found them. By the beach.' She looked Ana dead in the eyes, the moon reflecting in them. Her face was manic. 'They're dead. Not just dead though... massacred.' She broke down. Ana was dimly aware of

Ricky shuffling about behind them. She continued to ignore him.

'What do you mean?' asked Ana, trying to control the rising panic in her voice.

'Murdered,' whispered Rachel. 'Oh god, she'd been gutted. Something attacked me. I think I killed it.'

'What do you mean "something"?'

Rachel sniffed loudly, tears streaming down her cheeks. 'It looked like a man...but it wasn't. It...I don't know, I can't explain.'

Ana held her sister tightly. 'It's okay, it's okay. It's gone now.' She knew how hollow that sounded. She wanted to believe it herself but couldn't, her breath coming in gasps, seconds away from a full-bore panic attack. Behind her there was a crash. She turned to see Ricky wildly searching for something.

'What are you doing?' said Ana, her voice a pale facsimile of its usual self. He slammed a cartridge into the flare gun and aimed it at Ana's head. Time came to a standstill as Ana stared down the barrel of the weapon.

'Ricky, no,' she said.

She was too tired and too confused to do anything.

She closed her eyes as Ricky squeezed the trigger.

18

THE FLARE ROCKETED PAST HER FACE, SINGEING HER HAIR.

Oh good, he missed, was the first thought that flashed through Ana's mind as she smelt the burning follicles. Then came the shriek from behind her, the sound of a thousand voices coming from one mouth. She whipped her head round in time to see a strange semi-translucent silhouette pinwheeling on the edge of the deck, hands raised to its head, the flare buried in its mouth. It took a step backwards, flames sparking like a Catherine wheel, until the flare burst into life with an almighty explosion. The deck was showered with blood, bone and a thick, phlegmy mucus that must have been the remains of the thing's head.

It stopped, staggered and toppled overboard, splashing into the sea.

No one moved.

'What the fuck was that?' whispered Ana. She turned to Ricky who held the smoking gun in limp, trembling hands. It slipped from his grasp, clattering to the deck.

'Oh Jesus I killed him,' he said.

Ana wiped warm liquid from her face. The smell was revolting.

A wet slapping sound turned their heads.

Something was climbing the ladder. A hand clutched the rail, sinuous fingers wrapping around the metal bar. Ana dragged Rachel towards Ricky, still frozen in place, a useless statue.

Behind them the creature clambered on board, the water running down its emaciated body. It dropped onto all fours and faced them, sizing them up, searching for the biggest threat.

'We need a weapon,' shouted Ana. 'Ricky, wake the fuck up.' He just stared at his empty hands like they were the first ones he had ever seen. 'Ricky!' she screamed. The thing crouched down, spreading its body wide. Ana's eyes darted across the boat for something, anything she could use to defend herself.

'Where's the harpoon?' asked Rachel in a frenzy, scrambling to her feet. 'Find it!'

The creature, perhaps assuming that the male would be the most dangerous predator onboard, dashed forwards and threw itself onto Ricky, the pair of them tumbling onto the deck. Ricky howled in agony as his head hit the wooden flooring with a crunch. At least it seemed to rouse him from his torpor, his arms coming up swinging, landing soft blows on the creature's arms and torso. Spittle leaked from its chin as the beast opened its mouth wide, baring the tiny sharpened pebbles of its teeth. Ricky held his arms in front of his face as the thing leaned forwards and fastened its jaws onto his forearm. It sounded like someone taking a bite of an apple as the teeth tore into his skin and muscle and came away a chunk of flesh. It spat the meat to one side and raised its head again, blood pouring from between the ragged jaws.

It gave Ana just enough time to act.

She tossed aside water bottles and life jackets until her hands found the harpoon gun. She grabbed it and ran towards the creature. She considered firing but was afraid she'd miss.

This was not the time to leave things to chance.

Instead, she slammed the spike of the harpoon upwards into the open mouth of the monster, the tip rupturing the soft palate. The creature fell backwards, writhing on the deck. Ana lunged forward and grabbed the gun, her fingers searching for the trigger. The creature cast its arms out, reaching for her, the harpoon keeping it at a safe distance. Ana levered the weapon until it pointed upwards, and then she squeezed, ejecting the sharpened metal at immense velocity. It blasted forth from the skull of the beast and disappeared into the night, leaving a gaping hole in the back of its head.

The creature twitched, shuddered and died.

Peace was momentarily restored. Ana sat down heavily, placing a hand over her heart, feeling the intense rhythmic beating subside like it was running out of battery.

The silence was at once beautiful and terrifying.

'I told you it wasn't human,' said Rachel from behind her.

It was not helpful.

Ricky sat up, clutching at the bleeding wound on his arm and whimpering softly.

'What was that?' he said.

No one had a good answer.

'I dunno, but I killed one on the beach,' said a dazed-looking Rachel.

'And we just killed two more,' said Ana, not taking her

eyes from the corpse, not even for a second. She realised she was whispering. They all were.

'How many are there?' asked Ricky.

'I don't know,' replied Rachel.

'I don't wanna find out,' said Ana. Her whole body felt numb. She clenched and unclenched her toes and fingers, closing her eyes to try to think straight. It was no use. She crawled towards the cadaver. It was lying on its back, mouth locked in an eternal scream, the harpoon gun jutting out between its teeth. She prodded the body with her foot.

'What is it?' asked Rachel. Ana merely shrugged. It certainly looked human. The proportions were mostly correct at least. The skin was stretched taut over the bones, so much so that she could see the veins and musculature beneath. But it had two arms and two legs. Below the arms, on the torso, were two more small nubs. She checked the other side and found the same, two stubby under-developed limbs, the missing-link in a bizarre and hitherto unknown evolutionary chain.

'It's so pale, like it's never seen the sun.' She squinted at the chest. Was something moving in there?

'Rach, is your phone still working?' Rachel removed it from her armband and checked. Two percent battery. She sidled over to Ana, keeping as far away from the body as possible, and handed her the phone.

'Careful,' said Rachel. 'The one I killed had something living in it.'

'That's what I want to check.'

Ana swiped on the lock screen and brought up the torch function. She switched it on and turned the beam to the corpse. Up close she could see the ribcage, and below it the intestines. The bones were shrivelled and worn look-ing, the guts stringy and purple. There was definitely something moving inside. It scurried away to avoid the light.

'Spiders. When I killed it, spiders came out. Lots of them.'

Ana involuntarily jumped back. She looked at her sister. 'That's not possible.'

'None of this is possible. Just keep away from it, okay? Please?'

Ana nodded. 'No fucking problem.'

The phone died and only then did she realise how dark it had become. The sun was long gone and now only the moonlight cast its pearly glow on the island.

Rachel tended to Ricky. She wrapped the neon vest tightly around his arm to try to stem the blood loss. Ana thought about telling Rachel that Ricky had tried to assault her and decided not to. This was neither the time nor the place. Plus, he currently wore the shell-shocked expression of a returning Vietnam vet.

'We need to get out of here,' she said.

'And go where?' asked her sister.

'We're safe here,' said Ricky, grimacing as the makeshift bandage tightened over his arm.

'No. They know we're here. We've fired enough fucking flares for the whole island to see. We have to move. What if a hundred of those things come for us? What are we gonna do, hide downstairs and not answer the door?' She tried to control the panic in her voice.

'Maybe there aren't any more of them?'

'Oh yeah? You wanna take that chance? Fine, you stay here and me and Rachel will go.'

'Ana!' said Rachel, surprised at the vehemence of Ana's voice. She hadn't seen her sister this assertive in a long, long time.

'No Rach, I'm serious. We're sitting ducks out here on this floating death trap.'

'Where do you suggest we go?'

Ana thought for a moment. Why was she suddenly in charge?

Because someone has to be.

She pointed to the outline of the abandoned building on the hill.

'Up there.'

'What, we just trek through the jungle in the middle of the night, yeah? Great fucking plan,' snapped Ricky. 'Ow!' he shouted as Rachel tightened the bandage with unnecessary force.

'Sorry,' she said coldly.

'At least they won't know we're there. And it'll give us a good vantage point of the island. We can wait there til morning and weigh our options.'

'I agree,' said Rachel. 'The more time we waste here, the higher the chance that more of those things will come along.'

'And what if that's where they live?' said Ricky.

Ana hadn't thought of that. She wanted more time to think, but time was now an unaffordable luxury. 'Then we'll just have to cross that bridge when we come to it. I don't think it will be. After all, the smoke was coming from the other end of the island.'

'You think those things can create fire?' asked Rachel.

Ana shrugged. 'I dunno Rach, I'm not a scientist.' She sighed, her shoulders going limp. The fight was leaving her again, the adrenaline wearing off. 'But yeah, probably. They're more human than anything else I think. It's like they've been...*infected*, or mutated in some way. I can't explain it.'

'Then that's it settled,' said Rachel. 'We'll grab as much water as we can carry and head on up.'

'I'm not sure I can make it,' said Ricky, looking for sympathy.

'Fuck off Ricky, it bit your arm not your leg. Be a fucking man for once,' said Ana.

She looked up towards the hill. They had no weapons, no torches. Nothing except for some bottles of water and a grim determination to survive.

She hoped it would be enough.

19

At the far end of the island, the fire roared again.

Lisa watched the flames, her arms manacled to a wooden pole above her head, the rusted edges scratching at her wrists. Darren lay undisturbed by the fire, his mushed-up body now little more than an inconvenience. His screams rang through her head. They had beaten his body until it was a broken mess, bringing their clubs down long after he had died, beating him to a pulp.

Darren.

Her friend.

Now they moved furtively through the shadows, avoiding the yellow light of the flames.

She tried to count how many. Ten, twenty, thirty...there were too many. As far as she could tell, they were all male. Most were naked, their scrawny penises dangling limply between malnourished legs. Some wore clothes, decaying tee-shirts clinging on by a thread, jeans worn through at the knees, and pockets that hung in tatters like flesh from a wound.

She wondered if Bret had escaped. It was her only

chance, and she clung to it with grim determination. Glancing down at her cleavage, she saw the small baggie of pills still tucked into her bra. She longed for one, just one, to take the edge off the brain-twisting madness that surrounded her. Several of the creatures, or whatever they were, came towards the fire, dragging something. A sob caught in her throat as her last vestige of hope set sail.

Bret.

'No,' she whimpered as they dragged his carcass by the legs and dumped it next to Darren's. Lisa wanted to make it all go away, but she couldn't tear her eyes from the grisly tableaux. One of the men stepped forward. What had once been a pair of overalls were draped around him like a shroud, stopping just above his genitals. A small hoop earring glinted in the firelight, dangling from a drooping lobe.

He carried an axe.

From a frayed pocket he pulled a pair of sunglasses; they looked like Ray-Bans, but were probably knock-offs. Lisa could have laughed at the absurdity had it not all been so terrifying. He kicked at Bret's arms, spreading them out until he lay like Jesus awaiting the crucifixion. The others formed a semi-circle, watching expectantly. The Pale Man in the sunglasses raised the axe ceremonially, letting it hang in the air for several seconds, before issuing a guttural shriek. His followers responded in kind, the sound rising to a shrill cacophony until The Pale Man brought the tool down on Bret's shoulder joint, severing the limb. Lisa screamed in horror as the bone cracked and gave way but no one paid her any attention. She pulled at her bonds but the steel cuffs dug in further, warm rivulets of blood running down her bare arms. The Pale Man raised the axe again and this time she did look away, hearing the thump as the axe hit the ground. Again, one blow was all it took.

'Why are you doing this?' she shouted, barely recognising her own voice. She sounded older somehow, a haggard old crone. Another man picked up the two severed arms as Bret's face stared at her through lifeless, sunken eyes.

Soon another man appeared carrying the strange spider-like totem, resting it flat in the dirt beside Bret. The top two skeletal limbs were wrenched from their fixings and discarded into the fire, replaced by Bret's appendages. Another man stepped forward, carrying a hammer and nails as The Pale Man looked on. Was he smiling? Lisa wanted to faint, to black out...to *die*, even, but the blissful ignorance of sleep evaded her. She closed her eyes and willed herself to wake up in bed somewhere. Anywhere but here, with this cosmic madness surrounding her. She heard the hammering of nails into soft flesh and the gruesome splintering of bone. There was a cheer and when she opened her eyes, the ghastly idol had two new, fresh limbs attached to it. The Pale Man turned his attention to Darren and at this point Lisa came close to losing her mind.

She prayed.

Lisa had never been religious; the only figure she deified was Howard Marks. But Welsh drug-smugglers weren't going to help her now, so she prayed to a God, a higher power, for divine intervention.

She may as well have prayed to Cheech and Chong for all the good it did.

When she looked back, Darren's limbs were affixed above Bret's on the obscene idol. Her friend's bodies were then picked up and tossed onto the fire, the stench of burning bodies filling the air like a noxious chemical.

Two men came towards her.

'No, no,' she muttered repeatedly. 'Please, no, leave me alone, no, no...'

One of them carried an enormous pair of bolt-cutters. Her body went limp with fear. Bolt-cutters? Primitive savages didn't wield tools like this! They should carry spears and blow poison darts, like in the movies.

Ah, the movies. This must be some kind of karma for watching all those sick movies with Darren and Bret. What torture was in store for her?

Behind the men the fire glowed, the dancing light visible through their bodies like a lava-lamp. Things moved around inside them like specks of dust on a projector screen.

Would they hang her up with meathooks through her breasts, like in that film *Cannibal Ferox*? Or would they shove a pole up her snatch until it came through her mouth, spit-roasted for all eternity, like in *Cannibal Holocaust*?

No longer concerned about the restraints that dug into her skin, Lisa screamed until her throat was raw. The men advanced, and she wondered where the twin blades of the bolt-cutter were going to settle. Her nose? Tongue?

Her nipples?

The man disappeared behind her, the cutters scraping along the ground leaving a deep groove. Her mind reeled at the possibilities. Her Achilles' tendon? Or the base of her spine? Both would immobilise her. She supposed if she had to choose, she would opt for her Achilles.

Ha! It was like that party game, Would You Rather, except life-threatening and all too real.

Then came the snipping sound, the cutters squealing as they clamped shut. Lisa tensed her body.

She dropped to the ground, her wrists freed from the chains. The first thing she did was laugh, a high-pitched, manic cackle. She rubbed her hands, avoiding the peeling, torn skin of her wrists.

Everything was going to be okay.

They had allowed her to live.

Her mind became a whirlwind of outrageous fantasies. She imagined them worshipping her as a queen. She would sit atop a throne of skulls in a diaphanous white gown, a ring of human intestine fashioned into a crown adorning her hair, the gruesome creatures bringing her human sacrifices as she ruled over them with an apathetic sneer.

She fished the baggie out of her bra and swallowed one of the tablets, then took another for good measure.

After all, it was a celebration.

Fuck it, she popped a third one down the gullet.

Then she was kicked onto her back, four of the men pinioning her arms and legs. They needn't have bothered, she was far beyond struggling now. A weary acceptance of her fate insidiously crept into her head, jostling for position with her deranged fantasy. How far could the gossamer thin fabric of her mind stretch before snapping once and for all?

A long strip of metal rested in the fire next to her. She could see Bret's face aflame, his melted eyeballs dribbling down his cheeks, which were black and charred and bubbling, his mouth open in a rictus grin that ridiculed her from beyond the grave.

The Pale Man pulled the metal bar from the fire and brandished it towards Lisa. The end was so yellow it was almost white. White hot. That was a saying, wasn't it? She had never understood it, not until now. The tip of the bar opened out into an intricate engraving, like a cattle brand.

How funny. There were no cows here! She laughed, and laughed, and laughed.

She finally blacked out, escaping into the sweet nirvana of delirium.

It didn't last.

The scorching metal pressed against her abdomen and a searing pain unlike any Lisa had ever experienced jolted her from out of one bad dream and into another. Her skin sizzled and burnt and her limbs jerked wildly, the men struggling to hold her steady. She saw smoke and smelt her own flesh as it popped and smouldered, the brand pushing harder onto her stomach until it practically scalded her intestines.

Lisa screamed.

The men cheered.

The first sacrifice in a long time was almost ready.

20

PAUL CHECKED HIS PHONE, THE SIGNAL BLINKING monotonously. It hadn't moved since midday, but now appeared to be travelling inland.

'How long?' he asked Chakrit.

'Soon, soon,' the man replied sleepily, reclining on the deck and smoking another cigarette. 'Half hour or so.'

'It looks like they're on the move,' said Paul.

He nervously scratched the fat neck of the pug. Docile, chubby and constantly craving attention; it reminded him of Ana.

The moonlight cascaded across the rippling sea. Under different circumstances it would be beautiful. Rachel would be taking photos for her Instagram and cooing over how lovely it was. Ana would be whining about putting their phones away and enjoying it with their eyes.

'When are you ever going to look at those photos again?' she would say. She was a real pain in the arse sometimes. But she was Rachel's sister, so he had to put up with her. The trip had been his idea. He had planned it to get away from Ana and her melodrama. So she couldn't handle the pressure of being an adult. Big deal. Sink or swim. She had tried to kill herself. So what?

'Look, she needs professional help,' Paul had suggested to Rachel. 'Taking her on holiday with us is just going to be a drag.'

They had a huge fight about it, the kind that ended in Rachel storming out of the house, telling him she was going to stay with Ana. Paul had been pissed. So pissed, in fact, that he called his ex and spent the night with her. Just one more indiscretion that Rachel was unaware of. Silly cow. He decided there and then to dump her when they got back to Scotland. They had been together almost a year now, and that was more commitment than Paul was used to.

Still, think of the sex he would get tonight for rescuing her. She wouldn't be able to say no to anything.

'You smiling? Happy?' asked Chakrit.

'Just passing the time,' he said. 'Just passing the time.'

'You think Paul will come?' asked Ana. She was out of breath and stopped for a moment to lean against a tree, spreading her legs slightly to ease the pain where her thighs rubbed. Rachel stopped too, happy to rest for a while. They had been hiking uphill for what felt like hours but really could only have been thirty minutes. The jungle was an oven, the trees refusing to let the night chill enter their domain, and the ground underfoot was treacherous. Marshy terrain gave way to streams, which in turn led to knotted roots and razor sharp grass. The worst thing was the light, or lack of it. Moonlight occasionally muscled its way through the leaves, but mostly they were walking in pitch black. At any moment they could step off a cliff edge and not know until the inevitable.

It was why Ana had insisted Ricky go first.

'He'll be on his way,' said Rachel. 'Thank goodness for that tracker app. Knowing Paul, he'll have commandeered a cruise liner and he'll be standing at the front in a sailor's cap and smoking a pipe.'

'Yeah, then he'll be all "I rescued you Rachel. Now bend over and let me fuck up the arse. You owe me this much."'

'If he can get us off this island, he can fuck me anywhere he wants.'

'Fair enough,' agreed Ana. 'I bet he's thinking the same thing right now.'

Rachel launched into a spot-on impersonation of Paul. 'You know Rach, anytime we're apart, just look at the moon, and you'll know I'm looking at the same moon and thinking about taking you up the shitter.'

'And I thought romance was dead.'

Rachel smiled. It felt good to do so. She took her sister's hand. 'I'm scared, Ana. I'm fucking terrified.'

Ana squeezed her back. 'Me too. But if I had to be stuck on an island, I'm glad it's with you.'

'What are you two doing back there?' shouted Ricky.

'Fuck off,' Ana shouted back, hearing him fighting through the undergrowth. 'I'm sorry for what I—'

Rachel put her hand to Ana's parched lips. 'Don't. Don't apologise for anything. I'm the one who's sorry. I'm sorry I wasn't there for you. I'm—'

'Guys, seriously, come on! I've found a road!'

Rachel sighed and Ana pulled her towards her and hugged her tight. 'I love you,' she said.

'Love you more,' said Rachel. 'Come on, let's see what that asshole is talking about.'

They tramped their way up through the vegetation until they caught up with Ricky, his neon paint catching the moon's rays. He stood by the remains of a track, only noticeable by the way the trees parted to allow access. Once upon a time it had been used by vehicles, for the middle section was completely overgrown, but on either side was a deep groove that bore traces of wear and tear.

'There's only one place this could lead,' announced Ricky.

'How's your arm?' asked Rachel. He held it up for them to see. The blood had stopped at least. It had coagulated around the wound, forming a crusty red shell. 'Is it sore?'

'Hurts like hell.'

'Then let's get moving. You first.'

'I knew you'd say that.'

Ana listened to the easy-going banter between them and once more debated internally whether to tell Rachel about Ricky. She decided now was not a good time.

Let's get off this fucking island first.

She looked out to sea from their new vantage point. She thought she could see something in the distance, near the horizon. A light?

'Ana, come on. We can't be far now. It'll be quicker if we stick to the track.'

'Okay,' she said, only half-listening. She glanced back, but the light was gone. It must have been her imagination.

21

HER DEMENTED FANTASY WAS COMING TRUE.

The mark on Lisa's belly was hot to the touch, the pain immense. Branded like cattle and left to writhe in agony by the fire, Lisa had crawled her way backwards and leaned against the nightmarish wooden idol that bore her friends' severed limbs.

Now the men proceeded towards her, carrying a white robe, or at least an old bit of tarpaulin with a hole cut in it.

They were going to crown her their queen.

She remembered a film Darren had shown her once, *White Cannibal Queen* or something. A guy had lost his daughter in the jungle and when he went back years later to find her she had become the high priestess of the tribe, a gorgeous blonde that ruled over the land. They had gotten real high and laughed all the way through it, and now here it was, a stark reality. Life truly is stranger than fiction.

Two of the men hoisted her into a standing position. Her panties were roughly tugged down over her hips and one of the men struggled with her bra.

'Fucking men,' she sighed, reaching behind and

undoing the clasp. She dropped her shoulders and the garment fell to the ground. She stepped out of her undies and waited, naked, while the men with the tarpaulin advanced.

The drugs were taking effect. This was the good stuff, the kind they had all taken last night, the same pills she had sold that weaselly little bastard Ricky.

Last night.

Was that really all it was? Had it not even been twenty-four hours since they had been dancing and drinking on Koh Phangan beach? Today would have been a day of rest, and they had a waterfall trek booked for tomorrow.

Guess they would miss that.

I wonder if we can get a refund, thought Lisa. She laughed too hard and too long.

She thought of her suitcase lying in the hostel. Her clothes, her makeup, her bag of weed. Holiday essentials.

It would all go to waste.

They placed the tarpaulin over Lisa's head. It sat like a poncho as one of the men tied a string around her waist.

Lisa smiled. Had she gone mad, or were the drugs even better than she remembered, or was this whole thing just comically ridiculous? She figured it was a combination of all three.

'I will be your queen,' she announced. 'Your white cannibal queen. I shall rule over you with poise and dignity.'

The men ignored her.

She raised her arms and spread them wide, tilting her head back.

'I will be your queen!' she shouted. The men turned her around, two of them flanking her, the others lining up behind. They took her by the arms and walked her away from the village. Lisa felt like a macabre Pied Piper. 'Bring me my flute,' she demanded, 'And I will play you a tune. We shall dance until the sun comes up.'

They left the fire behind, walking slowly past the worn, ruined buildings towards the edge of the clearing. Black clouds gathered in the sky; an ominous portent, or just weather doing what weather does? The terrain hardened as they climbed a gentle slope, the mud giving way to cracked black earth. The trees, too, seemed to become more and more wizened, the utter absence of leaves allowing them to hunch forwards in all their petrified glory.

The well-trodden path led towards two trees in particular, ones that towered over the rest. They were unlike anything Lisa had ever seen, except perhaps on one of her occasional LSD trips. An enormous spider web hung between them like a lace curtain, obscuring what lay beyond. Someone prodded Lisa in the back with a knife, urging her onwards.

Queen Lisa of the Cannibals, knowing no such thing as fear, walked forwards into the web. It snapped and fell, draping over her, a bridal veil for the damned.

The men cheered.

Lisa smiled.

They continued.

'Take me to my throne,' said Lisa, dizziness and nausea jostling for pole position in her mind. 'Your queen must rest now.'

She raked the webs off her face to better see, but the path was free of obstacles.

Small stones had been carefully laid out along either side of the pathway. The surrounding jungle looked impenetrable, a wall of twisted white limbs and roots that plunged several feet out of the ground, twisting and coiling around each other, their decaying forms spiralling outwards with grasping hands that clutched at thin air. They moved as she watched, the trees themselves seeming to breathe as she passed, their trunks gently pulsing.

Then the smell hit Lisa. The stench of rotting, putrefying meat.

It was enough to briefly shatter her illusion, but not quite enough to snap her back to reality. To her left was a pit, but she couldn't tell how deep it was - there were too many corpses in it for an accurate guess. Behind her the men carried the charred remains of Bret and Darren, their crispy bodies rudely bundled into the pit atop the others.

'Hi guys,' said Lisa dreamily. 'I'm the queen now.' She smiled and Bret's horrified face gazed back at her, one side melted away to the bone, the black craters of his eye sockets giving him a skull-like aspect. Darren's head had avoided the worst of the flames, but still hung like a loose sack. His glassy doll's eyes never moved, yet he managed to wink at her in his inimitable way. She smiled back. It was just like old times.

I'm so proud of you, Lisa. You were always my queen.

'Thanks, Daz. Guess I'll see ya on the other side.'

Stygian clouds rolled across the sky, obscuring the moon and plunging the barren landscape into darkness. A lone light flickered in the distance, a sight to warm the heart of the weary traveller.

Lisa said goodbye to her friends and carried on the infernal procession. The wind picked up and billowed her tarpaulin gown around her waist, her silken veil sticking to her hair and face. The light grew stronger as they neared a sheer rock face that led up hundreds of feet towards the abandoned buildings that crowned the island. Ageing, decrepit vehicles and construction materials littered the ground; shovels, pick-axes, even a pneumatic drill. The diggers were dilapidated and rusted and covered in bird shit, the flat tyres sunk deep into the mud.

The firelight fluttered within a deep gash in the rock. A cave, man-made if the great heaps of rubble were anything to go by.

'My castle awaits,' sighed Lisa as the men led her into the mountain, the entrance greedily swallowing her up. Nearby, thunder pealed and lightning tore the sky asunder as Lisa stood in the man-made tunnel and looked at her feet. The cave floor was fifteen feet down a steep incline. She checked for a ladder or a rope, but she needn't have bothered. Two firm hands on the small of her back shoved her, and she stepped forwards, trying to maintain her balance, but to no avail. Her feet skidded out from under her and she fell on her ass and slid down into the belly of the cave.

'Hey!' she shouted as she thumped onto the hard rock. 'This is no way to treat your queen!'

But the men had already left.

She was alone.

22

'OH SHIT, WAS THAT THUNDER?'

A jagged finger of lightning forked its way across the horizon in answer to Ana's question.

'Think it's heading our way?' asked Rachel.

Ana put her index finger in her mouth and licked it, then held it up in the air.

'What are you doing?' asked her sister.

'Dad used to do this, remember? You can tell which way the wind's blowing by feeling the breeze on your finger.'

Rachel waited a sufficient amount of time before asking, 'So is it?'

Ana looked thoughtful. 'I have no fucking idea,' she said. Rachel laughed, surprising them both.

'Come on,' she said. They walked hand in hand up the old road. The temperature had dropped dramatically since they stepped out onto the track, the increased altitude not helping matters, their lack of clothing becoming ever more apparent. The mosquitoes were out in hordes now, and Ana slapped a hand onto her thigh, squashing one.

'I would give literally anything for some Deet right now,' she said.

Rachel nodded appreciatively. 'And a pair of comfy shoes,' she added.

'What about a steak? A big, fat, juicy steak?'

Rachel hit her on the arm. 'Stop it. I'm so hungry.'

'I dunno. I think I lost my appetite when that thing's head exploded.'

Rachel smiled grimly. 'How can you joke about that?'

Ana shrugged. 'What else are we supposed to do? Sit and cry?'

Rachel stopped walking. Up ahead Ricky trudged on regardless. 'Maybe we should? I mean, how the fuck are we gonna get out of this? How are we gonna get off this island?' Her voice cracked. 'What if we die here?'

Ana touched her sister's face. It was wet with tears. 'We're not gonna die here. No fucking way. Not with bloody Rambo looking after us,' she said, gesturing at Ricky. 'Paul will be on his way with the fucking marines. We just have to stay focused, that's all. And stick together. I don't give a shit about Ricky, but you and me...we need to stick together.'

Rachel wrapped her arms around Ana, a hug of desperate, unconditional love.

'Hurry up, we're almost there,' shouted Ricky.

'Keep your voice down,' hissed Ana. 'Fucking master of stealth.'

The first drops of rain began to fall. Within seconds the mosquitos had dispersed and the cool water muscled its way through the trees. Ana leaned her head back and opened her mouth, letting the rain drops hit her tongue and dribble down her chin. She turned back, wondering how far they had come, half-expecting to see the boat a few hundred yards away, mocking their futile escape.

But the boat was far behind them now, hidden by a near-impenetrable wall of vegetation. It was as if the jungle was closing in on them. She watched, waiting for the sinuous limbs of the trees to warp and tangle with each other, blocking off the way they came, forcing them onwards.

There's no point staring. It only happens when you're not watching.

'Come on, Ana,' said Rachel, tugging on her arm. Reluctantly, Ana turned away and renewed their ascent.

A few minutes later, the heavens opened fully.

The storm had arrived.

23

THE ISLAND ROSE UP FROM THE SHADOWS LIKE SOME unnameable thing from Lovecraftian lore, a colossal sea creature from the very depths of the ocean.

'That's it,' said Chakrit, nudging Paul awake.

'That's what?' said Paul, rubbing the sleep from his bleary eyes and following Chakrit's unwavering gaze.

'Koh Wai. The forgotten island.'

Paul snapped to attention and sat up. He squinted out to sea. There it was alright, through the murk and gloom, shrouded in fog. The island.

The wind picked up, and soon torrents of rain lashed down, the droplets bouncing as they struck the deck. Paul gripped a rail with one hand to steady himself as the sea became choppier, waves crashing against the little fishing boat. He tried to ignore the inclement weather, instead focusing on the island. He didn't like the look of the place. Oh sure, during the day it was probably some exotic paradise, but right now, in the late evening, it took on a sinister characteristic. The old man piloting the boat called down in Thai, his voice almost lost in the wind. Chakrit shouted back at him then turned to Paul.

'This is as far as we go.'

'Why? Is the sea too dangerous?'

Chakrit averted his eyes. 'Something like that. We take dinghy.'

'What? With those waves?'

'Don't worry. It has a motor.'

A six foot wave ploughed into the side of the boat, tilting them at an obscene angle. Paul's feet slid out from under him and he gripped the rail harder.

'A motor,' he snarled, as the boat temporarily righted itself. 'I didn't come out here to die, Chakrit.'

Chakrit replied, the elements drowning out his voice. It sounded like, 'You may not have a choice.' Paul didn't ask him to repeat himself. Using the handrail, the pair worked their way around the boat to the dinghy, which floated alongside them, a heavy rope holding it in place. Chakrit held it tight as Paul climbed the railing and lowered himself into the dinghy, gripping onto the handles for dear life, the ocean spray drenching him with salt water. Chakrit untied the rope and leapt overboard, landing next to Paul. He gunned the engine and nothing happened.

'What's wrong?' asked Paul. Chakrit didn't answer. He yanked the cord again. This time the motor briefly whirred into life then promptly gave up the ghost.

'Nothing,' said the young Thai man, as he pulled the cord a third time, the engine roaring and, this time, not stopping. 'Hold on,' he said.

Paul did just that as they motored off towards the island, leaving the fishing boat and Chakrit's uncle behind.

'It gets rough now.'

'Don't worry about that,' grimaced Paul as water

splashed into the dinghy. There was at least three inches of water in the boat already.

This better be worth it, he thought.

He looked back and saw the old man standing on the prow of the boat watching them through the downpour. There was something eerie about the way he stood there in the lashing rain, like he didn't expect to see them again.

The island drew closer.

24

LISA STUMBLED DOWN THE TUNNEL, GRINNING INANELY.

She heard rain spattering outside, running down the slope and pooling at the bottom. She had tried to climb back out but the lichen-coated rock was too slippery.

No problem-o.

The walls were lined with flaming torches that danced madly in the howling wind that shuddered through the passageway. She tried to remove one from its metal holder, but it wouldn't budge. She watched the flames for a while as they flickered and spat, the heat on her skin a pleasant distraction. After a while it was time to move on, though the flame continued to sparkle in front of her eyes.

She walked some more, stopping at the next torch and watching it. She realised she could no longer hear the rain. She kept going.

Viridescent creepers lined the walls, and ugly purple flowers bloomed from cracks. Everywhere Lisa looked she thought she saw faces leering at her, jealous of her hand-crafted regal tarpaulin. She waved dismissively at the imaginary people.

Her foot kicked something soft and she looked down at what used to be a person. Male or female, she couldn't say. It had been turned inside out.

'Hello,' she said to the ragged mess. When there was no response, she resumed her doomed journey. More strange plants dotted the path. She crouched down next to one, the pink and purple flowers shimmering in the trembling light of the torches. She had never seen anything like them. They seemed to be breathing. She noticed that they turned to follow her as she walked past.

This place was funny. Funny-weird *and* funny-haha. She giggled as a long blue plant hissed at her. It was coiled like a garden hose, but unfurled slightly as she got closer, the petals opening wide to reveal a leafy tongue running over the tiny knives of its teeth.

'Well fuck *that*,' she said, and carried on walking.

The walls gradually smoothed out, growing wider until they opened out into a chamber. No, not a chamber. A cavern.

It was gigantic, so tall she couldn't see the roof.

The rock beneath her feet gave way to something soft. Lisa thought it best not to look down and see what she was standing on. She had a pretty good idea.

'Honey, I'm home,' she called out, her voice echoing through the cavern. Nothing happened. She felt wonderful, and also very sick. She scratched at the dry patches at the side of her mouth until they bled.

'It's me, your white cannibal queen. Furnish me with wine and grapes, and be quick about it. Your Royal Highness aches for a bath.' She stumbled and fell to her knees, coming face to face with a skull.

'Who the fuck are you?' she demanded.

She lifted the skull and pitched it across the cavern.

Above her something awoke.

'Come out, come out, wherever you are.'

It started to move.

She didn't like it here. She didn't like it one bit. Were the drugs wearing off, or was reality threatening to boot the door down? She found her drugs, still tucked snugly into her cleavage, and swallowed the last pill.

'Hurry up. I need to take a royal shit.'

A sound, the sensation of movement from far away. But not too far.

Not far enough.

She turned in circles, searching for the way she had come in, for the comforting glow of the torches. Her eyelids felt heavy but she no longer wanted to be here. She hadn't asked to be their queen. They had no right to crown her.

'That's it, I'm leaving.' She bit down hard on the inside of her cheek as she spoke, the words barely legible. Only Darren had ever been able to understand her when she was this high, and would have to translate for anyone present. But Darren wasn't here anymore.

Darren was dead.

Bret was dead.

And then she saw it, blocking the exit. Waiting for her.

The fantasy collapsed like the wreckage of a flaming building. Suddenly sober, she realised she was standing on human flesh and bone. She knew she wasn't the White Cannibal Queen. That was just a dumb movie. This was real life, and yet somehow it also wasn't. Because this sort of thing only happened in movies, right?

'Oh god. Oh god no, no, you can't be real...' She lumbered backwards and fell.

It moved closer.

Lisa's heart stopped for a few seconds. She froze.

'Oh god you can't be real oh god you can't be real oh god you can't be real oh...'

But it was real.

Lisa screamed until she could scream no more.

Only then did her nightmare truly begin.

'IT'S A HOTEL,' EXCLAIMED RACHEL.

'It would have been,' said Ricky, 'If they had ever finished it.'

They had reached the top of the hill and now stood panting in what was nearly a driveway, Ana bent over with her hands on her knees. She had never been a big hiker. The imposing facade of the reception awaited its first ever customers.

The rain lashed down, bouncing off the dirt, and a brief burst of lightning momentarily illuminated the empty building. It was designed in typically gaudy style to resemble a Thai temple. It could have been stunning, with golden spires reaching for the sky and miniature pagodas lining the walls. A narrow bridge led to the entrance over what was intended as a koi pond. The roof was multi-tiered in the traditional style of a Buddhist temple and carved figures decorated the exterior.

Now though, without constant care and attention, the colours had faded. Moss and creepers slithered up the wall, vanishing into cracks while a tree lay blocking the entrance, a victim of one of Thailand's many tropical storms. The carved figures showed signs of wear, the wood splintered into thin lines where tiny plants and insects now made their home. To one side lay a pile of bamboo scaffolding that had collapsed after years of neglect.

Beyond the reception the yellowing apartment blocks stood watch, four storeys of empty rooms and broken dreams.

'Let's go inside,' said Ricky.

'Yeah, good idea,' said Ana.

But none of them moved. The rain soaked their skin, their flimsy underwear doing nothing to protect them from the torrential downpour, the water dripping from the tips of their noses.

'You first, Ricky,' shivered Rachel.

'Why always me?'

'Because you're a big, tough man,' said Ana, still trying to catch her breath.

'Cunt,' he muttered, and without another word he hopped over the fallen tree. The girls followed, reaching the stone bridge that led into the lobby of the resort. Filthy water filled the koi pond, crooked white branches jutting out from the brown murk. Ana stopped at the entrance, afraid they were being followed. Through the gloom and the rain she couldn't see much of anything. The trees swayed and loose leaves and scattered branches rolled by like tumbleweed.

They went inside.

Around the same time, Paul and Chakrit were doing their own investigating on the deck of old Prama's boat, still wedged on the sandbank not far from shore, deserted and eerily quiet.

'Rachel? Ana? You guys here?' shouted Paul, his voice lost in the wind, the rain drumming off his face.

'Let's try downstairs,' suggested Chakrit. He handed Paul the flashlight and unsheathed an eight-inch hunting knife from his belt.

'What the fuck do you need that for?'

Chakrit ignored him. They kept low and crept towards the wooden hatch that led below deck. Chakrit carefully lifted it and sidled down the steps, gripping the knife in his rain slicked hand, his heart beating in his ears. The water poured down the stairs like a miniature waterfall.

He slowly, so-very-slowly opened the door at the foot of the stairs. A boxy room, a stained mattress at one side and a girly calendar on the wall. Another door led to a toilet, vomit caked around the rim. Paul walked behind Chakrit, shining the torch over his shoulder.

'Nothing here.'

Paul's jaw clenched. 'So where are they?'

'Maybe they seek shelter?'

'They had shelter here.'

'Not enough room.'

'Great. That's just fucking great.' Paul kicked at the wall. The sound was hollow and unsatisfying. 'So where would they have gone?'

Chakrit let out a deep, painful sigh. 'Uphill. To old hotel. You check your phone?'

'Yeah. It says she's on the island, but it doesn't really narrow it down. Phone's almost dead anyway, had to move it to low-power mode.' He waited for Chakrit to suggest something. 'So what now?'

'We go uphill. But my friend, there could be much danger. In Thai jungle, everything wants you dead.'

'I'll be okay. I just wanna find Rach and get off this island. Her clothes were on the beach, you know. I mean, her shoes and everything. You think she'll be okay?'

Chakrit paused. 'Come on, let's go.'

Paul blocked his route. 'You never answered my question.'

The men locked stares as the rain thrummed off the deck. Paul stood a good three inches taller than Chakrit. The smaller man smiled. 'Thai jungle very dangerous. If she sticks to the path, she'll be okay.'

'That's assuming there *are* paths here.'

Chakrit shoved past Paul, easily knocking him aside, and headed up the stairs. Paul waited, surveying the scene. There was nothing to indicate that anyone had been on the boat apart from an overflowing ashtray, and Rachel didn't smoke. Fuck, he wasn't even sure what he was looking for. It's not as if they had any clothes to leave lying around.

'Mr Paul!'

It was Chakrit. Paul left behind the empty room and climbed back out into the rain.

'Bring the torch. Shine here.'

Paul didn't like being told what to do, but he supposed Chakrit was the expert. The deck was slippery, and he gripped the railing as he made his way towards Chakrit.

There was something lying at his feet. Against his better judgement, Paul illuminated the unmoving lump.

'What the fuck is that?' he asked, running the beam up the pale white body, the harpoon gun still wedged between its teeth.

Chakrit shook his head in disbelief. 'And who killed it?'

The two men looked at each other.

Above them the thunder roared.

It sounded like laughter.

At least the inside of the hotel offered some shelter. Sure, there were plenty of holes in the roof where water cascaded in and the floor was damp with puddles, but it was better than being in the jungle.

Less exposed.

Palm leaves criss-crossed the floor like scars, and bags of cement lay piled in the corner, abandoned and forgotten. There was a huge stone desk by the wall. Presumably it would have been the reception desk, but unfinished and unadorned it reminded Ana of a sacrificial altar.

She sneezed.

'You okay, sis?'

Ana nodded. 'Just cold.' She sneezed again, the sound bouncing off the bare walls. She rubbed her temples, leaning against the wall for balance.

The voices were back and stronger than ever. Taunting, laughing, sighing, moaning. She only understood two of the words.

Help me.

The rest was nonsense, gibberish.

She dug her nails into the palms of her hands, pressing them in, bursting the skin. It helped to quieten the voices.

Pain always helped.

'Should we start a fire?' asked Ricky.

'I dunno,' said Rachel. 'Would that not give away our location?'

'But don't we want to be found? By a rescue team, I mean?'

'We're fucked either way,' grimaced Ana. 'Might as well be warm.'

'And for all we know, Darren and the others are still out there. Maybe they'll see the smoke and come find us,' said Ricky.

Ana was unconvinced. Rachel just looked down at her hands.

'Come on then, let's get this fire going,' said Ana, stooping to gather a small armful of wood. 'How well does bamboo burn? There's no shortage of that.'

'I guess we'll find out,' said Rachel. 'Ricky, grab as much as you can from that pile round the front.'

'I can't carry it all myself. My arm is all messed up, remember?'

'Shit. Fine, I'll help. You okay in here, Ana?'

'Don't have much choice, do I?'

Rachel sighed. 'I guess not.'

She was so tired. She hoped the bamboo would keep them going all night.

Presuming they made it that long.

The rain showed no signs of abating as Ricky stepped out of the lobby onto the bridge.

'Careful,' he said, holding out his hand for Rachel.

'Thanks, but I'm perfectly capable of walking.'

Snooty bitch.

Were all Scottish girls as prissy as these two? He decided never to go and find out. He also decided never to go travelling again. From now on, his holidays were going to be along the California coastline, where the weather was good and the bitches were hot. Still, he couldn't complain about his current view, Rachel's shapely ass bouncing as she jogged through the downpour to the bamboo, the polka dot panties clinging like a second skin. The long rods of wood were drenched, and she looked around for some that were sheltered from the rain.

'Shit, it's too wet, Ricky. We need to find some dry wood.'

'What about out back? There's gotta be something in those other buildings. They looked more finished than this one. Maybe they've got tables and chairs and things.'

Rachel considered the idea. Ricky's heartbeat quickened.

'Okay,' she said. 'But let's hurry, I don't want to leave Ana alone too long.'

'Uh, yeah, sure,' he replied, barely listening, watching the way the rain dripped down her spine and rolled over the curve of her ass as she crouched by the bamboo. They would be alone soon.

Just the two of them.

Rachel went first, taking the long way round the lobby. Ricky stayed close behind, watching, feeling the stirring in his groin.

A thousand thoughts ran through his head. He had killed a man today. Was it even a man? It was something. A living, breathing creature, and he had blown its head clean off with a flare gun. The idea appalled him, repulsed him, and yet...

He felt strong. Powerful.

A real man.

He had been in fights before. Plenty of them, always one-sided fights that ended with him on the ground, bleeding and sobbing. He had never understood why people picked on him.

Now, finally, he did. It was because hurting someone

gave you power. It made you ten-feet tall. For the first time
in his life, he felt like a real man. But he hadn't just beaten
up some loser. No, he had killed. Taken a life. Wiped
someone from existence.

Death was a turn-on. Who knew?

Of course, the joke was ultimately on himself. Soon, it
would be his turn. And Rachel's. And Ana's. There was no
way in hell they were getting off this island.

Delaying the inevitable, that's all they were doing.

He pictured the creature's head exploding again.
Suddenly he wanted to cry. What was happening? Why him,
why now? Why couldn't Ana have just fucked him back on
the boat? Or better yet, back on Koh Phangan. And Rachel
too, though he knew she was out of his league.

That bitch. It was her fault they were all here. If she had
just given him what he deserved, none of this would have
happened.

They slopped their way through the mud towards the
apartment blocks. Ricky nodded in satisfaction. He was
right; they were in better condition than the reception. Even
the roofs looked intact. He saw Rachel smile to herself like it
had been her fucking suggestion.

What was she planning?

Those girls were only looking out for themselves. He
knew it. They whispered behind his back all the way up the
hill. Were they planning on killing him? Maybe that was
why they were building a fire; something to roast his flesh
over. Even if they were rescued, he knew they wouldn't let
him off the island.

Well fuck them.

Ahead of him, Rachel broke into a trot and he adjusted
his shorts to give his erection room to breathe.

They were using him. Letting him go first through the

jungle. He had saved their lives, and how did they thank him? Not by spreading their legs, which would have been the decent thing to do.

Well, if he was going to die, he would take them down with him. And if they were all going to die, why not have a little fun first?

Ana wondered why she hadn't just gone with Rachel and Ricky. She was alone in the vast, empty lobby, but there were sounds from all around. The constant drip-drip of the rain coming through the ceiling. The wind battering the walls hard enough to dislodge the plaster, the unusual-looking birds that roosted far above her in the beams of the roof, squawking and ruffling their feathers.

And the voices, of course.

They were back with a vengeance. Perhaps they had never really gone away? She had buried them in a shallow grave, but they had risen like the undead and sought her out again.

Stress, her doctor had said. The stress of looking after her ailing mother, of tending to a dying woman. So why had it all started months before they even knew her mum was sick?

The doctor could not explain that one.

Ana grabbed bricks from a large pile and laid them in a circle, then arranged the small bundle of kindling she had gathered into a pyramid. There was no point in trying to light it yet. The fire would be out in seconds. She needed the others to bring back plenty more, hopefully some nice, dry fuel wood. She listened to the storm and wondered if they would find any.

She heard wet feet slapping behind her, slowly, rhyth-
mically.

Ana froze.

She tried to ignore it, thinking instead of going to Girl
Guide Camp with Rachel when they were younger. It was
where Ana had learnt to build a fire. She would help the
Guide leaders by gathering the wood and constructing it,
though she wasn't allowed to use the matches to light it.

The footsteps behind her continued their inexorable
journey.

She remembered holding Rachel's hand during the
ghost stories, and how they had tried to out-sing each other
during the campfire songs, always a competition to see who
could be the loudest.

Help me.

The footsteps stopped. Ana swallowed hard but didn't
turn round.

'You're not real. Leave me alone.'

The steps resumed, growing louder, plodding towards
her.

'Please, stop. Just go.'

Ana.

Her whole body tensed as if bracing itself for impact.
'No,' she said.

Look at me, Ana.

'Please, no.' She turned her head, scanning the bare and
decrepit walls of the resort until she saw it.

Rachel, or a ghastly, inhuman copy of her. The cadav-
erous doppelgänger fell to its knees, limbs jutting out at
inhuman angles, the pale, dead skin so tight over the bones
that it was torn in several places. There was no blood, just
thick, oozing white sap.

It's all your fault, said Rachel, as she held both hands in front of her gut and plunged the talon-like nails in, ripping the dry, powdery flesh apart and giving Ana a glimpse of the black nightmare inside her, coiled and deadly.

The apartment block materialised through the sheets of rain, an enormous weather-beaten U-shaped edifice, the paint peeling and cracked and yellowing.

'There has to be some kind of furniture in here,' shouted Rachel. She wondered how Ana was getting on and wished they had stuck together. When did splitting up ever yield good results?

She stopped suddenly, caught on something, like her panties had snagged on a nail.

She felt an odd sensation at the base of her spine as Ricky grabbed the waistband of her knickers and yanked her backwards, catching a momentary glimpse of her bare ass as he did so.

'Hey!' she yelled as he twirled her round to face him. He planted a hard kiss on her lips as one hand found the plump flesh of her ass and roughly squeezed it, his hard-on pressing through his shorts into the wet flesh of her belly. She wriggled free and fell backwards into the mud, the rain pressing her hair to her face. She swept it away and looked at the bedraggled figure above her.

'What the fuck are you doing, arsehole?' she demanded. Ricky stroked the tentpole in his shorts without seeming to realise he was doing so.

'We're all gonna die here, you know that?' he said matter-of-factly. 'You wanna die a virgin?'

Rachel laughed bitterly. 'You're barking up the wrong tree, pal. I've not been a virgin for a long, long time.'

She tried to get to her feet and Ricky kicked her in the ribs. 'What the fuck!' she cried as he forced himself down on top of her, pinning her arms down into the dirt.

'We're gonna die Rachel,' he shouted over the thunder. 'All of us. I could have made it real special for you, but you fucked up. Still, I'm a nice guy. I'm gonna give you another shot. If we can't make love at a time like this, when can we?'

'You're a fucking nutter!' she roared, throwing her knee up into his groin with all the force she could muster. He yelped like a soprano and she shoved him off, splashing backwards through the filth until she ran out of ground and fell several feet, landing on her back in soft mud. Where was she?

Lightning flashed again.

A large pit, probably intended as a swimming pool but just as unfinished as the rest of the place. A mud bath, more like. She struggled to her feet, hands sinking into the sludge.

Ricky appeared at the lip of the excavation. He pulled his underwear off and nursed his aching testicles, his erection undiminished.

'Fucking bitch!' he cried, jumping in after her.

'Ricky, stop!'

But he wouldn't. Not any more. Things were too far gone now. They were in the endgame. She was his by right. He would fuck her and then kill her. Or kill her then fuck her, whichever came first.

No one was around to see.

No one was around to judge him.

She could scream all she wanted. And afterwards, he would go back for Ana. Why not? They would all be dead soon. All of them. There were no morals anymore. No such thing as right or wrong in this situation.

There was only live or die.

And once, just once, he wanted to wipe that smug, self-satisfied little smirk from Ana's fucking moon-face.

The mud sucked at his feet and he sank up to his knees. He pulled them out one at a time with a squelching sound as Rachel kept going backwards, trying to get up, trying to run, or find a way to defend herself. He was gaining on her. She slithered on, the howling wind stinging her eyes, the rain making progress slow, almost impossible. She turned her back on him and tried to get to her feet, then screamed as her knickers were dragged down to her knees. She tripped on them and collapsed face-first into the mud. Then Ricky was on her, manhandling her onto her back. His eyes blazed with fury, his tongue poking out the side of his mouth in a parody of concentration.

'No! Ana! Help!' she called, but her words were lost in the storm. She felt the tip of his penis nudging her thigh as he tried to guide it in.

Running out of time, she lashed out and caught her assailant on the bridge of the nose. Even over the gale-force wind she heard it crack.

'Ow! You bitch,' he shouted, restraining her arms with one hand as he raised the other to his broken nose. He stared at his fingers — it was hard to tell where the mud ended and the blood began — then tightened his fist and rammed it onto Rachel's face. Her vision exploded in stars and colours. He struck her again and almost came right there. Then he briefly let go of her, afraid to ruin their special moment. She reached for his injured arm and raked the makeshift bandage down, finding the deep wound and stabbing her fingers into it. Her nails scraped the exposed bone and came away with meaty chunks of flesh beneath them. Ricky howled in agony and she took the opportunity to draw back her fist and punch him in the throat, leaving the knuckle of her index finger sticking out. It caught him in the Adam's apple, and he rolled backwards, gargling blood and shrieking obscenities.

Rachel managed to stand and shakily faced Ricky. She didn't even recognise him; a man possessed, eyes hungry with lust and madness.

'Why are you doing this?' she wailed, her feet squelching with each step as she backed up, not realising how close she was to the hole in the middle, the hole that decades ago had swallowed up a young Thai construction worker called Arama and unleashed hell on the remote island of Koh Wai.

'I'm doing this because your body is mine by right,' snarled Ricky, the bandage on his arm fluttering in the wind like a sad flag, blood pouring from his nose and arm. 'I saved your life!'

Rachel shuffled backwards until her heels hung over the edge of the abyss. She felt wind caressing her legs and back and realised that one more step would send her hurtling down into fuck-knows-where.

Ricky came for her, his erection leading the charge.

Rachel dodged to the side and kicked out, aiming at his shins.

His legs struck her ankle, sending shooting pains through Rachel's leg, but it was worth it.

Because Ricky fell forwards, the pit opening up before him like a black hole of insanity.

He groped wildly as he fell and caught a handful of Rachel's hair, dragging her with him. For one heart-stopping moment she thought she was falling until a searing pain in her scalp told her otherwise.

Ricky, clutching a filthy clump of Rachel's locks, vanished.

She listened as his thin, reedy scream faded into the distance, her heart pounding. She waited. There was nothing.

She ran a hand over her head and found the bald patch where Ricky had torn her hair out at the roots, then hauled her mud-caked knickers back up. Flipping onto her belly, she slid across the mud to where Ricky had fallen.

She stared down into the abyss but could see nothing.

'I hope you die, you fucking wanker,' she spat. She got to her feet.

She had to find Ana.

The ground had swallowed him whole, and now he was falling. Was this what it was like to die? An eternity of tumbling through a black, empty void? He came, his own semen splattering his face as he floated into the darkness. He would have been sick, but his stomach was still somewhere on the surface trying to catch up.

And then he stopped.

Something soft and springy had broken his fall. He lay still, then after a while opened his eyes. Far above him the night sky was a navy blue against the awful round blackness of...of wherever he was now. This cave. He tried to move but couldn't. Had he broken his neck? No, he could wiggle his fingers and toes.

He was not paralysed, just stuck on something.

He started to laugh at his own good fortune.

The clouds parted above him and the moon's celestial beam streamed into the cavern.

All around him were webs. Thick, monstrous spiderwebs spanning as far as he could see in a giant funnel, vanishing below into a chasm. Animals and birds were trapped there, most long dead and stripped of flesh, leaving only a rotting skeleton.

He stopped laughing.

'Help,' rasped Ricky, his head spinning, the taste of his own semen on his tongue.

From far, far below came a clicking noise, like nails dropped on a hardwood floor. Ricky swallowed, inadvertently gulping a mouthful of his own cum. He struggled, pulled, thrashed, screamed.

The shadows stirred.

It was coming for him.

The clouds shifted and the moonlight faded away until all around was sheer emptiness.

Click-click-click-click.

Ricky's stomach lurched and he vomited over himself. He tried to scream but this time nothing came out.

Click-click-click-click.

He could sense its presence, his jaw opening and closing, eyes blinking madly, head shaking from side to side. A shape loomed up over him. He could smell it, feel its foul, unearthly breath on his face, as coarse hairs brushed his frigid, naked limbs.

Click-click.

Just when Ricky thought he could take no more, the clouds parted again, allowing the moonlight to penetrate the inky surroundings. Ricky saw his own face reflected in hundreds of swollen, inhuman eyes. He saw the fangs, dripping with venom. They plunged into his stomach, the massive creature now mercifully blocking the light. Ricky's whole body shuddered as the fangs withdrew, rending his flesh like the world's worst autopsy and leaving a gaping hole in his torso.

As his life slipped away, Ricky was sure he felt hands - human hands - rooting around in his stomach, scooping out handfuls of his intestines. Some of them slipped out of the creature's grip and slopped back down onto Ricky's prone body, somehow finding their way back into the ravaged stomach cavity.

Oh hi, guts, he thought. *Good to see you again.*

And then once again the moonlight was gone, leaving nothing in its wake but death and madness.

26

THEY HAD BEEN AWAY TOO LONG AND ANA WAS WORRIED. HOW long did it take to gather wood for the fire?

The apparition was long gone, if it was ever really there to begin with. She shuddered at the memory.

Rachel.

Only it wasn't. Rachel was safe, she hoped. She was with Ricky. They'd be back any minute now, with armfuls of wood, enough to start a fire. It wasn't much to ask, was it?

She peered out through the rain at the worsening weather, watching as it turned into a full-blown tropical storm, the trees rocking violently, shedding broken, splintered branches. Should she call out? What if they were injured? Or worse? She should be ready.

Thankfully, weapons were not hard to find. Tools lay scattered across the floor, as if the men who had been wielding them had taken flight at a moment's notice. She picked up a screwdriver then discarded it. Too short. She lifted a pitchfork. Too bulky, too unwieldy.

Why was it so hard to choose a suitable weapon?

She settled on a wrench. The weight was about right.

Not too heavy that she couldn't swing it quickly, but enough to crush a skull should the need arise.

Enough to crush a skull.

What the fuck was happening? Yesterday she had been just arriving at the Full Moon Party. A week ago she had been sipping a margarita with Rachel and Paul in Edinburgh Airport, waiting on their flight. And now here she was thinking about how best to bash someone's brains in. She didn't know whether to laugh or cry.

You can get through this.

Bullshit. It had only been a year since she tried to take her own life. How far had she really come since then?

Well, she had killed that monster on the boat. When the time had come, she had been able to act. But that had been instinct. Now she had time to consider what was going on. Could she do it again? Could she fight?

Could she *kill*?

Only one way to find out.

She might not have to. Paul was on his way, wasn't he? Ana couldn't be sure. She didn't trust Paul. Although she had never mentioned it to her sister, she hadn't liked him from the moment she had met him. Wandering eyes. Too many "late nights" at work. But Rachel liked him and Ana felt it wasn't her place to say anything. Not while their own relationship was still on the mend.

A sound. Scraping metal. Ana whirled in its direction.

Nothing there. She was getting jumpy. The wind screeched through the empty window panes.

No, not empty.

Something was watching her from the window.

She clutched the wrench in both hands and took a few steps back. Cold eyes regarded her from a clear frame on the second storey. She blinked away the rain. How the hell did it get up there? It came through slowly, deliberately.

'Rachel,' whispered Ana. She looked back but there was still no sign of her.

When she turned back the creature was gone. Her imagination again? She looked around, heart-rate increasing by the second. Too many shadows. She felt exposed, too out in the open. Why had they stayed here rather than head to the apartments? Hell, why hadn't they just remained on the boat?

Because if you had, you'd be dead by now.

It was on the ceiling. She saw it, her mind struggling to register it as fact. It moved along on its hands and feet, never once dropping its gaze, leaving a trail of sticky prints along the wall.

'You can't be real,' she whispered. The thing on the ceiling just watched, clinging to the shadows. She struggled to make out details, its pallid skin glistening anaemically in the darkness.

Watching.

Waiting.

'What do you want?' hissed Ana through gritted teeth.

She couldn't do it. Not by herself. She didn't want to die here, not like this. Not alone.

Not alone.

Behind her, feet thudded off concrete and she surprised herself by spinning, swinging the wrench with all her might. As she did so, she had the terrifying realisation that it could well be Rachel, and tried to halt the swing.

It wasn't Rachel.

The creature put up an arm to block the wrench. Despite the decrease in power caused by Ana's uncertainty, the dry twigs of its radius and ulna bones still snapped on impact. The creature stepped back, roaring as its arm dangled uselessly, Ana taking the opportunity to backhand the fucker, smashing the beast hard in the ribs. It went down like a sack of potatoes. She glanced at the ceiling. The other one was on the move. She raised the wrench, turning her attention back to the downed beast. It scuttled backwards, leaping onto the wall and running, scaling the vertical incline with ease.

'Jesus Christ, you can't! It's not fair!' cried Ana. Another one entered through a different window. 'Fuck off! Just fuck off!' She backed up further until she slammed into a wall. She looked up and saw a face leering over the frame of the window directly above her. One of the creatures pounded towards her and she threw the wrench with both hands then turned and ran. She heard a soft crack but was already on her way out by then.

She did not stop to check on her handiwork.

Ana didn't care where she was going as long as it was away from the lobby. She barrelled down a corridor, electrical cables hanging from the ceiling like cobras. She batted them out of the way. The corridor ended in a T junction and she chose left, slipping on the wet floor but not falling, smashing her shoulder off the brick wall and continuing on. She chanced a look back and saw the creatures following her, some on the floor, others on the walls and ceiling. Her legs ached, her body cried out to stop. Taking a right, she found herself among the ghostly remains of the bamboo scaffolding.

'Rachel!' she yelled into the storm, never stopping running. It was a futile gesture.

Up ahead were the apartments, or at least the shell of what they would have been. To the left, slightly closer, lay an unfinished restaurant. She dodged the half-dug swimming pool, narrowly avoided falling in and headed towards the restaurant. The place looked empty and she hurtled through the doorway, throwing herself over the counter. She bumped off the floor hard, winding herself.

She paused, trying to catch her breath before moving on.

Moving on where, exactly?

There was nowhere else to hide. The restaurant had a counter and some booths but no furniture. A door presumably led to the kitchen area, but what if it was a dead-end? Careful to avoid being spotted, she raised her head above the countertop and watched. Some of the mutants raced by the window and she ducked back down, waiting for them to pass.

The seconds ticked by interminably, but her heart rate showed little sign of slowing. The counter was cool against her back and she began to regain what was left of her composure. She had to find Rachel, that was the most important thing. Find her and get off the island. Even if they had to fashion a raft out of logs and palm leaves, they would escape together, the last surviving members of the Logan family.

Satisfied that enough time had elapsed, she squirmed her way to the edge of the counter. Listening carefully and hearing nothing except the relentless barrage of the elements, she peered round the counter and almost came face-to-face with a creature.

She jerked her head back. Had it seen her?

She waited, wishing she still had the wrench, trying to figure out how many were in here with her.

Could she hear two sets of footsteps, or one creature on all-fours?

Just one, she thought. It rasped and wheezed. She heard

its skin brushing off the other side of the counter and she bristled, her whole body tensing up.

Ana closed her eyes. If she saw even a shadow move, she knew she would scream. Her nose itched and she shivered, the rain soaking through her underwear.

She was about to sneeze.

Shit.

How to stop it? She put both hands over her mouth, as if that would do anything to mask the sound. She hitched in a tight breath, trying to keep it under control.

There was no way round it; she was going to sneeze.

In other words, she was well and truly fucked.

She had one chance. The backdoor. If she could get far enough away, then the creature might not hear her. Of course, she had no idea where it currently was, or what direction it was looking in. One more sharp intake of breath and she made her mind up.

As stealthily as possible, she made her way back to the edge of the counter, adrenaline building to a crescendo, and made a dash for it, never looking back. She raced through a long corridor, and after rounding a corner, the kitchen area. Large steel sinks had already been installed, but the rest of the room was bare.

She sneezed, trying to muffle the noise, glad of the release.

It wasn't enough.

The creature shrieked and the door to the corridor flew open and smashed off the wall. It was coming for her. Ana had seconds to decide on a plan of action. There were no hiding places. Nothing to defend herself with. She heard the creature barrelling down the corridor.

Her only chance was the window. At least it was free of glass.

Ana bolted for the escape route just as the creature made its way into the room. She heard the wet smack of its hands and feet on the floor but refused to turn round, instead leaping for the enormous steel sink, hauling her weary body up and into it. Half-a-second later the creature hit the sink head-first, denting the metal. Two shrivelled hands appeared on the rim of the sink, followed by a head. It gazed at her with expressionless eyes and Ana sat up as best she could, reaching both hands out to the monster, grabbing the back of its soft, white head and wrenching it towards her. Caught unawares, the creature offered little resistance, allowing its face to be smashed into the edge of the sink.

It pulled back, a vicious dent in its skull where the nose once was. Ana yanked it forwards again, white goo showering over her and spilling into the sink, the creatures face disintegrating in her hands. She slammed it towards her once more for luck, and this time the skull shattered and crumbled in her hands and she let go, the inert body dropping from view. She sat upright, letting the adrenaline surge through her for a moment before getting to her feet and squeezing her arse through the window frame, landing on the overgrown grass. The rain spattered down.

She was outside again.

Keeping low, she glanced around and saw she was near an amphitheatre, the tiered seats overlooking a sizeable stage where bored tourists could sit and watch traditional Thai dancing and singing while gorging themselves on all-inclusive food and drink. A small tree was growing from the centre of the stage, and hanging from the branches were human skulls. They dangled languorously from cords, spinning one way and then back again like a monstrous baby's mobile.

Ana picked a bone from the grass. It looked like a femur, good and strong. In lieu of a better weapon, it would have to do. She checked for movement on the stage but couldn't see anything.

A hand on her shoulder. She swung without thinking, almost taking Rachel's head clean off. The girl dodged backwards and the bone whistled harmlessly through the air.

'Oh god I'm sorry!' said Ana, but Rachel barely noticed.

'Ricky's dead,' she panted. Ana looked her sister up and down. She was caked in mud, her hair plastered to her face.

'Did you kill him?'

'Yeah, I think I did.'

Ana nodded. 'What now?'

Rachel didn't answer. Instead she grabbed Ana by the hand and dragged her away from the grisly amphitheatre towards the apartment buildings, their feet splattering in the mud, horizontal rain hammering their bodies. Overhead, lightning crashed again, the thunder following promptly afterwards, the whole island seeming to shake under the force of the mighty elements.

Ana struggled to keep up with her sister. Rachel's naturally athletic build made running for her life a lot easier. Ana, on the other hand, was short of breath. Her thighs chafed mercilessly and her ankles threatened to give up at any moment. She pressed an arm across her chest to stop her tits swinging about so much, wishing she had on a more supportive bra rather than this stupid lace one. The only sexy underwear she had brought on holiday, and she was wearing it because she thought she might get some from Ricky. Look how that little encounter turned out.

From now on, if I ever got out of this, I'm wearing nothing but sports bras and granny pants for the rest of my life.

She fought through it, her lungs wailing in protest as she

tried in vain to match her sister's pace, heading for sanctuary within the walls of the decrepit apartment block.

Ana never once dared to look back over her shoulder.
Ironically, had she done so, she would have seen nothing
out of the ordinary. The creatures were nowhere to
be found.

27

RACHEL REACHED THE DOORWAY AND WAITED FOR ANA TO catch up. Beyond lay dense, yawning darkness.

Uninviting didn't quite cover it.

Rather than offering a haven of safety, the empty building instead filled the girls with dread. They had no torch, no light of any kind. There could be anything in there.

Anything.

Ana arrived, collapsing into an embrace with her sister. She looked back, checking for the creatures, the rain stinging her eyes.

'Come on, let's go,' she rasped.

'Yeah,' agreed Rachel uneasily. 'Okay.'

Hand in hand they shuffled into the gloom of the corridor, past a reception desk and several doors until they reached a wall and went left, leaving behind the last of the moonlight. From here on, it was like walking blindfolded.

'Stairs,' warned Rachel as the floor disappeared beneath her. She pointed her foot like a ballerina to find the next step down, her toes dipping into shallow water. 'I think it's flooded. Be careful.'

Ana followed, descending the stairs until she joined Rachel in stagnant water that rose to her waist. They waded onwards, hands out, feeling for potential obstructions, trying their best to ignore the rank odour that permeated the building.

'Where are we?'

Rachel shook her head. 'Beats me. Should we keep going?'

'We can't go back out there. There's too many of those things.'

'What are they?'

'I don't know, Rach. It's like they're almost human, but not quite.'

'Or maybe they used to be?' said Rachel, sending a shiver down both their spines. Liquid drizzled from the ceiling. The room smelled like an old well, Ana wrinkling her nose in disgust. Something brushed past her leg and she jumped.

'Fuck!'

'What?'

Ana froze.

'What is it?' asked Rachel again.

'Rach…I don't think we're alone.'

A heavy silence fell, broken only by the drip-drip of the water.

'You're being paranoid,' Rachel whispered.

'Something touched my leg.'

'Bollocks. Come on, let's get out of here.'

'Wait a second.'

'What?'

'Just wait!' snapped Ana. They stood in silence for several seconds.

'Okay, we can go now,' announced Ana.

'Did you just pee?' asked Rachel.

Ana thought for a moment, deciding whether to tell the truth.

'Yeah,' she said. This was no time for lies.

'In the water that I'm standing in?'

'Aye.'

'That's disgusting.'

Ana almost laughed. 'You've gotta be joking.'

'I'm just saying, you could have warned me,' sulked Rachel.

'I thought we had bigger fish to fry.'

They went on, deeper into the bowels of the building. It was like a sensory deprivation experiment. But wasn't that supposed to relax you and eliminate anxiety? Ana had once had a dream in which she was walking through a morgue to identify her mother's body, but as she walked the lights went out one-by-one. Then, in the darkness, the corridor had narrowed, gradually drawing in on her until she could barely squeeze herself round the corners. She remembered that dream as they slipped further into the abandoned apartments. At least this time she wasn't alone.

'Why did you do it?' asked Rachel after a while, her voice echoing through the enclosed space.

'Do what?'

'Try to kill yourself.'

'You know why,' said Ana. 'I was depressed. I had depression.'

'That's what you said at the time, and I didn't believe you then either.'

Ana stopped, the water sloshing around her naval.

'You really wanna talk about this now?'

'You got something better to do? This might be our last

chance,' said Rachel in a small voice. Ana was all out of reassurances.

'Shit, Rach, I can't explain it. I don't even understand it myself. None of it makes any sense. Remember the nightmares I used to have?'

'Yeah, you'd wake up screaming and dad would get real pissed that you'd wet the bed.'

'Yeah. By the way, thanks for telling the whole school about that.'

'Oh yeah. Sorry.'

'Doesn't matter. Anyway...I think I used to dream about what happened.'

'About killing yourself?'

'Yeah. I used to hear voices too, and see things, like nightmares, but while I was awake.'

Rachel took Ana's hand and squeezed it.

'What did the voices say?'

'I don't know. I didn't understand them, but in a way I think I did. Subconsciously or something. Listen, I told you it didn't make sense.'

'Jesus. So the voices told you to slit your wrists?'

'I'm not sure. Look, admittedly I was fucking hammered that night, but all I know is this; when I cut my wrists, it felt like...like I was fulfilling my destiny or something. Y'know, a prophecy or shit like that. It felt like what I was born to do. In that moment, I knew I was absolutely doing the right thing. I just didn't understand why. And then you saved me.'

'You make it sound like I messed things up.'

Ana shook her head, a gesture lost in the darkness. 'No, that's not it. Rach, I saw things too.' She waited for Rachel to laugh. When no laughter was forthcoming, she continued. 'I used to see mum. Only not her, like a weird version of her.'

'You mean like a ghost?'

'Something like that. But I saw her — it — while mum was still alive. She looked like she did the day she...the day she passed away.'

Rachel was silent for a long time. When she spoke, it was in a voice both reassuring and dismissive. 'There's no such thing as ghosts, Ana. We both know that.'

'I'm not saying she was a ghost. I just told you that mum was still alive. Hell, she wasn't even diagnosed yet. It was more like a vision or something. A premonition.'

'So now you're psychic?'

Ana could tell Rachel was struggling to control her tone.

'I'm just saying I saw her. She used to call out to me. Ask me for help. I didn't know what to do. I thought I was losing my mind. The doctors convinced me it was stress related, and I even started to believe it myself. But ever since we arrived here Rach, I've been hearing the voices again. I've been seeing things. Awful things. But it's not mum anymore.'

Rachel let go of her sister. 'Okay, stop it, you're freaking me out.'

'It's you, Rach. I've been seeing your ghost. You asked me for help, and I don't know how.'

Rachel wept. Was she to be the last sane one standing?

'Oh Ana,' she said, hugging her sister, burying her face in Ana's neck. Ana held her. She stroked Rachel's filthy, matted hair.

'Rach,' she cooed, 'Listen to me. I'm not mental, okay?'

'You are,' blubbered Rachel. 'You're seeing my ghost, but I'm right here in front of you. Can't you understand that?'

'I just need to get you off this island. You were right, I wasn't able to save mum. I knew she was going to die, but there was nothing I could do about it. But you...you I can help. I think if I can get us out of here, I can put an end to this.'

'You're insane,' said Rachel sadly. 'Everyone on this island is fucking insane.'

'Rach, seriously, I need you to stop crying and listen to me. Something bad is about to happen.'

'It's too late. My boyfriend isn't coming and my sister sees fucking ghosts. It can't get any worse.'

Ana wrapped her arms around Rachel. 'Rach, you have to be strong.'

'Why? Why bother?'

'Because they're in here with us.'

Rachel pulled away. 'Where? I can't see anything?' She raised her head.

'Ana...the ceiling's moving.'

Ana nodded. 'Yeah. Yeah it is.'

The creatures swarmed over the roof like maggots on a week-old corpse, covering it, clambering over each other, a writhing, twitching mass of limbs. One jumped down and splashed into the water nearby, then another.

As the bodies rained down around them, Ana held Rachel, pushing her head down into her chest.

'It's okay, Rach. It's okay. Everything is going to be okay.'

And then, so quietly as to be almost imperceptible, she said,

'This isn't how you die.'

28

ANA AWOKE, SITTING BOLT UPRIGHT IN SEMI-DARKNESS. FOR A moment she thought she was back on the boat again, half-expecting to turn round and see Ricky's stupid gormless face as he masturbated in the corner. Her skull pounded, a rhythmic drumming like something inside was trying to get out. She cast the ghoulish thought aside, raising her hands to her head, finding them restrained by thick shackles.

'Shit,' she sighed, the throbbing in her temples increasing. She tried to remember what had happened, but all that came to her was the splashing sound as the creatures dropped into the water that had surrounded them. Then she was no longer even aware of the darkness.

A steel band manacled her wrists together, affixed to the wall with a heavy chain. Outside the rain continued to pour, flowing in through the glassless window frame.

The strange cell was barren; no furniture, no weapons, just four walls, a window and a door.

She was alone.

'Rach?' she called out in desperation, but the only response was the relentless drizzle of the rain.

Ana stretched, feeling her joints pop. Then came the questions.

Where was she? Where was Rachel? And why was she chained up in a makeshift dungeon? She felt woozy and closed her eyes until the sensation passed. Then she cried a little, but found tears hard to come by and gave up. There were more pressing matters. She tugged on the chains, but they were going nowhere. All she succeeded in doing was digging the edges into her hands and peeling back some skin. Through the window she could see the tops of the trees, the massive hill behind them, and up top, the bones of the hotel complex.

So I'm not in the apartments anymore. They brought me here, wherever here is.

But why had they let her live?

Light played across the tree branches and she realised there was a fire outside. She sat, exhausted, waiting for inspiration to strike. She could hear a commotion outside, people working, sometimes talking. No, not talking, *speaking*; there was no conversational aspect to the harsh, sibilant tones of the language. She recognised it from her dreams. It was like the voices in her head.

This time was different though. She felt sure they were real. Normally the sounds boomed through her head like amplifiers in her brain. This time they were distant, almost as if they weren't meant for her ears.

She spotted a figure standing stock-still, facing the far corner.

'Rach?'

The girl in the corner didn't acknowledge her. She was naked, her skin sagging like sheets on a washing line. Something inside her moved, the skin bulging, stretching but not breaking.

'Are you real?' asked Ana.

The girl faded from view like a sun-bleached photograph.

'You couldn't make this shit up,' Ana said to herself. It gave her the giggles, which soon turned to full blown laughter, her shoulders shaking, stomach cramping, tears spilling down her bruised cheeks. She wept, huge wracking sobs from the pit of her soul, pounding the wall until her fists bled, screaming until her throat burned.

'Fuck you! Fuck you! Give me back my sister!'

Perhaps Rachel had been right. She was crazy. Everyone had been right all along. She was seeing things again. This was actually a padded cell back in Scotland, and she was simply imagining the chains and the rain and the bricks and the fire and the ghost girl with the thing inside her and the monsters and the island and—

There was a thump against the door, something slamming against it. What now? What fresh horror awaited?

Her survival instincts kicked in. She looked around for an escape route, or a weapon, or *anything*. Backing up into the corner, Ana tightened her fists and waited silently.

A key rattled in the lock.

Ana fixated on the door handle, watching as it began to turn. The door creaked open, letting in a thin sliver of light. Her jaw was clenched so tight that her teeth ground together.

Come on, hurry up. I'm not afraid.

She was, of course, but a little white lie never hurt anyone.

A dark shape slunk into the room, as stealthy as a shadow, and a torch beam flicked into Ana's face, momentarily blinding her. She held up her fists.

'Come on then, you fucker,' she croaked.

'Jesus Christ,' said Paul. 'Is that you, Ana?'

29

HE HARDLY RECOGNISED HER.

Ana's red hair was filthy and black, her puffy face smeared with tears and blood. Bruises dotted her arms and legs, shallow scars slashing across her body, the dried crimson mingling with mud and slime.

Ana blinked hard. Another mirage?

'Paul?' she managed.

He just stood there. She expected him to fade away too, just like the girl before.

'Jesus, what have they done to you?' he said. 'You look disgusting.'

It was definitely Paul.

He came to her, kneeling before her, putting his hands on her shoulders. For a second she thought he was going to hug her. Behind him another man dragged in a body, his lithe yet muscular frame carrying the unconscious (dead?) guard with ease. He dumped it on the floor and quietly closed the door.

'What the fuck is going on, Ana?' snarled Paul. Ana just

stared at him and he shook her, her head snapping back-wards. 'Where's Rach? For fuck's sake Ana, answer me!'

'Quiet,' said the other man with a strong Thai accent. 'They'll hear!'

Paul turned Ana's face up to his, shining the light into her blank eyes. 'Is she still alive?'

The other man handed her a bottle of water from his pack. 'Drink,' he said. She took the bottle and greedily glugged it down. It stung her lips and throat, but she didn't care. It was the greatest water she had ever tasted, at least until she choked and spat some of it out over Paul. Her throat felt so small. Paul wiped the residue from his face.

'Ana, stop fucking around. Where is Rachel? I've come a long way to find her, so you'd fucking better answer me, okay?'

'They took her,' she stammered in-between taking small sips from the bottle.

'Who did? Where, dammit?' He stood up and turned his back on her. 'Fuck's sake Ana, you're wasting my time. I've been through hell to get here, y'know.'

Ana stared into his eyes. 'You don't know what hell is,' she said.

Paul laughed. 'Great. Just great.' He knelt down beside her again and leaned in close. 'Listen you dumb bitch, if you don't tell me where Rachel is, right fucking now, then I can just leave you here. Don't think I wouldn't.'

A blood-curdling scream from outside shut them all up. A scream that Paul knew all too well.

'Rachel.'

He ran to the single window and looked out, leaving Ana shackled in the corner.

There, in the pouring rain, was Rachel. It was too bizarre for Paul to fully comprehend. She was stripped to her underwear and tied to a wooden pole, surrounded by a semi-circle of approximately thirty men. Behind them a fire blazed, the flames hungry and out of control. The men were strange, otherworldly, some clothed in ragged civilian clothes, others nude. They looked like they were about to perform some kind of ritual.

'What's happening?' asked Ana from the corner.

'I don't know,' snapped Paul. 'Chakrit, what's going on? Are they...are they going to sacrifice her?'

Instead of answering, Chakrit went to Ana, inspecting the metal band that held her wrists together. He brushed her hair back from her face.

'It's going to be okay,' he said.

'Please, help me,' she urged.

'I will,' said Chakrit. 'But you must trust me, understand?'

Chakrit placed his hands over Ana's. She nodded.

'I mean it,' he said. 'You trust me?'

'I do,' she replied, trying not to think of what was about to happen, of the inevitable pain.

He placed a thumb on one of her knuckles. 'This won't hurt,' he said, smiling. His voice was so soothing she almost believed him. Then he jerked hard on her metacarpal, popping the bone down and dislocating her thumb with an audible snap. He immediately clamped his hand over her mouth as she yelled in pain, using his free hand to yank the metal band off. He pulled her towards him and stifled her agonised wail on his chest, holding her there.

'I'm sorry,' he said, stroking her hair. 'I lied.'

Ana held her injured hand close. It throbbed, but pain was only temporary. Over the past twenty-four hours, she had become an expert on the subject. Chakrit helped her up and the three of them crowded round the window. The men disrobed Rachel, tearing her few remaining clothes off and discarding the flimsy garments into the fire. Ana could see her sister's mouth moving as she begged and pleaded with them to stop, but the elements drowned out the words themselves.

'You bastards,' said Ana as the unholy rite took place.

When Rachel was fully nude, one of the gaunt figures lifted a metal rod from the fire, the tip glowing yellow, and advanced on the helpless girl. Ana could take no more.

'Oh god, we have to help her,' she said, making her way to the door. The man that had arrived with Paul grabbed her by the arms.

'No! Too many! We wait,' he whispered.

'But they're going to kill her!'

'No. Not yet.'

'What do you mean?' snapped Ana. 'Who even are you? What do you know?'

The man refused to make eye contact. 'My name is Chakrit. I know nothing for sure. But if she was going to die, they do it already. I think they're preparing her.'

'For what?'

'To meet their god.'

Ana rubbed her eyes. She was so tired. She leaned up against the cool brick wall. 'You're not making any fucking sense.'

Paul finally spoke up, his voice wavering. 'Chakrit, you said your grandfather worked here. What exactly did he see?'

Outside Rachel screamed and Paul turned away. Only Ana watched as her sister was branded like livestock, the smoke rising from her belly as she bucked and thrashed, trying to escape. She felt useless. Pathetic.

Worthless.

Chakrit closed his eyes. 'My grandfather never speak of it. Not until the day he died. In the hospital, he took my father and grandmother and told them what he saw. He said something lived in the mountain. Something as old as the world; an evil thing, a demon. No one believed him, and he died with everyone thinking he's crazy.'

'It sounds like he was,' said Paul.

'No,' said Ana, turning to the two men, unable to face Rachel's torture any longer. 'There's something to that. Those...*things* out there. Those people. They're not normal. They can climb on walls.'

'Oh for fucks sake,' said Paul. 'Don't you start.'

'I know it sounds crazy, Paul, but I've seen it!'

'I believe you,' said Chakrit.

'Of course you fucking do,' sneered Paul. 'You're both mental.'

'Some things people are not meant to understand,' said Chakrit. 'Like why the men that work for my grandfather have become like this.'

Paul fixed him with a stare. 'You mean to tell me that these fucking savages are the men who were building the hotel?'

Chakrit nodded. 'I recognise one of grandfather's friends. Taught me to play poker. Now I see him out there. His skin change, he lose his hair, but still looks the same.' He shook his head in disbelief. 'My god, what *happened* here?'

Ana went back to the window. She watched as Rachel writhed in agony, the men cheering. She tried to crawl away but the men blocked her escape route, kicking her back into the mud. Two of them dragged her by the hair in front of the idol.

'Leave her alone you fuckers,' muttered Ana. 'Leave my sister the *fuck* alone.'

Two men held Rachel up, while a third draped a white sheet over her, then tied it with string. The men cheered again.

'We have to do something,' said Ana.

'We have to *wait*,' said Chakrit.

The men marched Rachel away from the fire, towards two huge, dead trees at the edge of the jungle.

'Where are they taking her?'

'We follow,' said Chakrit. 'Come on.'

'What about him?' asked Ana, pointing to the body of the guard.

Chakrit refused to meet her gaze. 'Don't worry. He's dead.'

Ana looked down at the fallen man and saw his head was facing the wrong way.

'Jesus,' was all she could say.

What was happening? Why had everything gone to shit?

Chakrit held the door for her, Paul pushing in front and hurrying down the stairs.

After you, she thought.

They passed through a large room lined with beds. It reminded Ana of a military camp, except in terrible disarray. Webs coated the walls and she firmly averted her gaze, focusing on Chakrit's back until they reached another door. Through this one was a staircase down which they crept warily, ready for any unwanted attention. Chakrit's eyes darted back and forth, searching for guards or sentries, but the village was empty. The fire still burned but there was no trace of life.

Chakrit looked off in the direction the men had taken Rachel, towards the two trees that looked older than time itself. Was it Ana's imagination, or had the branches between them intertwined since allowing passage to Rachel and the men?

'You ready?' Chakrit asked them.

'Yeah,' said Ana. 'We can follow their tracks, keep a safe distance.'

'Fuck that,' said Paul. Ana turned to him.

'What?'

He backed up. 'Look, this wasn't the plan, y'know? I thought I was just coming to pick you guys up. I didn't realise I was walking into a fucking B-movie.'

Ana shook her head. 'But you've come this far...'

'I know Ana, but cults? Monsters? Sacrifices? Fuck *that* for a laugh. There's not a cunt on Earth worth *dying* for.' He had already started backing away, the branches of the trees sliding past his face and obscuring him from sight. Ana stepped after him.

'Are you fucking serious? That's your girlfriend — my sister — back there. We can't leave her!'

'No. I can. I really can.' He shrugged, the jungle beginning to swallow him up. 'We've not even been going out a year. I'm not going to risk my life for someone I hardly know.'

Ana moved forward and Chakrit held her back. 'Hardly know? You bastard. You're the real fucking monster here, you cunt.'

Paul half-smiled. 'Listen, good luck, honestly. But I'm heading back to the boat, okay? I'll wait for you there.'

'You're a coward.'

'I'm smart.' And with that, he vanished into the jungle, never once looking back. Ana seethed with anger and Chakrit put a hand on her shoulder. Without thinking she brushed it off.

'Forget him,' said Chakrit. 'I help you, okay?'

She looked him dead in the eyes. 'Why? You don't even know me.'

He smiled at her. 'Why not? Good karma.' The smile fell from his face and his eyes glazed over. 'Also, I need to find out what made my grandfather crazy. I need to find it and kill it.' He turned to Ana. 'If you'll allow me.'

Ana's whole body ached. Her arms were tired, her legs worn. All she wanted was a hot meal and a bath. Instead, she picked up a discarded machete from the ground. She caught her own reflection in the blade but hardly recognised the woman that stared back at her.

'Okay,' she said quietly. 'Let's do this.'

Several years ago, she thought she had lost her sister for good.

She wasn't about to lose her again.

30

THIS WAS OFFICIALLY A BAD IDEA.

Dating Rachel. Going on holiday. The Full Moon Party. Coming to this island on some half-assed rescue mission. The entire last year had been one big Bad Idea. And now here he was, traipsing through the jungle without food, water or weapons, totally lost. Paul figured as long as he followed a straight line downhill, he would eventually come to the sea. Problem was, he kept getting turned around. The vegetation would get too thick, or gigantic spiderwebs would block his path. He did not want to meet whatever spun *those* webs.

His thoughts turned to Rachel. Poor Rachel. She was done for. His conscience told him he should turn back and save her. Would she do the same for him? Of course not. Out here, self-preservation is the name of the game. And all that effort just so that he might get to to ram his cock up her tight little arsehole.

It was almost worth it...but not quite.

And anyway, at least one of them had to get home to warn the world about the island and its tribe of cannibals, or whatever the fuck they were. Someone also had to reap the rewards. He would make the cover of the papers, maybe even get on TV.

LONE SURVIVOR OF JUNGLE MASSACRE TELLS OF HIS DARING ESCAPE

He would bend the truth a little, tell of how he bravely fought off hordes of tribesmen in a desperate bid to protect his lover. He would tell how he planned on proposing to her when they got home. A lie here or there wouldn't matter; after all, who would ever know?

Chakrit's uncle might be a problem. How long would he wait before taking Paul back to the mainland? Well, if Paul told him Chakrit was dead, not long at all.

He smiled at the Machiavellian nature of his plan. Sometimes he surprised even himself. Now, if he could just get back to the boat, everything would be fine, but the problem with the jungle is that it all looks the same. Paul was more of a city kid. He liked street signs and roads and traffic, buildings and lights and pedestrians. He found nature disturbing.

Thick green vines blocked his path and he brushed them aside. He heard the soft sound of the sea in the distance, the waves pushing forwards then calmly withdrawing. With any luck, he would come out near the dinghy. He tried not to think about what was happening with Rachel right now. He hoped she wasn't suffering. Sometimes death is the lesser of two evils, he figured.

He should have stayed on Koh Phangan. He could've had a quickie in the morning with that slut he won in the bet, then hooked up with some drunk tourist by now. Hell, so what if he had to pay for it? A fuck was a fuck, and he bet those Thai girls could teach even *him* a thing or two.

The rain slowed, granting Paul a brief respite from the elements. Ahead there was a break in the trees and beyond it, the moon reflecting off the ocean, the water sparkling like scattered diamonds.

'Yes,' he said, speeding up. His watch told him it was almost midnight. He spotted a light in the distance, bobbing on the water. The boat was close. Branches scratched his face and arms and in his haste he stepped on a loose root and slipped. His hands shot out for balance, but it was too late. Plunging forwards headfirst, sliding down an incline towards a dark crevice, Paul covered his head as he disappeared through a hole, spiralling down and catching on something, jolting to a halt in mid-air. He dangled there, upside-down, the blood rushing to his head as he tried to get his bearings.

'Fuck! Help! Someone help me!'

It was pitch black wherever he was, the stars glimmering through the tapered crack above him. What was he caught on? With no idea how high up he was, Paul carefully unbuttoned a pocket and his phone slid out. He caught it before it could shatter on the rocks below and switched it on. Five percent battery. Just enough power to activate the torch and find a way out.

His hands were slippery with sweat as he worked the touch screen, his stress level rising as he slowly spun in a circle. He lifted his head to ease the mounting pressure and switched on the torch. The crack in the ceiling was about six foot above him, his leg ensnared on a white, gauzy cord that wrapped itself around his ankle.

A web. The strength of it had to be immense to hold his weight. He remembered the giant ones in the jungle and panicked as he sensed movement below him. Fighting every urge in his body, he shined the torch and tilted his head to look down.

Another Bad Idea.

The ground was a seething mass of spiders, a thick carpet that stretched as far as he could see. Hundreds, thousands of them, big and small, thick and thin. Some were covered in hair, while others looked like tiny skeletons. They climbed on top of each other, forming an obscene arachnid pyramid, working their way towards his face. They spilled from cracks and gaps in the rock, piling onto each other, more and more, a ceaseless torrent. Paul screamed, helpless, twirling upside down by one leg as they rose towards him.

He tried to swat them away with his phone but it slipped from his greasy palm and vanished in the sea of insects, the light obscured immediately, leaving him suspended in near-total darkness. He reached up, clutching at his leg, trying to pull himself away from the horror below. Their tiny bodies rubbed together, a sickening sound that burrowed into his brain, and then his hand slipped and his head swung down and something brushed his forehead.

They were getting closer.

'Oh god, help me, please!' he screamed.

The web gave way. Not entirely, just a couple of inches.

It was enough.

Paul's head plunged into the mass of bodies, their legs probing, crawling on his wretched, shrieking face. He shook, lifted his head, tried to force them off, but more came, his head now dipped into the heaving mass up to his eyeballs, their grotesque legs crawling all over him. He couldn't stop screaming, even when one squirmed into his open mouth. He thrust his jaws shut, catching several of its legs between his teeth. In response, fangs sank into his tongue, tearing away at the soft pink. Blood filled his mouth, and that, combined with the taste of the spider, made him vomit. The tiny monsters covered his entire head like a constantly shifting mask, biting and tearing at whatever flesh was available. He felt his eyelid being torn away, one of the spiders biting and pulling at his eyeball, the soft orb rupturing, white fluid gushing from the socket. He clamped his jaw shut, but they ate away at his cheeks, the flesh offering little resistance.

And then they were in his mouth, in his throat, biting him, choking him. With one final massive effort Paul thrust his head out of quagmire and roared in abject horror, a roar that carried across the bay, reaching as far as Chakrit's uncle on the deck of the fishing boat, who gripped his shotgun and said a silent prayer.

It was several minutes before the screaming finally stopped.

31

THEY KEPT A SAFE DISTANCE, MOVING ONLY WHEN THE TROOP of men dropped out of sight, sticking to the dense undergrowth wherever possible. Using the moonlight to guide them, Ana and Chakrit followed the well-trodden path as it wound uphill towards an unknown destination.

The rain had slowed to a drizzle, but the clouds hung thick and foreboding, threatening another deluge before the night's end. The jungle was curiously silent save for the distant footsteps of the tribe and the occasional shout from Rachel. Ana wished to call out to her, to let her know they were not far behind. She must be so frightened. She wondered if Chakrit was too. He seemed calm, rolling a cigarette whenever they drew too close as if he was waiting at a bus stop. The knife poked out of the back of his shorts, sometimes catching the glint of the moon on its sharpened blade.

Chakrit stopped, holding up a hand for her to do the same. Ana could see the men ahead, glimpses of their bald heads in the distance. She crouched, wishing for some clothes. She was far beyond modesty by now, but it would be nice to have something to protect her from the thorns and leaves that scratched at her exposed skin. If Paul had been a gentleman, he would have given her his shirt, instead of running off like a frightened little boy. What was he even doing wearing a Beyonce shirt in the first place?

If she ever got her hands on him, she would kill him.

Chakrit moved on, his feet padding on the soft earth. He paused, sniffing the air. Ana smelt it too, the most vile odour ever to assail her nostrils. Chakrit, keeping low, crossed to the other side of the path and beckoned her over. She crept over to his side, pinching her nose shut and breathing through her mouth. Chakrit waited several minutes until he was sure the men were far enough away, then took out his torch and flicked it on.

They found themselves perched on the rim of a pit filled with dozens of dead bodies. Ana quickly turned away, her stomach reeling, then forced herself to look back. Was Rachel in there?

Chakrit moved the beam across the bodies like a search-light, pausing whenever he alighted on a corpse that looked fresh enough to be recent.

She saw Bret, his limbs hacked from his body, eyes staring into space. Darren too, though she only recognised him by his underwear. His head was unrecognisable, crushed to a pulp. They lay on a bed of bloated, green flesh and rotting carcasses, skeletal limbs jutting out from underneath like springs from an old sofa. She couldn't see Lisa anywhere. Maybe she had escaped?

Chakrit switched the flashlight off and swore in Thai.

'Someone's coming.'

Ana heard it too. Was it from in front of them or behind? It was impossible to tell. Sound travelled oddly here. They had to hide. She glanced back. The trees were too far. Could they make it? In her periphery she could see a light approaching. Chakrit placed a hand on the small of her back and she knew what was coming. It was their only chance. He pushed, and she slid forwards into the loathsome pit.

'Hide,' said Chakrit as he joined her.

Ana reached out and grabbed one of the bodies, finding it surprisingly insubstantial. Her hands touched the rubbery skin and she gagged.

The light approached the clearing. A flaming torch.

Almost out of time, she lifted the delicate body and scooched down underneath it until she was lying on top of another, her hands touching the white bone of a skull, small patches of flesh still clinging on. She was sure she would be sick. She chanced a look to her right but couldn't see Chakrit. The man with the torch came closer, reaching the edge of the pit and stopping there, holding out the torch. Ana froze, holding her breath, her mind numb with terror. She looked down, fearful of making eye contact with the man, his light source brightening the pit, allowing Ana to stare right into the blackened face of a corpse, its eyes sealed shut, the white teeth shocking against the discoloured flesh.

She was going to vomit. Her stomach turned somersaults, jerking her body, and she closed her eyes, not wanting to know if the man had spotted her. Her body tensed, fighting the urge to spray stomach acids all over the face of the ancient carcass beneath her and run shrieking from this place into warm, hellish oblivion.

One time — she must have been about seven or eight — she and Rachel had played hide and seek in their grandma's house, a colossal three-storey Victorian monstrosity. Rachel had been doing the seeking, Ana tearing up the stairs as her sister loudly raced through the numbers up to one-hundred as fast as she could.

'Ready or not, here I come!'

Ana was on the second floor, heart beating, excitement building. She almost went into the lounge then remembered the door always banged shut, so ran past it and headed into one of the spare rooms. She ignored the bed and headed for the grand oak wardrobe, sliding her way in and tenderly closing the door behind her, keeping it slightly ajar, allowing a shard of light to find its way in. There she had sat, tension building in her gut, listening to her sister go from room to room, crying 'gotcha!' every time she burst through a door.

Hide and seek was not Ana's forte. She usually got too excited and started to laugh as her sister got nearer, giving away her position, the excitement and fear too much for her to take. This time in the wardrobe was different.

Because she wasn't alone.

She made the mistake of glancing up, the light allowing her a glimpse of something moving towards her. A spider. In retrospect it was tiny, a house spider, but to Ana it was enormous, a terrifying eight-legged monstrosity come to suck her blood and drag her back to its web next to the flies as a warning to other little girls playing hide and seek.

She slid down onto her back, rigid with fear, staring up as it descended, unable to cry out. She wanted to run but her legs wouldn't respond so she lay there, watching the spider's inexorable journey until Rachel burst open the door and cried 'Gotcha!' and she ran screaming from the wardrobe and down the stairs into her grandmother's arms.

The stakes were higher now, but the terror felt the same. How long was the man going to stand there? What was he looking for? Had he heard them, or perhaps seen Chakrit's torchlight?

She waited.

And waited.

There were more footsteps. She tried to think happy thoughts but kept coming back to being trapped in the wardrobe, her first childhood taste of adult horrors, and the weeks of nightmares that inevitably followed. Still, they weren't a patch on the nightmares that had plagued her for most of her adult life.

The men were coming back. She could hear them. Unlike earlier, when they had walked in deathly silence, this time they talked in the same unfamiliar language she had heard in her dreams.

She waited some more.

The corpse on top of her moved. What if it wasn't dead? What if this pit was full of people waiting to die but unable to, kept alive by some kind of mad sorcery?

'We go now,' said Chakrit, lifting the body from her and letting it fall to the side. He held out a hand which she gratefully took, her feet struggling to find purchase on the ghoulish remains.

'Are they gone?'

'For now.'

'Was Rachel with them? My sister?'

'No.'

'Then she can't be far.'

Chakrit climbed out of the pit first, then helped Ana. They sat on the verge for a moment, then Ana turned and spewed. Chakrit knelt by her, one hand resting on her back.

She finished and got to her feet.

'You okay?' asked Chakrit.

'Sure. Just crawled out of a mass grave, but sure, I'm okay.'

'You're strong. Stronger than your friend.'

'Paul is no friend of mine.'

'Good. Me neither. Let's go.'

They started down the path again, Chakrit taking the knife from his shorts and crouching low. Further ahead they could see a light penetrating the darkness.

A cave entrance.

The end was in sight.

Ana and Chakrit peered out from the deep foliage, surveying the scene for any unwanted surprises. The cave itself stood only about six feet high, then sloped down rapidly. Deep inside, something burned.

'What now?' whispered Ana.

'Not many options.'

'No turning back,' agreed Ana. 'She has to be in there.'

Though not quite worthy of celebration yet, the situation was at least less dire than it had been for a while. Since the attack on the boat, things had gone from bad to worse to fucking nightmarish. Their fruitless trek up the hill had led to Ricky's death and their capture and imprisonment. Then Rachel had been tortured and taken and Paul had hotfooted it back to the boat, leaving her with a man she didn't know. At the time, she had been running on empty, ready to give in and give up at the slightest provocation. Now she felt reinvigorated.

Okay, she still felt like shit, but at least she was closing in on her sister. It was a considerable improvement over a few hours ago. All they had to do now was sneak into the cave, rescue Rachel from inside and get back down to the boat, where Chakrit's uncle waited to whisk them all to safety.

Easy, right?

'Ready?' asked Chakrit.

She took a deep breath. 'As ready as I'll ever be.'

She leaned forward and kissed him softly on the cheek. 'I just want to say thanks. Thanks for helping me. You didn't have to do any of this.'

'It not over yet.'

'I know.'

'You've done well. Survived a long time.'

She realised she was still holding onto his muscular arm and let go.

'Come on,' she said, walking away. 'You're making me blush. Let's find my sister and get the fuck out of here.'

They walked silently together into the cave, not knowing what horrors lay in store in that vast, underground cavern, where ancient evil slumbered and nightmares came shockingly true.

Their appointment with madness awaited.

32

THE ENTRANCE TO THE CAVE IMMEDIATELY GAVE WAY TO A polished slope that descended into the bowels of the hill, the torchlight ahead of them flickering grimly in the gloom. Chakrit went first, crouching at the top of the slope and letting gravity do the work. Ana followed, sliding down after him. The first thing she noticed was the chilly underground air on her skin. The second was the smell. It wasn't as bad as the mass grave — how could it be? — but it was pungent nonetheless.

She stood by Chakrit and cast a glance back up to the mouth of the cave.

'How will we get out?' she wondered aloud.

'We find a way.'

She nodded. He was a man of few words. Regardless, she wanted to talk. Talking made things more normal, like they were out a nice stroll in the countryside. It distracted from the fear that gnawed at her like a rat, its teeth sharpened and deadly. The fear of the unknown.

The fear of death.

Together they walked, their steps tentative and soundless. The rocks jabbed into Ana's feet with each step. They reached the first torch. Chakrit tried to pull it out of its receptacle, but it wouldn't budge. He shone the flashlight around the cave. It was getting bigger, the ceiling now at least three times as tall as Ana. Moisture dripped from ancient stalactites, splashing in small pools by her feet. She thought of her Geography teacher in high school explaining how to remember the difference between stalactites and stalagmites.

'When the mites go up, the tites go down.'

The class had groaned at the bad pun, but it had stuck with her all these years. She couldn't quote Shakespeare or recall any maths other than basic arithmetic, but she would always know what a stalactite was.

'Fucking useless.'

'What?' said Chakrit, without stopping.

'Oh, sorry, I didn't realise I said that out loud.'

'We should be quiet now. I think we're getting close.'

'Close to what? Rachel?'

'Close to whatever did this,' he said, flashing the beam on the ground. A desiccated corpse lay at his feet, its jaw locked in perpetual agony, the purple skin dried up and hardened like an old raisin. He stepped around the corpse, his fingers wrapped around the hunting knife. Ana followed, glad to leave the foul body behind.

Without warning the tunnel opened up, as if the walls had simply fallen away, leaving them in total darkness save for the minimal light cast from the flashlight, the oppressive shadows hungrily swallowing up the beam. Unable to find anything to focus the light on, Chakrit instead shined the torch above them. He didn't like what he found.

'My god,' he said.

Ana watched as Chakrit moved the beam around, his

hands noticeably shaking. Above them were webs, nothing but webs, criss-crossing over each other. But they were also different; thicker, fluid dripping off them in pale globs. They were strung along randomly at first before rising out of sight in a cylindrical shape.

'What made that?' said Ana.

'Look.'

Ana followed the beam as it picked out strange shapes dotted around the web. Cocoons. Some were empty, as if having burst open. Others looked untouched, with bony arms and rotten limbs protruding outwards. They reminded Ana of the old tabletop game Pop Up Pirate. She almost laughed. She had been dragged to the very precipice of insanity already today, and now she stood teetering on the edge. She stifled the giggle, afraid it would send her hurtling into mindlessness.

'Is your sister one of them?' he asked, using the torch to pick out the frozen and long-dead victims one at a time.

'I can't see. I don't know.'

She couldn't think. My god, those people were *cocooned*.

What the fuck had done that to them? What creature on Earth would be big enough to spin these giant webs?

She panicked. 'Rachel! Rachel where are you!' she yelled.

'Ana? Is that you?' The world seemed to stop. Ana's heart leapt. She tried to speak but the words wouldn't come. *'They made me their queen, Ana. It's all going to be okay.'*

She fell to her knees. It wasn't Rachel. That unmistakable Australian accent belonged to Lisa.

'Ana? You there? Ana?'

She sat down, sobbing into her arm. Chakrit knelt by her side.

'You know her?' he whispered.

'Is someone there? I hear voices.'

She wept. Chakrit put his arm round her.

'They made me their queen! I'm the white cannibal queen! Just like in the movie!'

'You have to stop crying,' urged Chakrit.

'I can't. I'm done. I give up. I can't take this anymore.'

He pressed his palm to her mouth. 'It's awake.'

Ana looked at him. In the all-consuming darkness, only the grim, fearful whites of his eyes were visible.

'Look! Here he comes now, to bring me to ecstasy!'

Chakrit arced the beam up towards Lisa's shrill voice, picking her out. She had not been cocooned yet. She lay on a web, stark naked.

'Come to me.'

She writhed on the web, her body drenched in dark blood.

'Come to me, my king.'

Ana gripped Chakrit's bicep. They both peered up into the darkness. From far away came a sound.

Click-click-click.

It grew closer. Ana thought she could see something moving up there.

'My God, I am your queen. Come to me!'

Click-click-click.

It was getting louder.

'COME TO ME!' screamed Lisa.

And then it did.

33

FROM OUT OF THE SHADOWS IT CAME.

A crawling, monstrous horror, its eight legs clicking as it drew in on its prey. Ana's heart stopped for what felt like an eternity as it emerged fully into the path of the beam in all its monstrous, obscene glory.

It's a spider, she thought, though she knew it wasn't. Her mind raced, making connections, sorting fantasy from reality, trying to acclimate her brain to this fresh horror. A spider was the closest thing from nature that it resembled, and so she settled on that. How else to explain the unexplainable?

The bulbous, shimmering body. Eight legs. The webs.

A spider. A giant fucking monster spider. And yet it was so much more.

Her mind reeled.

Its legs were sinewy, the red muscle exposed as if the skin had been carefully peeled back, ending in sharpened talons that dripped with venom, wet and terrible. It wore a strange white shroud, streaked and dyed with the blood of a thousand victims. It moved from wall to web, easily navigating the treacherous material it had spun so deftly over the centuries.

Lisa fell silent as the massive creature paused before her, hovering over her prone, naked body, hundreds of tiny, bead-like eyes catching the reflection of Chakrit's torch. The front four stalk-like legs reared up, revealing the underside of its body and then the flesh began to part, splitting open with a wretched sound that filled the cavern, the muscle stretching and tearing until it burst open and a mass of thin, reedy tentacles squirmed their way out, finding Lisa's arms and legs and coiling around her limbs, binding her. Blood gushed from the creature's open wound, showering Lisa in gore, spilling down her body and splashing on the ground in great dollops of blood and tissue.

'We have to go,' said Ana, surprised to hear her own voice. Her nails dug into Chakrit's arm, miniature paths of blood running freely and dripping from his bicep.

The creature's legs spasmed, the joints cracking like shotgun blasts as they turned back on themselves and the ragged hole in its stomach billowed as if something was trying to get out.

'Chakrit, please.'

Two hands, red and savage and inhuman, slopped out of the hole, grasping either side. More tentacles thrashed the air, dancing and spitting like electrical cables, whipping Lisa's defenceless body. A head appeared, or something resembling one, featureless and distended, the bloated mass splitting open and disgorging its contents onto Lisa with an inhuman roar, its own hands reaching up and pulling at the sagging mess of a skull, stripping the putrid muscle back. Beneath it, finally, a long, bone-like proboscis.

Ana snatched the torch from Chakrit's hands and shone it directly into his eyes. He turned to her, suddenly snapping out of his fear-induced lethargy. From somewhere above them, in the dark, came an infernal slurping. Neither of them looked.

Ana released Chakrit's arm.

'Run,' she said.

34

ANA SWEPT THE TORCHLIGHT LEFT AND RIGHT, LOOKING FOR an exit, somewhere to hide, anything. She thought they were heading back in the direction they had come from, but in the dark it was easy to lose your bearings. The ground was uneven, stalagmites jutting out from the ground like knives.

When the mites go up, the tites go down.

Leaving the infernal beast and the gruesome noises behind, they ran into the beyond, unable to find the exit, or a wall, or anything that might indicate a way out. Lost in the eternal nighttime of the cave, Ana felt like falling to her knees and screaming.

'Ana.'

A weak voice. A croak. Instantly recognisable.

'Rach?'

Ana whirled on the spot, the beam lighting nothing but glistening webs stretched taut above her like white rainbows of horror.

'Keep talking Rach, I can't find you,' she said, the panic manifest in her voice.

'Over here. I'm over here.'

She listened, shutting out the awful noise of the creature. Rachel sounded exhausted, like every word was an immense effort. Ana knew the feeling.

She swung the torch, the light catching something on the ground.

A pool of blood, dark and tranquil.

She ran towards it, looking up above her, not caring if she tripped and fell.

There she was, suspended above them on the web, drenched in sticky red fluid.

'I found you!' shouted Ana, her heart pumping like she had just snorted several lines of cocaine.

'Keep your voice down,' barked Chakrit. 'I cut her loose.' He wrenched the torch from Ana and pointed the beam at the web, identifying where it angled downwards to its lowest point. Ana had no time to react, finding herself in darkness as Chakrit raced out of sight. In her mind, the cave was closing in.

'We're gonna get you out of here,' she said, hoping she was right. The web moved, one corner dropping. She could see the light in the distance, hear Chakrit's panting as he raced to find another accessible part of the web to sever.

Where was the spider?

What had it done to Lisa?

Ana reached up to Rachel. She could almost touch her sister's foot. She wanted desperately to feel her, to truly believe they were together, and that escape was within their grasp. With a loud snap another corner of the web broke, Rachel falling further, dangling in front of Ana. Like Lisa, she too was naked and drenched in blood. Ana grabbed her sister by the waist, her face pressing into the girl's belly.

Rachel cried out in pain as Ana tried to tug her free, the web beginning to give way.

Then it did, depositing Rachel on top of her sister. They fell to the ground together, entangled in each other's limbs, both crying now, joy or terror or madness; neither was sure, nor convinced it mattered.

The cavern lit up, the clouds far above them dispersing, allowing a single beam of moonlight to flood through the hole in the ceiling. They lay still, Ana holding Rachel.

'Is that your blood?'

'Some of it,' replied the dazed girl, her words slurred and indistinct. Nasty red welts scarred her bare back where the web had held her. Ana searched for Chakrit's torch and saw it coming towards them.

'We're getting you out of here.'

'It won't let us leave.'

Ana stroked her sister's blood-soaked hair.

'It's going to be okay, I promise. I'll never leave you, Rach. Never.'

The torch was getting closer, the beam flashing wildly from side to side.

'Run!' screamed Chakrit. 'It's right above you!'

It's not that Ana didn't believe him. It's just the perfectly natural human instinct to want to *look*. Like if someone shouts *He's got a gun* and instead of dropping to the floor you have a peek first to see precisely *who* has the gun.

It's why she looked up when she really shouldn't have.

The spider was descending, coming for her. For an instant she was eight again and back in the wardrobe in her grandmother's house, unable to move, unable to breathe, her body stiffening. It was even bigger than she had thought. It looked large enough to crush an elephant in its putrid, bleeding legs.

I'm going to die.

It didn't matter. She just hoped it would be quick.

I'm going to die.

Turned out Rachel needn't have bothered saving her life last year. It was simply delaying the inevitable.

Rachel.

I'm going to die, and so is Rachel.

'No!' yelled Ana, the enormous spider slinking down towards them on its white silk cord, thick jets of blood pumping from the gash on its belly. She watched as its legs folded back on themselves again, those strange long fingers breaking through the body, turning to fists that tore the spider's underside apart, a shower of plasma erupting from the dangling monster. She saw her own reflection staring back at her in the creatures eyes, her face scarlet with some-one's blood.

She found her final hidden reserve of strength, clutching Rachel under her arms and dragging her backwards, away from the creeping menace. It dropped quickly, landing hard on the rock and blocking the light from Chakrit's torch.

'Chakrit!' shouted Ana.

'Get out!' he called back.

The spider hesitated.

'Can you move?' said Ana to Rachel. 'I need you to move.'

'I can do it,' she replied. It was all Ana needed to hear. She yanked Rachel to her feet, took her hand and ran, their bare feet slapping off stone, never once stopping to look back. Chakrit was yelling something in Thai. Distracting the creature, giving them a chance to escape. Ana wanted to cry but she didn't have time. He was a fucking hero.

She didn't know where they were going, but she could

see a light source ahead of her. The corridor with the flaming torches?

What else could it be?

They headed straight for it.

35

HIS GRANDFATHER HAD BEEN TELLING THE TRUTH.

All these years carrying the dreadful secret with him, and when he had revealed the mystery of the island to his family, they hadn't believed him. They should all be ashamed. There had been no laughter; there was too much respect for old Prachya, and no one could hypothesize an alternative, better reason for the island's abandonment. Chakrit's own father had told him the story when he turned fourteen, before handing him his first beer. Together on the fishing boat, drifting aimlessly out to sea, they had gotten drunk together for the first time.

And now here it stood, colossal and evil, the thing from his grandfather's fairy story, the beast that had haunted his dreams until he passed on.

Just as he described.

It was real, and coming straight for him.

He hoped the girls had found their way out.

'I'm not afraid of you,' lied Chakrit, his fist closed over the handle of the knife in a death-grip. What use would a blade be against a creature of this magnitude? Escape was his only chance. But where was the exit? The gigantic arachnid just stood there, watching with its many eyes. It started towards him, the vaguely humanoid shape that protruded from its belly hanging like a sagging sack of flesh, the lifeless hands scraping off the rocks and leaving a thick trail of blood. Its movements were sluggish, obviously suffering from the repercussions of what it had done to the other girl in the web, the one that Ana recognised. This must be why the men on the island had taken Rachel first and kept Ana for later. The creature must need time to recover from...from whatever the fuck it was doing.

Chakrit ran, trying to zig and zag between rocky outcrops and stalagmites. And behind him, the bizarre mental torture of the *click-click-click* of the feet. The torch picked out a vast pool of blood. He looked up and saw what was left of Lisa, her remains spread out across the web. It was all he needed to know. He had his bearings now.

He pushed his body to the limit, every muscle crying out for mercy, feet pounding, heart racing, never once looking back. Chakrit swerved left and noticed the fire burning in the tunnel. He doubled his efforts to the point where his body could take no more. As he reached the tunnel entrance, something oily wrapped around his wrist, tugging him back.

Tentacles.

It must be close.

They tightened, digging into his skin and drawing fresh blood. He yelped, bringing the knife up and slashing through the membranous cords. They hissed as he sliced them, a foul-smelling gas issuing from the severed stumps, and then he found himself in the tunnel. Up ahead — *way* up ahead — moonlight and potential safety. It was too narrow for the spider to fit through. He looked around for Ana and Rachel but could find no trace of them.

Tentacles coiled round his ankle like rat tails. Chakrit bent to slice them but he wasn't quick enough. They went taut and he lost his footing and crashed to the ground. He tried to get back to his feet but they pulled, dragging him over rocks that gashed and cut his skin, out of the tunnel and back towards the infernal creature. He stabbed his knife into the ground and held on, shining the torch back into the cavern.

The spider was barely ten feet away. The revolting skin-less humanoid that hung from the spider's belly had two fleshy hands on the attenuated tentacles and was winding them in like a fisherman with his catch of the day. It was too strong. Chakrit forced his way to his feet and lunged for the flaming torch affixed to the wall.

He gripped it with both hands, letting the knife and the flashlight fall. The tentacles dug into his ankle, pulling tighter, stripping the flesh from his leg. He roared, fingers tightening over the torch until he felt his whole body shake, his knuckles whitening. He couldn't hold on much longer, the spider's breath hitting him like an Arctic wind.

The wall fixing for the torch moved, one nail tearing out of the rock as Chakrit edged ever closer to death. He thought of his uncle waiting on the boat for him. Little Grub the pug would be there too, sheltering from the cold.

How long would they wait?

More tentacles, lengthy probing fingers that coiled around his other foot, burning as they sliced easily through Chakrit's skin, pulling him until he was horizontal. The Upside-Down man strained hard on the veiny cables, and Chakrit knew he couldn't take much more, his fingers slip-ping. Then the torch came loose, tearing free of the fixings and Chakrit dropped to the ground, jolting his coccyx, inching towards the spider, his back scraping along the jagged points of the cave, torch in hand.

The great beast reared up again on its hind legs, the bony proboscis bursting free from the Upside-Down man's soft, balloon-like head, the tip sharp and cruel, hovering ready to strike. Chakrit thrust the torch forwards and the spider withdrew, stepping backwards, almost falling. He put the torch to his own leg, the tentacles fizzing and popping as they burst and fell away, not caring that the flames licked and caressed his own savaged ankle, the smell of burning meat assaulting his nostrils. And then, as quickly as it had come, the spider disappeared into the sanctity of the cavern, leaving Chakrit breathless and horrified.

From deep within he heard screams.

The girls were still in there.

And it was coming for them.

Chakrit pounded his fist off the wall. He didn't know if he could walk, his legs badly damaged in the attack. Only shock was keeping him conscious now, and the pain at bay.

Over his shoulder the exit beckoned, the eerie stillness welcoming.

Once more his thoughts came back to his uncle, and of Grub, then of Ana and Rachel, trapped somewhere in the recesses of an unnatural hell.

He had a decision to make.

36

'YOU OKAY?' ASKED ANA, HOLDING UP RACHEL'S LIMP BODY, helping her walk. She didn't answer. 'We're almost there. I can see the lights.'

Somewhere in the cavern Chakrit screamed and Ana's blood ran cold.

'Water,' said Rachel, oblivious to everything around her.

'Soon, I promise. We gotta get out of here first.'

The light was getting stronger. Ana already knew this wasn't the way she had come in. This light was steady, not flickering, and cast a deep red glow that spilled out through a small opening in the wall.

'Where's Paul?'

Ana considered the question carefully. 'He's safe. He's waiting for us at the boat.'

'You saw him?'

'Yes. He rescued me.' That was all she wanted to say on the matter. Luckily, Rachel asked no more questions, and they soon found themselves at the entrance to another tunnel. A way out? Ana hoped so. It was like a fucking anthill in here. Rachel stumbled, and Ana helped her upright again. They were both exhausted.

'Through here,' grunted Ana, putting Rachel's arm over her shoulder and holding it tight. The ceiling was low, and both girls had to stoop to make it through.

'I don't feel well.'

'I know. But we have to keep going.'

'No, inside. I'm burning.'

'Please Rach, we have to go before it comes back.'

Ahead of them the red light glowed like a beacon. But was it bringing them to safety?

They rounded a corner and Ana stopped, almost letting Rachel slip from her grasp.

'What the fuck,' she gasped.

It was a room.

She paused, taking in the absurd details. The angular walls, the sharp corners and clean, straight lines, the marble floor. It was the ultimate incongruity in this cave of hopeless nightmares, a man-made chamber nestled in a subterranean cavern.

Towards the back of the room the ceiling curved upwards into an arch, reminding Ana of a cathedral. Intricate carvings lined the walls, depicting a variety of sinister creatures that sent her already fragile mind spinning at the ghastly implications. Stone pews faced away from the entrance, separated by an aisle, each one bedecked in detailed carvings. It was the work of disturbed master craftsmen. Hieroglyphic words engraved on the walls meant little to Ana, carved as they were in some obscene, ancient tongue.

The aisle led to a huge circular pit, from which the scarlet light emanated, highlighting the ethereal dance of the vaporous mists that rose from within, and beyond that, set into the wall, were seven doors of solid oak.

She sat Rachel down on one of the monolithic stone pews. The blood on her skin was drying and forming a hardened shell that cracked as she moved.

'Stay there,' she said, as if Rachel had a choice.

She ambled down the aisle in a grotesque parody of matrimony, her eyes fixed on the circular pit.

Strange bas-relief sculptures watched her from the walls, the work exquisite and chillingly lifelike, though bearing little resemblance to anything that had ever set foot on this planet.

Ana shuddered as she drew nearer. The light was coming from below. How many levels could this hellish dungeon contain?

'You okay Rach?' she called back.

'Yes,' came the weak reply. 'Hurry. It burns.'

Against her better judgement, Ana quickened her pace, wearing her trepidation like a funeral gown. The pit radiated heat like an out-of-control furnace and she stepped to the edge.

There was a crashing sound as the tunnel wall started caving in, rubble tumbling to the ground and rocks breaking.

The spider had found them, and now it was trying to get through.

Time's up.

This chamber was important in some grand cosmic scheme, but she wasn't going to find out why, not today, maybe not ever. She had to get back to Rachel and get them out of here. She refused to let Rachel die. She *couldn't* let her die. The thought was the only thing keeping her going.

As she turned back towards her sister, something caught

her eye, deep in the pit, and she looked down, catching a fleeting glimpse of what lay beneath. A glimpse was all she needed. Any longer and there may have been no coming back, zero chance of psychological recovery.

It carried on forever, like looking through an inter-dimensional telescope to a realm where madness ruled and sanity was the stuff of fantasy. Deep in the pit of her frazzled brain, it registered with her. She had seen this place before.

The great vista stretched out over the horizon, a maddening collage of cyclopean buildings rising from smouldering ruins, the spires and obelisks scraping reddened skies or rising up and out of sight, the whole place coated in thick webs, the screams of those caught in them echoing across aeons, time nothing more than a sick joke played on the eternally damned. The spiders — hundreds of them — waited with damnable patience, perched next to their prey, some feeding, others simply watching. They lined the pit all the way down, an army of sentient monsters, their eyes hungry with mad desire.

The last thing she saw before she turned away from that half-glimpse of another place and time was a solitary spider leg emerging from the clouds and coming to rest on a cathedral, the ground quaking, the stone structure collapsing on top of the unseen congregation, the beast's colossal form thankfully hidden by the perpetual storm clouds. It must have been hundreds and hundreds of feet tall...

'Ana, it's coming!'

Her vision spiralled, and she stepped backwards to prevent herself toppling over into the pit.

That wasn't our world

Dazed, she turned to Rachel.

The walls were lined with spiders

Rachel shuffled her way towards Ana, her eyes wide with fear.

It was taller than the fucking clouds

'Help!'

Snap out of it

'Ana!'

Snap out of it, it wasn't real, it can't be real

'Ana, it's breaking through the walls.'

'Okay,' whispered Ana. Then, louder, 'Okay!' She willed her legs to work, carrying her away from the pit and towards her sister.

They lined the walls like moss

Rachel fell, Ana catching her in her open arms. The walls shook. One of the carvings, a hideous beast resembling a winged octopus, split up the middle, a black snake slithering towards the high ceiling before splitting in two and continuing its journey.

'What are we gonna do?' she asked Ana.

Rock crumbled overhead and crashed down next to them, dust clouding before their eyes as dirt and earth poured in from the widening fissures.

'I don't know,' she said, her eyes darting frenziedly around the room.

Two sinewy legs poked through, raking deep grooves in the ground, the spider scrambling for grip as it forced its way through. The walls didn't look like they would hold out much longer.

'What about down there?' said Rachel, pointing towards the pit.

'No. There's nothing there.'

If only that were true.

The spider hauled itself through the gap, its shroud catching on the rocks and tearing free, the exposed musculature of its foul body throbbing and pulsing in lurid symphony. The sides of the tunnel gave way as it dragged its grotesque frame into the chamber.

Ana stepped in front of Rachel.

'Go away!' she shouted as the spider crept towards her, the blank, lifeless eyes locked onto their target. 'What do you fucking want?'

One leg lashed out, catching her in the stomach and launching her across the room. She smacked into the wall and dropped to the floor like a rag doll. Ana picked herself up, head swooning in delirium, her vision swimming in and out of focus. She put a hand to the back of her hand and it came away slick with dark blood.

The spider raised itself, towering over Rachel. The round egg-like belly squirmed, the muscle quivering and parting as the familiar red hands spread the flesh apart and a figure — it wasn't a man, not really — writhed his way through. This time though, he emerged fully, stepping out of and away from the spider. He stood on wobbling legs as the now-empty vessel behind him shuddered and froze, a ship without a captain.

The bleeding man staggered towards them like a toddler, shoulders swaying, knees buckling, head lolling from side to side like a puppet with its strings cut. He weaved his way over the treacherous terrain until he stood mere inches from Rachel and slumped down onto one knee before her. It looked like he was about to propose. He held out one drooping, gory paw and placed it gently on Rachel's stomach, rubbing it across her belly with the soothing caress of a lover. Then he lifted his sagging head back and issued a laugh that chilled Ana to her very marrow. From somewhere — she thought it may have been from deep within the red pit — came another laugh, a high-pitched cackling. Then another, and another, until the cave was alive with mocking, cruel howling. The man stopped abruptly and looked at Ana through the black pits of its eyes.

She stood her ground, fists clenched and wiped away a solitary tear.

'I'm not afraid of you, you fuckin' wee bastard. I've killed hundreds of your friends over the years. Fucking stamped on them, washed them down the plughole, whatever. Is this your revenge? Huh? Come on then, you cunt. Come on!'

The bloody, monstrous figure stood a moment, then walked backwards, following the trail of his own blood towards the body of the spider. He turned and faced it, then entered the bulging sac of its belly, partly disintegrating as he did so, chunks of meat hitting the ground.

Seconds later, the spider awoke, raising itself up. It pivoted, turned and left, bundling its way through the gap, leaving Rachel and Ana alone in the chamber.

Ana stood, speechless, trying to process what had just happened. She looked at Rachel, at the bloody handprint on her belly. Her swollen, inflamed belly.

Oh god. Oh no, please...

A distant cry. 'Ana?'

'Chakrit?'

'Hurry, we don't have much time!' He emerged into the chamber, staggering on his damaged legs, somehow dripping wet. Ana ran to Rachel first, lifting her, escape at the forefront of her mind.

'What happened?' she asked. 'Where did it go?'

'Distracted. Come on!'

'I thought you were dead,' said Ana.

'Almost. Hurry!'

They navigated the damaged tunnel towards the main cavern. The giant funnel web was ablaze with fire, the whole place lit up like a Christmas tree in Hell. The spider perched beneath it, howling in rage as centuries of work crisped and melted before its many eyes, the cocoons sizzling and popping, showering the creature with thousands of tiny flaming spiderlings. They were dead before they hit the ground. The fire spread across the web like a fuse on a stick of dynamite. It was almost hypnotic to watch.

Chakrit held the torch that had caused the carnage, dodging the flaming debris that rained down from above.

'This way,' he said, beckoning them on. 'I found a way out!'

They ran, following Chakrit's lead until Ana could see the flames playing across a rippling surface. Water!

'In here. A tunnel,' panted an out-of-breath Chakrit. 'Should take us out.'

'Should?' asked Ana doubtfully. She could hear the dreadful clicking of the spider's feet echoing through the cavern, could see its shadow darting about the remnants of its web, its *home*.

They stopped at a pool by the edge of the cavern, Chakrit plunging in, heedless of any potential dangers. He floated there as Ana lowered Rachel into his waiting arms. The cold water caused Rachel's eyes to briefly flicker open. She looked at Ana and smiled.

'Thank you,' she said.

The smile died on her lips. Ana saw something in her sister's eyes. Fear. She seemed to be looking through Ana, or beyond her. The realisation hit her and she prepared for the inevitable. Chakrit saw it too and called out, but it was too late.

It was far, far too late.

The spider descended and, in the blink of an eye, Ana was gone.

37

Her world went black.

Ana was on her back, fleshy digits clawing at her face, reaching for her throat. The Upside-down Man was trying to kill her. The body of the spider loomed over her, eclipsing the inferno that raged overhead. She fought back, punching and kicking.

The Upside-down Man's drooping head slapped off her face so she dug her nails in, tearing the soft tissue to shreds. It had little effect. The body buckled and the tip of the bony proboscis protruded outwards, aimed at her chest. She wrapped both hands around the monstrous appendage, wrestling it away from her, gelatinous sap oozing from the tip. The spider lowered its body, the Upside-down Man pressing against her, his exposed muscle wet to the touch. The proboscis lifted slightly, then drove towards her. Ana rolled left, the piercing implement stabbing into the hard rock. She drew back a foot and aimed a hard kick at it. The spider roared in pain.

She had found a weakness.

Lashing out again with her heel, the spider tried to rear

up, but the proboscis was firmly entrenched in the ground. Another blow brought a snapping sound, and a fourth broke it in two. Hot liquid bubbled from the splintered bone as the spider scurried backwards, the hands of the Upside-down Man taking her firmly by the shoulders, dragging her body along the ground.

Rachel and Chakrit watched helplessly from the water as the spider ran, Ana bouncing and smashing off the rocks below, unable to escape the grip of the strange mutant that lived within the spider.

It was heading for the wall.

As Ana's feet lifted into the air, she looked down and saw the rocky ground receding into the distance.

One thought ran through her mind.

Jesus fucking Christ.

Fear had left her. Once you've been dragged up a wall by a skinless man in the belly of a spider, not much remains to be afraid of. It was replaced by a desperate need to survive.

And anger.

'Put me down! Let me go!' she shouted, lashing out at the grotesque skinless man.

The broken proboscis stabbed into her belly. She barely noticed, raking her hands down the man's body, scratching and tearing. Her fingers slipped in-between chunks of flesh and she tore them out, handfuls of putrid muscle and sinew, her hands burrowing further. The Upside-down Man crumbled, his torso falling apart as Ana yanked out hunks of meat, his hands still gripping her as if they were working independently. The spider slowed, its movements becoming jerky, the muscles spasming. As it started back down the wall to safety, Ana plunged her hands into the Upside-down Man's throat, reaching in and finding long ropes of intestines. The spider leapt from the wall, twirling in midair, its double-jointed legs popping back so that it landed upside down. It should have thrown Ana clear, but she was elbow deep in spider guts.

The spider scuttled around the cavern, trying to shake her loose. She pulled a coil of intestine out. When it stuck, she put it in her mouth and bit down on the rubbery tissue, grinding her teeth until it severed, coppery liquid spilling down her throat. The body of the man now almost empty, Ana did the only thing left to do. She forced her way into the belly of the spider through the gaping hole.

Using her hands as shovels, she ripped and tore and dug, spooning out fistfuls of lumpy black flesh, burrowing her own head inside, feeling the blood washing over her as she plunged into darkness.

Chakrit held Rachel, watching powerlessly as Ana battled the giant spider.

In a frenzy, it came for them, its movements erratic and uncertain. He hauled himself and Rachel out of the pool, grabbing the remnants of the flaming torch, trying to hold the giant insect at bay.

'Get up,' he shouted at Rachel. She was curled into a foetal position, clutching her stomach.

The spider came for them, staggering like a drunkard. Ana was somewhere inside, only her frantically kicking legs visible, the rest of her buried deep in the belly of the beast. Rachel didn't move, either unable or unwilling to. If Chakrit left her, he might be able to escape through the underwater tunnel. Then again, he had no idea if it even led outside. He could be getting them all killed.

Run or go on the offensive? He only had a split-second to

decide, the spider bearing down on him like an eighteen-wheeler with the brakes cut. He jumped over Rachel and threw himself at the spider, ramming the torch into its beady, doll-like eyes. They popped, expelling gouts of an acrid, foul mucus over Chakrit. The spider whipped a leg at him, catching him with a serrated talon, slicing across his chest. He fell back, landing heavily and letting go of the makeshift lantern. It bounced from his hand and hit the water with a splash and a fizz as the light was permanently extinguished.

Chakrit shuffled backwards. He saw Rachel, unmoving. Was she dead?

The spider approached.

If Ana thought the spider smelled bad on the outside, then she was unprepared for the noxious internal stench that invaded her lungs.

It was warm inside. The image of Luke Skywalker inside a Tauntaun popped into her head and she laughed, a high-pitched psychotic gurgle.

A crazy thought; was there any other kind in this situation? Her grip on reality was tenuous at best. A few more minutes and it would be game over. But before that happened, she had one simple goal.

To kill this motherfucking spider. To rip its goddam heart out of its chest and drive a fucking stake through it. Her screams were muffled inside the lacuna of the spider but she kept them up anyway, blood and matter sloshing into her mouth and choking her as her hands rooted around the internal organs. There were no bones, the exterior exposed muscle acting as an exoskeleton. Veins tangled around her as the loud timpani of its heart echoed through the cramped space.

She was drawn to the sound.

Reaching forwards as if trapped in quicksand, Ana touched the beating muscle and squeezed it with every last ounce of strength she possessed. The heart beat faster, almost as if it was trying to shake her off, but she wouldn't let go.

Couldn't.

Her life, and that of her sister, depended on it. She tightened her grip, reaching both arms around until the tips of her fingers touched, clasping her hands and squashing the giant organ, harder and harder and harder until the pressure became too much and it burst in a vile explosion of blood and tissue.

The spider twitched violently as if it had touched an electrical cable.

Its movements became stilted and unpredictable, crawling one direction and then another until the legs gave way and it dropped. It tried to rear up, to crawl away. The body twitched once, twice and then stopped.

Far above, the webs still burned, smoke rippling out through the hole in the ceiling.

The spider lay still.

Chakrit touched the wound on his chest. Not too deep. He'd live. He took Rachel's arm and she stirred with a soft moan.

'Is it dead?' she asked, her eyes firmly shut.

'I think so.'

'Where's my sister?' She tried to sit up. 'Ana?' she called

out, getting to her feet, using Chakrit for leverage. He too stood, ignoring the raw pain that chafed his ankles. Together they stumbled towards the cold, dead body of the spider.

'Is she in there?' asked Rachel.

Chakrit felt for his hunting knife, then remembered it was somewhere near the cave entrance. He needed to cut the spider open. If there was a chance that Ana was still alive in there, he had to take it.

The spider shook slightly and they both froze. Something was moving inside. The flesh wobbled, and a fist emerged from the spider's belly, bursting through the tough meat, followed by another. Chakrit stepped in front of Rachel, shielding her, digging deep for hidden reserves of courage he wasn't even sure he possessed. Then Ana's head slipped out from between the folds of flesh. She pushed herself away from the carcass, sat atop it for a moment, then rolled to one side and landed heavily on the dirt, drenched in blood and gasping for air.

She stopped suddenly, looking around, the whites of her eyes contrasting against the dark red blood of the creature that she wore like a death-mask.

Ana took several deep breaths, her heart rate slowing, normal service resuming. 'What happened?' she breathed, torment writ large on her face, her eyes darting back and forth in pain and confusion.

'You did it, Ana. You killed it,' said Rachel.

Ana looked at her own gore-encrusted hands as Rachel came and sat by her side, holding her sister close, letting Ana weep on her shoulder. After a while Ana looked at Rachel and took her face in both hands.

'I think I'm losing my mind,' she said.

'That's okay,' said Rachel sadly. 'I think we all are.'

Ana relaxed, her body sinking into Rachel. The burning ashes of the web rained down like winter snow, catching in their hair. Bodies fell from the sky as the web disintegrated, dried-up husks hitting the ground in puffs of smoke and dead skin.

Chakrit settled his weary bones down opposite them. He pulled out a metal tin and started rolling a smoke. Ricky's disembowelled corpse landed nearby. None of them noticed.

'Is it over?' asked Ana.

Chakrit stared at his shaking hands, unsure. He looked like the walking dead. 'I think so,' was all he could say.

'Your grandfather was right,' said Ana, wiping the blood from her face, revealing her glazed and feverish expression.

Chakrit nodded. He lit the cigarette. It had never tasted so good, the chemicals giving him a head-rush. Ana stroked Rachel's hair. It was crisp and matted with blood. Rachel's eyes were closed, her breathing slow but steady.

'Will the boat still be there?' sighed Ana.

'Uncle will wait.'

More silence.

'What was that thing?' asked Chakrit, drawing on his cigarette and exhaling the fumes through his nostrils.

'I was hoping you'd know.'

Chakrit laughed dryly and mumbled something in Thai. He saw Ana looking at him. He smiled at her through his broken and bruised face. 'I just apologised to grandfather. My family dishonoured him.'

'Not you, Chakrit,' said Ana. 'Not you.'

He looked down at his feet, unsure of how to take this outpouring of sincerity. 'Man is not alone in the universe. There's more out there than we can possibly know. More than we would ever *want* to know. I guess some secrets are best left buried.'

Suddenly he looked at her, his face a mixture of panic and alarm.

'You hear that?'

She did.

A rumbling, a distant hum that gradually built in intensity until it filled the cavern, bouncing off the walls, surrounding them. Rachel's eyes snapped open. Chakrit flicked his half-smoked cigarette away and leapt to his feet, wincing at the pain in his ankles.

'We go *now*,' he said. No one disagreed.

The rumble increased in volume until the whole cavern began shaking, dislodging rocks in the ceiling. The fires were almost out now, the last vestiges of light snuffed out. Soon darkness would reign once more.

Ana coughed up a mouthful of blood and let Chakrit help her up. A boulder crashed down nearby, sharpened stalactites falling like huge, deadly icicles.

Click-click-click.

'What the fuck?'

Click-click-click-click-click-click-click-click-click.

It was a noise they were all intimately familiar with. One they had briefly hoped they would never hear again.

They turned as one towards the chamber with the pit, the red light streaming out through the broken tunnel, black shadows playing across the walls. Ana's hand tightened over Rachel's.

They lined the walls.

'They're coming,' she said.

38

So close.

To end like this after all they had been through.

You had to laugh.

They were pouring out, spilling over the lip of the pit in a great tidal wave of nightmares, a gruesome obscenity from another place and time. Dozens, hundreds of the beasts erupting forth like a geyser. The ground underfoot shook mightily.

Chakrit hoisted Rachel's prone body over his shoulder in a fireman's lift and grabbed Ana's limp hand. 'Run!' he bellowed. Fighting every urge in her body, she did, forcing her legs to work through sheer willpower. Chakrit took the lead and she tried to keep up, the red light from the pit illuminating the cavern and glinting off the pool of water ahead of them. Ana narrowed her eyes and focused on it, their one chance.

Safety. Sanctuary.

Possibly.

A stalactite ploughed into the rock mere feet from her, showering her with tiny shattered pebbles. She kept her head down and ran. Behind her the noise intensified, indiscernible screeches and roars and that damnable clicking sound, the wild cacophony grating on her frayed nerves.

Not far now. She was losing ground on Chakrit and Rachel, the pool impossibly far away, and then without even realising it she was falling, for a brief second, and then splashing, engulfed in the cool water, her head beneath the surface, momentarily unable to breathe. Her feet touched the rocks below and she pushed herself up until her head broke the surface and she could look into Chakrit's wild, frightened eyes. He glanced over her shoulder.

'Deep breaths,' he snapped, forcing down great lungfuls of air, and then he was gone, taking Rachel with him, leaving Ana alone. She copied him, and as the red light vanished behind something enormous she ducked her head under the water and swam, hands in front of her, feeling for obstacles and obstructions. It was pitch black and a brief, maddening flashback to being inside the guts of the spider washed over her. She wrestled it away, thrashing her legs to gain forward momentum. Her head struck a low rock but she kept swimming, stopping for nothing. She tried to remain as close to the ceiling of the tunnel as possible, praying for an air pocket. Already her lungs felt like they might burst.

Her escape route was narrowing, the roof dropping lower and lower until the rounded stones massaged her back, and she used her hands to grip the bed and pull herself along. She started to panic, keeping her mouth shut, knowing that letting the water in would surely finish her off for good. The tiny cave forked and Ana chose the right-hand side without thinking. How long had she been underwater? Thirty seconds? A minute? How long could she keep under? She had to breathe soon. Had to.

Her shoulders scraped off the sides. There was barely enough room for her to kick her legs anymore so she concentrated on her hands, gripping the walls and thrusting herself onwards. Her throat started to burn, her heartbeat out of control.

She knew she was going to die. Should she just open her mouth and get it over with?

Her hands slowed, her grip lessening. A bright white light appeared before her and suddenly she couldn't feel the surrounding rock anymore. She was floating, sailing through the water as if caught in a current, moving towards the light.

I'm dead, she thought, relaxing her muscles.

Then her head was above water and the cool night air was on her face and she breathed in huge, wracking gasps of air, her senses slowly returning. She opened her eyes as she floated serenely down the river, flanked by trees on either side, great hulking sentinels marking her progress. Behind her lay the mountain. She shifted her weight and turned round, searching, but there was no sign of Chakrit or Rachel. She thought of the fork in the tunnel, of her split-second decision to take the right-hand side. What if...

No. No what ifs. Ahead of her the water roared and instinctively she knew it was a waterfall. She tried to swim to the side but the banks were too steep and she was too tired, too utterly, hopelessly exhausted. She gave up, letting the river carry her like a broken tree trunk, drifting, drifting, and then falling, falling.

39

THE WORKERS' VILLAGE WAS IN CHAOS.

The men ran in circles, searching for Ana, her cell empty except for the guard lying in a pool of blood, his neck broken. Some followed footprints leading out to sea, Paul's hideously desiccated corpse the fool's gold at the end of the macabre rainbow. They split up, searching the six buildings, leaving no nook or cranny unexplored. A party of the men headed up the hill to the resort. She couldn't have gone far. She had to still be on the island!

The Pale Man in the sunglasses paced back and forth. It would be daylight soon. Daylight was no use. It was too bright for them, they would have to stick to the shadows. They would be at a disadvantage.

The Great Uabhas would be angry. He grabbed two of the men and instructed them, in that hideous, primordial language, to investigate the cave. The men, knowing no such thing as free will, obeyed, grabbing their tools and setting off through the petrified jungle, past the mass grave and neglected diggers, until they reached the entrance, the one they themselves had dug all those years ago, acting under that strange impulse that constantly whispered to them, that demanded loyalty, demanded sacrifice.

They stood at the entrance, listening to the rumbling tremor from within, feeling the ground tremble beneath their feet. The men stared at each other.

The whispering had stopped.

For the first time in as long as they could remember, their heads were clear, unencumbered by the malevolent, wicked voices that cackled and taunted them even in their dreams. One of the men let the pick-axe fall from his hand, where it hit the earth with a soft thud.

'Kasem,' he said. The other man turned to him. He smiled. 'I remember now. My name is Kasem.' He dropped to his knees and cried. 'What have we done?' he said. He clutched at his face, tearing deep scars across his cheeks, his long-dormant memories flooding back. His wife's smiling visage, the laughter of his children, the hubbub of the marketplace, his childhood on the shrimp farm, his first car. Then he remembered what came after it.

The way the men had begged for their lives as he lopped their arms off, the women screaming in unutterable horror as they were stripped and branded and taken to that lair of cosmic terror, the pit he had stared into and given up his life for, that glimpse of other worlds, dreadful places where faceless beasts roamed and ancient civilisations waited to rise again.

It was too late for prayers and incantations.

The spell was broken.

The time of reckoning had arrived.

He would answer for his crimes and accept punishment, knowing it would never truly be enough to atone for the dreadful sins they had perpetrated. Kasem closed his eyes and sat. His old friend, Narong, did the same, crossing his legs and awaiting oblivion, the sudden wave of memories nearly driving him mad. He dimly recalled that hazy September morning, when he had watched from the scaffolding as the two boats sailed away, almost crashing into each other, one of them taking half of the dock with it. They had run down the hill after them, setting off flares, screaming and shouting, but the people on the boats had chosen not to notice them.

That was when the voices had begun, a language none of the men had ever heard before, yet one they all understood. They had begun work on the tunnel that same morning, digging tirelessly over two long days, barely sleeping or eating, until they had broken through to the chamber of the Great Uabhas.

The next day, the first of the rescue boats had arrived. By then, everything had changed.

Narong took Kasem's hand and squeezed it. 'I'm sorry,' he said. Kasem withdrew his hand, clawing at his own eyeballs, forcing his fingers beneath the eyelids and gripping the soft orbs, crushing them until juices flowed down his hands and cheeks and into his mouth, horrified and ashamed at what he had become, a vessel for a cruel and bygone god. He deserved to die. They all did.

The spiders erupted forth from the cave entrance, crushing the men beneath their heavy bodies, heading towards the village, toppling trees as they travelled, the trunks splintering under the weight of the giant insects.

They were legion, and the carnage was absolute.

Within minutes, the village was a bloodbath, awash with torn limbs and savaged bodies.

None were spared.

40

ANA AWOKE TO THE HEAT OF THE EARLY MORNING SUN
in agony.

Every inch of her body was bruised or cut. Her joints
throbbed, her head ached, her stomach rebelled. The blood
that coated her had hardened into a parched riverbed and
she picked at it absently like a scab.

She looked up into the cloudless sky and wondered for a
moment whether the whole thing had been a drunken
nightmare, and this was the hangover from hell. Her sleep
had been fitful and fraught with terrors. She woke at one
point to the sound of screaming, of men in the very depths
of despair being slaughtered, unsure whether it was real or
part of her dreams.

To her right Chakrit pissed against a tree, the urine
striking the bark the only sound for miles around. He
turned, zipping his fly and noticed her staring. She looked
away hurriedly. He staggered towards her and sat. The
wound on his chest looked nasty, from above one nipple to
below the other. His legs were worse. The skin from one

ankle had been stripped clean like peeled fruit, the muscle raw and tender.

'Hey,' said Ana, her voice pitiful and small. Her stomach rumbled, and she realised she hadn't eaten in over twenty-four hours.

'Hey,' he said back, neither in the mood for small talk.

They had slept all night, after Chakrit had pulled Ana's unconscious body from the lagoon. The last thing she remembered was the third waterfall. According to Chakrit, there were several more, the last of which fed into the lagoon. It burbled away behind them and now they sat, the sun hot on their faces, two broken people who have glimpsed Hell and lived to tell the tale. Rachel lay curled up in the shade, the only one of them who hadn't slept a wink all night. It wasn't just the pain in her belly. It was the voices, the whispering...

'Those men...' started Ana.

'No worries anymore.'

Ana nodded. She got to her feet, her body wailing in protest, and looked out across the clear blue lagoon.

'I think you're right,' she said.

Ana peeled off her bra and knickers and stepped into the refreshing water. She smelled like a mixture of rotting corpses and spider guts; not exactly a desirable aroma. The water came to below her breasts and she dipped her head under and kept it there, the water at first stinging and then soothing her aches. When she surfaced, Chakrit was just getting in. He too was naked. Ana lay back, only her face breaking the surface, and closed her eyes.

Rachel was curled up on the edge of the lagoon. When Ana was done, she went to her sister, helped her sit and washed away as much of the blood as possible. She cupped handfuls of water and poured it onto Rachel's hair. She cleaned her face, then her breasts and belly. She noticed the brand on her flesh, an unintelligible squiggle that would scar her for life. Next to it was a small hole where it looked like she had been stabbed.

'My god,' gasped Ana. Her sister looked as pale as a corpse. Her lips were blue, her eyes milky. Ana knew Rachel was dying. If she could just get her back to the mainland in time, get her to a doctor...

Maybe.

'Rach, can you walk?'

'Mmm-hmm,' she said, though it hurt her to do so.

A shadow fell over her. Ana turned to see Chakrit, stripped to his blood-soaked underwear. He held out his shorts and Ana took them.

'For your sister,' he said, walking away.

She helped Rachel slip them on and fastened the belt.

'Where's Paul,' wheezed Rachel as Ana helped her to her feet.

'At the boat, Rach. We'll see him soon.'

Rachel scratched at her belly and looked Ana in the eyes for the last time. 'Take me home. Please,' she pleaded.

The sun beat down.

41

THE FISHING BOAT BOBBED ON THE SEA LIKE A CHILD'S BATH toy and Ana felt her knees go weak. It was too good to be true, wasn't it? A man stood on the deck, a lone silhouette against the burning sun. Chakrit's uncle, their saviour, waiting for them, to rescue them, to take them home.

Home. What a wonderful, perfect word that was. It conjured up images of her and Rachel laughing, playing in the shared garden, Ana helping her sister up when she fell off the swing, their mother calling for them to come inside because dinner was on the table and it looked like it was about to rain and if it did they'd catch their death of cold. She thought of the room she and Rachel had shared until Ana had turned thirteen, and the constant battle over who got to put up their posters, Ana wanting Green Day and Rachel fighting for Backstreet Boys. Rachel had won, of course. She always did.

Not long now.

The battered-looking yellow dinghy lounged on the sand, lapping up the rays of the sun, the useless craft they had arrived on still embedded in the sandbank near shore.

Let it rot there. Let it serve as a warning for other unlucky trespassers.

Rachel could barely keep her eyes open, never mind walk, so they laid her in the life-raft and dragged it over the sand into the water. It was a struggle, but they managed. The prospect of survival does extraordinary things for morale. Ana wondered why the small boat was still here. Had Paul not made it back? Was he still roaming the island, lost and disorientated?

Good. Fuck him.

Chakrit tugged the cord on the outboard motor and it caught on the second try, sputtering to life. As the dinghy rocked on the waves, heading towards the fishing boat, Ana took one last look at the island, expecting to see it brooding with unrestrained menace.

Instead, she saw the idyllic paradise it should have been. The unfinished resort still stood vigil, a sad reminder of mankind's insignificance in the face of the unknown. She thought of what lay below it in that hollowed-out hill, of the infernal pit secured within the chamber, and all the horrors therein. It all seemed so absurd now, little more than a campfire tale. She looked at the slight swell of Rachel's belly, and wondered what she carried in there that was so important.

Important enough to spare her life.

Someone can help her. Someone will be able to get it out and kill it and Rachel will be fine and everything can go back to normal.

It was a pipe dream.

But without hope, we have nothing. It's what gets us through the day.

Hope.

Such an empty word. She clasped Rachel's cold hand.

'Rach,' she whispered.

'Yeah,' came the delayed response.

'Hang on. We're almost there.'

She turned away from the island. The boat was close. She heard music playing from a radio, an oldies station, Frank Sinatra singing about *The Wee Small Hours of the Morning*. God, music! Was there a sweeter sound on Earth? Her spirits lifted. Even Rachel's eyes fluttered open at the sound.

'Are we home?' she asked, her hand weakly clutching Ana's.

'Not yet, Rach. Soon. We're almost at the boat.'

'Is Paul there?'

'Yeah, he's there,' said Ana, her eyes brimming with tears.

'What about mum?'

Ana looked out to sea, biting down on her lip.

'Yeah, Rach. Mum's there too. We'll all be together real soon.'

'Good. I'm so tired.'

Chakrit averted his eyes and Ana was thankful for his discretion. The remainder of the short trip passed in merciful silence until the dinghy reached the boat with a bump. The old Thai man casually tossed a rope down to Chakrit, who tied it to the metal ring on the nose of the small craft and put a hand on the three-rung ladder to steady it.

'I go first, you pass her to me,' he said to Ana. She could see the relief in his eyes. No doubt a celebratory smoke would soon be on the cards.

She nodded, too tired to talk, sitting and watching as Chakrit climbed the ladder with difficulty. His ankle was badly infected and needed urgent medical attention, the thick dark blood congealing around his wounds. His uncle held out a hand and hoisted Chakrit up and onto the deck. One down, two to go.

The old man helped Chakrit sit then looked over the edge at the two near-naked girls in the boat, both scarred and scratched and beaten almost beyond recognition. Rachel didn't stir, though Ana could see her chest rising and falling at painfully long intervals. The old man pointed at them and said something. Ana tried to smile at him. The man put his head in his hands. When he took them away, Ana could have sworn he was crying. He reached down and picked up a shotgun, carefully raising it. He muttered a quiet prayer and pointed it right at them.

She had no time to react.

He fired.

42

THE REPORT OF THE GUN WAS LOUD ENOUGH TO ROUSE THE slumbering birds from their nests in the trees, taking flight immediately and heading for the other side of the island in a squawk of beating wings and fluttering feathers.

Ana flinched, expecting the gunshot to blast her to shreds. Instead it fired harmlessly into the water. She looked up and saw the man was gone. There were shouts, curses and the thump of fists on flesh. Without thinking, she put two hands on the ladder and started climbing. The shotgun went off again and this time the air above her head rippled.

That was too close.

Chakrit and his uncle rolled on the deck in a flurry of limbs. Chakrit clearly had the advantage of youth and strength, but he was badly injured, his uncle landing a few strong blows to his nephew's head. This was no ordinary fight. This was a life or death struggle. The old man brought a sharp fist down into Chakrit's eye socket with a sickening thud. In the corner a pug barked excitedly, drowning out Ol' Blue Eyes on the radio and completing the surreal scene. His tail was uncurled, ears drawn back.

Chakrit smashed his uncle in the teeth with an elbow, knocking him to one side. The man responded by punching Chakrit in his chest wound. He roared in pain and fell back, allowing his uncle time to get on top of him. He closed one hand around Chakrit's neck and used the other to pummel his chest, his hand coming away bloodier with each strike as the scar reopened.

Ana scrambled up the ladder and rolled onto the deck, ignoring the pain that flared through her body, reaching for the discarded shotgun, her agonised brain screaming at her to stop. She grabbed the weapon and aimed at the man's head. He ignored her.

'It's empty!' said Chakrit, his voice a strangulated cry. The man dazed Chakrit with a punch and released him, turning his attention to Ana.

A day or so ago, Ana would have shrieked in terror at a crazed man coming for her, fearful of being beaten or killed.

But this was not the same woman who had tried to kill herself last year. Something had fundamentally changed, a switch had been activated in her brain, a switch she had never dared acknowledge, let alone touch. She had faced death many times and overcome it, and this asshole was not going to be the one to break the chain. A few hours ago she had disembowelled a giant fucking spider.

This was just a man.

With no regard for her own personal safety, Ana rushed towards the man, surprising him. She could tell he was on the backfoot, that he had expected her to shrink back in fear. The eyes gave it away. They always do.

Gripping the empty gun with both hands, she thrust it in front of her, smashing the steel barrel into the man's face. It struck his nose and she heard the delicate organ shatter, saw the blood gush from his nostrils like two broken taps, pouring down his chest and splattering the deck. He reached his hands up to stem the flow and Ana, wasting no time, adjusted the shotgun in her hands, swinging it like a golf club, striking Chakrit's uncle between the legs. He dropped to his knees, his mouth open in a silent scream, and she brought the wooden butt down on his head with a crack.

As his eyes rolled back into his head, he dropped unconscious to the deck, the blood from his nose creating an ever-widening pool around his face. Ana spotted movement in her periphery.

The pug. It was coming straight for her, his claws clacking off the deck (*click-click-click*) and his jaws wide open.

'Please no,' said Ana, holding the gun like a baseball bat. Then the tiny dog slowed to a trot, jumping up at her legs, grinning, his tongue lolling out the side of his mouth.

The gun slipped from her hands and clattered to the deck.

She scooped the little dog up in her aching arms and let him lick the salty tears from her face.

43

HALF AN HOUR LATER THEY SET SAIL FOR KOH PHANGAN.

The radio was playing a scratchy, distorted version of an old Bobby Vinton song, one that Ana remembered her grandmother playing on the old record player. *I Love How You Love Me*, it was called, and though she hadn't heard it in about fifteen years, she still knew the words, every syllable and inflection. She and Rachel used to fall asleep to that album, the music bleeding through the walls as their granny, who was as deaf as a post but would never admit it, cranked the volume dial even higher.

She wondered if Rachel remembered.

She took a bandage from the onboard first aid kit and wrapped it around Chakrit's chest.

'You crying?' he asked.

Ana drew in a breath. 'It's this song. It takes me back.' She barely recognised her own voice.

'Takes you back?'

She clasped a safety pin into the already reddening bandage. 'Aye. To being a wee kid. Back when you were allowed to be stupid and silly and not care about anything.

Before the reality of adulthood crushes your childhood dreams and you realise you can't grow up to be an astronaut or a princess or a unicorn.'

Chakrit smiled and Ana smiled back as she dabbed at his ankles with a wet sponge. They were a write-off, particularly the left one. The white of the bone was visible between the angry red muscle. Still, she would wash it. It was the least she could do. Anything to create the illusion of hope.

Hope.

That word again. That lying, deceitful word.

Where was Rachel's hope? Ana heard her cough from below deck and imagined the specks of blood hitting the pillow. She had better check on her again, see if she had touched the water Ana had left next to the bed, draped in that stained, oily blanket, convulsions wracking her fragile body.

First, she had to check on Chakrit's uncle. She finished tending to Chakrit, then walked to the stern and watched the dinghy they towed behind them, the old man in it lying still.

Unconscious or Dead?

She hadn't hit him hard enough to kill him. Had she? No, he was sleeping it off, she was sure of it. He was safe there, and they were safe from him. When she turned back to Chakrit, he was checking the map and plotting a course for Koh Phangan. There was a hospital there, and that would be their first port of call, followed by the police, not an encounter either of them were relishing.

'No one's gonna believe us,' said Ana, sitting in the shade and counting her bruises.

Chakrit rolled them both a cigarette. He lit his first, then handed Ana the lighter.

'I know.'

'So what are we going to tell them?'

He shrugged. 'Whatever they want to hear. How's your sister?'

'Not good. How long til we get to the island?'

'Six hours maybe.'

'Shit.' She took a drag on the cigarette. It was her first one in ten years and it simultaneously repulsed and calmed her.

'She'll be okay. Good doctors in Thailand.'

She smiled weakly. 'Chakrit, what happened earlier? Why did your uncle try to kill us?'

He looked at his hands, the cigarette, out to sea, anywhere but at her. 'He's crazy. An old fool. He said he can't let you on, can't let you anywhere near the mainland. Said you had to stay.'

'Why?'

'He said you carried the mark.'

'The mark?'

'Yes. That thing they burn on her.' They sat in silence for a while, both thinking about the strange raised welts on Rachel's belly. Ana flashed back to watching from her cell window as the man had taken the piece of metal from the fire and advanced on Rachel, the tip glowing. She remembered the steam rising from her belly and blinked it away.

'You believe him?'

He shook his head. 'He's crazy. Believes ladies shouldn't sing while cooking, or else they will marry an old man.'

'Okay. That actually makes me feel a bit better.' She smiled. 'Thanks again, Chakrit. For everything.'

'Hey, you saved *my* life.'

'Will you visit me in hospital?'

He laughed; a soft, pleasant sound. 'You visit *me*.'

'We can get beds next to each other.'

'It's a deal,' he said.

Ana leaned forwards and kissed him. He responded by putting his arm around her and moving in closer. His mouth tasted faintly of blood, but so did hers, so who gives a shit. She placed a hand on his chest, accidentally pressing on his wound.

'Ow!'

'I'm sorry! Oh god, I'm sorry!'

But he was laughing, and so was she. She stopped herself before it turned to tears.

'What was that place?' she asked.

He gave it some thought. 'Some kind of Hell.'

'They're all dead. So many people. I guess Paul is too. I wonder what happened to him.'

Chakrit flicked his cigarette overboard. 'I hope it was painful.'

She stood up, feeling like an old lady rising from a chair in a nursing home, bones creaking and beads of sweat rolling down her forehead. 'I'm gonna check on Rach. Make sure she's drinking plenty water.'

He nodded. 'Want a cigarette?'

'Sure. Why not.' She started to go down the narrow stairs and paused. 'Chakrit?'

'Yes?'

She thought about their brief kiss, unsure of what she was about to say. She settled on, 'Nothing.'

He nodded, then leaned his head back and closed his eyes.

Ana watched him for a moment then descended the stained and water-damaged steps, thinking about Chakrit. He had all the qualities she liked in a man; handsome, easy-going and willing to fight giant spiders. Yup, he ticked all the boxes.

The noise of the engine increased with each step until she reached the bottom and was confronted by two doors. One led to a small toilet cubicle, the other to a sort-of bedroom. At least it was more welcoming than the last boat she had been on. There were maps and crates and a cooler, and some yellow raincoats hanging from nails hammered into the walls.

Grub the pug stood guard at the door. Well, he was fast asleep, but they weren't expecting many visitors. Ana stepped over the slumbering beast and sat by the bed. She placed the back of her hand on Rachel's forehead. She was burning up. Feverish. Ana pulled back the covers, damp with sweat and urine, and looked at the knotted flesh and bowing bones of her sister.

'Rach?'

'Uhhh.'

'Hang in there, okay?'

She poured water onto her cupped hand and dribbled it onto Rachel's lips, then on her face for good measure.

'Uhhh,' replied Rachel, her distended belly pressing against Chakrit's shorts. Careful not to touch the cauterised flesh, Ana undid the belt and slipped them down over her sister's legs. She tossed them to one side. Rachel's veins were dark, *black* almost, and streaking down her thighs from a nasty wound near her navel.

'We're almost there, Rach. Not far to go now.'

'Promise?'

'Aye, I promise.'

A claw-like hand settled on Ana's leg and she gently held it, the same way she had held her mother's hand as she lay dying in the hospital bed.

'I'm sorry Ana,' said Rachel, her voice hazy and confused.

'For what?' whispered Ana.

'For not being there. Before. With mum.'

'Rach, it's okay—'

'She's dead now, isn't she?'

Ana swallowed hard. 'Yes, she is.'

Rachel nodded, almost imperceptibly. 'I thought so, but I can't remember. Like my memories are...slipping away.' Ana nodded. She could say nothing, her face was frozen. 'I was scared, Ana. Scared of death. Scared of dying. I couldn't watch it happen to mum.'

'It's okay, Rach,' managed Ana, her lip trembling.

'Is she dead?'

'She is.'

'Oh. I used to be afraid of dying too, y'know. I ever tell you that?'

'No,' lied Ana, squeezing Rachel's hand without realising it.

'Hey, you're hurting me.'

'I'm sorry,' said Ana, relinquishing her grip.

'It's not so bad, you know.'

'What?'

Rachel almost smiled, her dry lips cracking. 'Dying, I mean. If this is what it's like, then it's not so bad.'

'You're not dying,' said Ana.

Rachel didn't reply.

In the dinghy, the man stirred. Easing himself up, he tenderly touched his nose and a sharp pain spread throughout his temple. Broken. Both nostrils were sealed with clotted blood and he had to breathe through his mouth. Also, his balls ached like a motherfucker.

He didn't blame the girl. He blamed himself. He had underestimated her resilience and paid the price. In a way, he admired her.

The dinghy was attached to the boat — *his* boat — by a cable. He glanced around, moving as furtively as his swollen testicles would allow, making sure no one was watching. The island was far behind them now. That accursed place! He should never have come. Never. But the white idiot had offered him so much money. More money than he had ever held before, now safely stashed away beneath a loose plank below deck. But what good was money if you never lived to spend it? He gripped the rope with both hands and started to reel himself in. He couldn't let them reach the mainland.

He couldn't let them live.

Chakrit sat alone on the deck. Ana had been gone some time now. Should he join her below deck? No, what good would that do? This was between family. He didn't think Rachel was going to make it; the mainland was too far away. Presuming, of course, he was taking them in the right direction. His uncle was the sailor in the family, not him. They could be heading for fucking Vietnam for all he knew.

He rolled another smoke and realised Ana had his lighter. No problem, he would wait. He gazed across the ocean, the crackle of the radio obscuring the soft footsteps of his uncle as he crept towards the discarded shotgun.

Chakrit heard the weapon being cracked open. His uncle thumbed the cartridges into place and snapped it shut.

With tears in his eyes, he said, 'I'm sorry, Chakrit.'

As a tortured scream rose up from below deck, he pulled

the trigger. From three feet away, the damage was absolute. Chakrit's head was blown to pieces, shards of skull and sticky brain matter splattering the walls like a Jackson Pollock. His hand, still clutching the cigarette, twitched once before the legs gave way and his headless body sagged to the ground.

~

Ana held Rachel's limp hand. It was as cold as a winter night.

'It hurts,' she moaned.

'Where?'

'Everywhere.'

'Drink some water.'

Rachel tried to shake her head. 'Hurts to drink.' She turned away from Ana, curling up into a tight ball, scratching at her belly, her face contorted. She was rapidly deteriorating.

'I'm sorry,' said Ana. 'I don't know how to help.'

Rachel mouthed something at her. Ana leaned in closer. 'What? I can't hear you.' She put her ear against Rachel's mouth.

'Kill me.'

Ana straightened up. 'Rach, don't say that, please.'

'Just end it.'

Ana put her head in her hands. 'I can't, and I won't.'

Rachel spasmed, her body stiffening. She cried out. In the doorway, the pug woke up and looked at them, emitting a low growl.

'Oh god, it hurts. It hurts!' gurgled Rachel. She retched and Ana turned her onto her side, where she vomited black, gangrenous slug-like tissue onto the pillow.

The dog was barking now, howling at them and backing away.

'Kill me! Kill me!' screamed Rachel, her voice breaking.

'I can't!' cried Ana. Rachel's body twisted and cracked, her limbs jutting out at weird angles. Ana tore the blanket from her and screamed, just as a shotgun blast went off above deck.

Rachel's belly was pulsating.

It stretched, the blueish-purple skin pulling taut.

The dog turned and ran.

There was something inside her sister.

And it was trying to get out.

44

ANA WALKED BACKWARDS, BUMPING INTO THE WALL, EYES WIDE and white and shocked. Rachel reached a crooked hand out to her.

'Kill me!' she roared, 'Kill me kill me kill me!'

Gouts of blood jettisoned from her mouth, spilling down her nude and gnarled body as whatever lay in her belly scratched and clawed. Rachel's ribcage burst with a violent crack, several white bones tearing out through her skin like branches on a long-dead tree, ichorous fluid spraying Ana from across the room.

Rachel's stomach ruptured in a welter of gore as a stalk-like protrusion tore its way out, then another, and another. She jerked, her body a useless marionette, the thing inside her the dreadful, chuckling puppeteer.

The legs — eight in total, of course — unfurled until they rested on the wooden floor, now slick with blood, loose intestines slopping around as the boat rocked. It tried to raise itself up, weak with the exertion of birth, its host body now a flat, lifeless husk with vacant eyes that stared at Ana through a mask of horrified anguish.

Someone was coming down the stairs.

Chakrit.

She ripped her eyes away from the monstrous creation just as Chakrit's uncle stepped into the room. He saw Ana and raised the shotgun, finger hovering over the trigger, before becoming aware of the scuttling presence in the corner. He swung the weapon towards the ruined mess of Rachel.

He saw it.

The gun slipped from his hands, hitting the floor and going off, blasting a hole in the wall right between Ana's knees.

The spider, growing with each passing second, was as big as a dog. It flung itself towards the man, cloaking his face with all eight legs, muffling his cries.

The legs dug in, tiny claws burrowing into the back of his head, splitting the skull. He slumped against the wall as the spider sank its fangs into his neck, the arterial-spray painting the walls a dark crimson.

Ana leapt over the body of Chakrit's uncle as he gurgled and wailed, the spider feasting on human flesh for the first time, and hit the stairs running, relying on sheer adrenaline to carry her up. She burst through the hatch and felt the sea air on her face, then turned and slipped on the pool of blood seeping from the shredded remains of Chakrit's neck, the stump of his vertebrae jutting out between the gristle.

There was no time to mourn.

The boat lurched back and forth as Ana struggled to her feet, cursing herself for not picking up the shotgun. Her mind raced. The pug bayed at her from the far end of the boat. She crawled towards him, away from what was left of Chakrit. The wood behind her creaked and splintered as the spider made its way upstairs. She searched for weapons, scanning the deck.

Chakrit's lighter was still tucked in the waistband of her panties, but how could it be any use against the abominable thing coming up the stairs? The pug stood next to a large wooden crate. Perhaps she could get some wood and set it on fire?

She didn't know much about spiders, particularly giant ones, but she assumed they were as flammable as any other living thing.

She slid her way over to the crate, ignoring the plaintive wail of the dog. A huge rusted padlock swayed from the lid.

'No!' she cried, hammering her fists on the box. She tried to prise it open; even a single thin plank was better than nothing. Looking over her shoulder, she saw the creature emerging, obliterating the narrow staircase as it reached the outside, already the size of a grown man. It spotted her, the feet clicking madly on the deck as it scurried forwards, ignoring the pug and launching itself towards her. Ana kicked away from the crate and the spider crashed into it, smashing it apart, small blue sticks rolling out and across the deck.

Dynamite.

The spider lurched unsteadily before coming at Ana again. A wave crashed into the side, sending both of them off-balance and the dynamite skittering across the deck. Ana lunged for it, outstretched fingers grasping at thin air as the sticks rolled one way then the next, her own feet, wet with blood, struggling to find maintain contact with the slippery deck.

I could throw myself overboard. Spiders can't swim.

Yeah, but can you swim back to shore?

Of course not. To do so would mean certain death. She would be killing herself again, only this time there was no one to save her.

The pug had stopped barking and was cowering near the broken staircase. She couldn't blame him.

The spider approached, its legs wobbling slightly.

Well, it has just been born.

The boat tipped, and the dynamite came rolling back down towards Ana. She stooped and grabbed one as the spider made its move, hurtling towards her. She threw herself onto her back, legs sticking up in the air, pressing into the spider's abdomen and keeping it at bay. The legs gouged at her, lacerating her already brutalised skin. She had the lighter in one hand, a stick of dynamite in the other, and a gargantuan flesh-hungry spider on top of her. She flipped the lighter open and tried desperately to get it to catch a flame. The spider brought a muscular leg down on her forearm, pressing it to the deck and putting the dynamite stick safely out of reach, betraying a malevolent intelligence behind the hundreds of tiny eyes. She struck flame with the lighter and held it up to the creature's stomach as it slathered drool from its jaws.

The creature's belly squirmed and undulated and Ana knew what was coming next. A hand, soft and red, tentatively reaching out, emerging up to the elbow. It found Ana's wrist and gripped it, pressing hard with its skinless thumb. She heard her ulna snap and she roared in pain, the lighter dropping from her now-useless hand, the fleshy digits keeping hold of her as the soggy tissue parted once more and the bulging sac of a head appeared. This one had more definition to it; a mouth, a nose and two black holes where the eyes should be. The mouth opened, unleashing an ear-splitting shriek that vibrated in the pit of Ana's stomach. The Upside-Down Man released her arm and reached for her throat. She moved her head, snapping her own mouth shut, trying to bite the creature, her own animal instincts kicking in.

Suddenly the pressure on Ana's good arm abated, and the hand on her neck slackened. She turned her head and saw the pug with its jaws clamped firmly over the spider's leg, scrambling backwards like it was determined to tear the limb clean off. The spider shook its appendage, but the little dog clung on fiercely, even as the spider slammed it into the deck.

Ana had one chance. She brought her free arm up in one fluid motion, slamming the stick of dynamite into the Upside-Down man's gaping mouth. It went straight in, the end bursting out the back of his head and wedging in tightly.

The spider waved its leg one more time, propelling the small dog overboard and into the ocean. It was only a second, but it was all the time Ana needed. With the spider momentarily distracted, she grabbed the fallen lighter with her good hand, flicked it and held the flame to the dynamite. It caught, the fuse sparking into life and she kicked with all her strength, pushing the spider back just far enough for her to roll out from under it.

The Upside-Down Man groped for the explosive, unwilling to go near the burning fuse. Ana ran, her bare feet smacking off the deck. She reached the rail and threw herself over as behind her the spider exploded. The heat of the blast scorched her back as she sailed through the air, splashing into the sea in a colossal belly-flop, followed closely by a rainstorm of blood and limbs spattering across the surface. Drifting under the water, she saw the yellow dinghy and swam for it, breaking the surface for a moment, in time to see the fire raging across the deck of the fishing boat, the fuses of the loose dynamite sticks catching and sparking. She ducked back under as they went off, explosions blasting across the boat sending wood and metal firing across the sky and into the sea, eradicating any trace that the boat had ever existed.

It was quiet under the water, mercifully so. In a way, Ana wished she could just stay there forever, cocooned in the tranquillity of the ocean, nestled in Mother Nature's womb.

She bobbed her head up and looked to where the boat once was. The craft was destroyed and whatever remained was sinking fast and taking her sister's body with it. With her last gasp of strength, she swam towards the dinghy, now floating freely, the rope that had bound it now a frazzled cord that trailed through the sea.

She reached the rescue boat and hauled herself up, fighting through the pain of her broken wrist. Wrapping one bruised and cut leg over the edge, she dragged her body up and flopped down into the dinghy, utterly spent.

Something scratched at the boat, clawing violently at it.

'You can't still be alive,' breathed Ana.

This was it then. Even after all that, after blowing it to smithereens with dynamite, it still came for her, a waking nightmare that crawled on eight wretched legs.

'Come and fucking get me then,' she sighed.

She lay there, unable to move, squinting into the sun, waiting for the half-burnt spider to clamber on board and finish her off, dragging her down into the fathomless depths.

With a splash it finally forced its way out of the water and landed in the dinghy. Ana closed her eyes. Small feet padded their way over to her as Grub the pug let out a sad whimper and curled up next to her, his wet fur soothing against Ana's aching, scalded skin. She put an arm over his shivering body and wept beneath the glare of the sun.

They slept for a long time.

45

ANA AWOKE TO GRUB'S ROUGH TONGUE LICKING HER CHEEK.

She groaned and sat up, every inch of her throbbing in dull agony, her near-nude body riddled with scars and angry purple bruises. Leaning over the side, she vomited into the sea.

She found a bottle of water tucked into the side of the rubber boat and remembered they had left one for Chakrit's uncle in case he woke up. She tried to unscrew the bottle cap, but her broken wrist hung limply from one arm. Instead, she clamped her teeth on the cap and managed to open it. She took a few small sips, then poured a small amount into her hand for Grub to gratefully lap up. She didn't know how long they had slept, but already the sun was setting. She welcomed the cool night air, her fair skin now blistered and bright red from sunburn.

'Should've brought my sun tan lotion,' she said to the dog, her voice a distant cousin twice-removed. He tilted his head at her.

The ocean spread out around the boat. No land, no other ships, just interminable blue everywhere she looked.

She crawled over to the outboard motor and tugged on the cord with her good hand. Nothing happened. She tried again and gave up, exhaustion setting in.

'What the fuck are we gonna do, pug?' she slurred. She ran her tongue over her teeth and realised she was missing a few. When had that happened?

She tried the engine one more time, putting every last bit of effort into it. The motor coughed, caught and died.

The pug sidled over to her and rested his chin on her thigh. She stroked his head, his tail curling with pleasure.

'I couldn't save her,' she said. 'I promised that I would, but I failed.'

No one could, the dog said. *But you gave it your best shot, and you can't do anymore than that.*

'But I promised her.'

You never stood a chance. But you fought, that's the important thing. Faced with adversity, you stood and faced it head on. Most people would have crumbled. But not you. Chakrit was right. You don't know how strong you really are.

The dog licked his nose.

'You're just saying that to be nice.'

No, I mean it. I'm sure that somewhere out there, your family is watching over you. And you know what? I think they're proud of you. Now scratch my chin, please.

Ana scratched his chin.

'Thanks pug. If it wasn't for you, I think I'd go completely mad.'

She laughed until her lungs hurt, then cried again. After a while she got bored with crying and lay down. The sun dipped below the horizon and night enveloped her.

When Grub woke her with his incessant barking, she tried to quieten him by petting his head. When that didn't work, she forced herself to sit up. It was still night and she was sore all over, especially a nasty wound in her stomach. She couldn't remember where she had gotten that particular one.

'What are you barking at?'

Look! Over there! I see lights!

'Don't fuck with me, please.'

No, look! Yellow lights!

'Now I know you're shitting me. Dogs are colour blind.'

But she looked anyway.

There they were. Far off in the night, through a wall of darkness. The lights of a boat, like fireflies in the night. She was too tired to be excited, so just rubbed Grub's head instead.

'We're gonna make it,' she said, scratching at her stomach. She gave the outboard motor one final try. She didn't know if it was the rest from her sleep, or the thrill of seeing another boat, or if it was plain luck, but the motor started on the first try.

The boat was far away, but they were going to reach it. They had to.

The motor purred as they sped across the water. Ana screwed up her face as a sharp pain gnawed at her guts. The dog's tail dropped and he shuffled backwards, growling at her.

'What's wrong?' she said, every word an effort. She tried to open the water bottle but this time couldn't manage, letting it fall into her lap.

The boat drew closer, one of the big tourist ships, like the one they had stolen the night of the party. How long ago had that been? Two nights? Three? It felt like a lifetime.

The low snarling from the pug continued.

Ana touched the wound on her abdomen, gently

caressing it with her fingers, tracing them around the circular puncture.

The spider. When the Upside-down Man had her in his grip, when they were halfway up the wall of the cave, it had pierced her with its broken proboscis. She must have blanked the whole thing out.

'Funny how that happens, huh?' she croaked, but Grub didn't answer. His tail was down, his lower teeth bared.

Ana winced at the burning sensation inside her. She thought of Rachel, in pieces, somewhere at the bottom of the sea.

'I'm sorry, Rach. I tried.'

She scratched her belly. The lights on the tourist boat drew closer. She heard someone shouting in Thai, or was it English? It didn't matter.

'You were right,' she said to her dead sister. 'It really does burn.' She rested a palm on her stomach and felt something move inside.

Beneath the sallow moon, she whispered into the cool night sky.

'I love you, sis,' was what she said.

AFTERWORD

This book was inspired by my honeymoon.

No wait, hear me out!

My wife and I travelled to Hong Kong and then Thailand for our honeymoon. It was perfect and wonderful, but I guess my mind is broken, because even with my wife for company and surrounded by white-sand beaches and tropical jungle, I just can't seem to switch off the horror.

Well, why would I want to?

There were three separate instances that formed the idea for The Forgotten Island. The first two happened at pretty much the same time. We were on a tour boat, identical to the one that Ana finds herself on. The boat cruised from Koh Samui to Koh Phangan, and on the way we passed an island, on top of which sat an abandoned building, almost hidden by the trees. That would probably have been enough, but seconds later I spotted smoke from a fire coming from further down the hill. I remember turning to my wife and saying, 'Imagine you were trapped on that island, and you followed the smoke hoping to find safety, but once you arrived you discovered the remains of your friends being roasted over a fire.'

I don't recall her reaction. Love was truly in the air.

The next night, the final piece of the puzzle slipped into place. We were dining in the resort, tucking into some mouth-watering Thai food, when I noticed a shadow above my wife's head. Something on the parasol.

Something huge.

Can you guess what it was?

I've never seen either of us move so fast. Fuckin' spiders, man. Fuckin' spiders.

Thanks for reading my book. I sincerely hope you enjoyed it. I couldn't have written it without the tireless support of my wife and family, as well as all you crazy folk on Twitter and Instagram. Special thanks to Bradley, Lysette and Sadie for their feedback and advice, and to Boris for being a good boy.

I'll leave you with my writing playlist. The entire book was written to the following movie soundtracks. Some of them are pretty hard to find, but I feel they form the ideal accompaniment to *The Forgotten Island*, and also give a pretty good indication of my influences.

Carlo Maria Cordio - *Absurd*

Glenn Paxton - *Dark Night of the Scarecrow*

Goblin - *Buio Omega*

John Carpenter & Alan Howarth - *Christine*

Libra - *Shock*

Marcello Giombini - *Anthropophagous The Beast*

Marcello Giombini - *The Beast in Space*
Marcello Giombini - *Erotic Nights of the Living Dead*
Martin Cooper & David A Hughes - *C.H.U.D*
Riz Ortolani - *Cannibal Holocaust*
Riz Ortolani - *Zeder*
Roberto Donati - *Cannibal Ferox*
Simon Boswell - *Stagefright*
Tangerine Dream - *Firestarter*
Tim Krog - *The Boogey Man*

ABOUT THE AUTHOR

David Sodergren lives in Scotland with his wife Heather and his best friend, Boris the Pug. A lifelong devotee of horror, he has several more books in various stages of development.

Find us at the following locations -

https://paperbacksandpugs.wordpress.com
https://twitter.com/paperbacksnpugs
https://www.instagram.com/paperbacksandpugs/

COMING IN 2019

NIGHT SHOOT - A novel of unrelenting slasher horror